Bite Your Tongue

Francesca Rendle-Short grew up in Queensland, the fifth of six children. She has worked variously as a radio producer, teacher, editor, freelance writer and arts journalist. She is the author of the novel *Imago* (Spinifex Press), the novella *Big Sister* (Redress Novellas), and co-author with Felicity Packard of the play *Us*. Her short fictions, photo-essays, exhibition text, and poetry for the page and for the wall, have been published in literary journals and magazines, online and in exhibitions. She has a Doctor of Creative Arts from the University of Wollongong and is the Program Director of Creative Writing at RMIT University. She lives in Melbourne.

Bite Your Tongue

Francesca Rendle-Short

First published by Spinifex Press 2011, Reprinted 2012 (twice)

Spinifex Press Pty Ltd
504 Queensberry St
North Melbourne, Victoria 3051
Australia
women@spinifexpress.com.au
www.spinifexpress.com.au

Copyright © Francesca Rendle-Short, 2011

All rights reserved. Without limiting the rights under copyright reserved above, no part of this publication may be reproduced, stored in or introduced into a retrieval system, or transmitted, in any form or by any means (electronic, mechanical, photocopying, recording or otherwise) without prior written permission of both the copyright owner and the above publisher of the book.

Copying for educational purposes
Information in this book may be reproduced in whole or part for study or training purposes, subject to acknowledgement of the source and providing no commercial usage or sale of material occurs. Where copies of part or whole of the book are made under part VB of the Copyright Act, the law requires that prescribed procedures be followed. For information contact the Copyright Agency Limited.

Edited by Sophie Cunningham
Cover design by Deb Snibson, MAPG
Typeset by Palmer Higgs
Printed by McPherson's Printing Group

The National Library of Australia Cataloguing-in-Publication data:
National Library of Australia Cataloguing-in-Publication entry (pbk)
Rendle-Short, Francesca.
Bite your tongue / Francesca Rendle-Short.
9781876756963 (pbk)
9781742197883 (ebook: ePub)
9781742197852 (ebook: pdf)
9781742197869 (ebook: Kindle)
Rendle-Short, Angel.
Families.
Queensland--Social life and customs--20th century.
306.85

 This publication is assisted by the Australia Council, the Australian Government's arts funding and advisory body.

For my mother, Angel
1920–2006

Also by Francesca Rendle-Short

Imago

Contents

It's a sin   7

The most secret of all places   55

Kill! Kill!   119

Don't ever tell   181

Wings ablaze   215

'The books leapt and danced like roasted birds, their wings ablaze with red and yellow feathers.'

Ray Bradbury, *Fahrenheit 451*

Prologue

My mother's name is Angel and she's buried near the Big Pineapple in Queensland outside a little town called Bli Bli. She waits, deep in the red earth of that Queensland countryside on a grassy hill with a view, facing east— just the way she instructed—ready to greet her saviour: ready to rise triumphant when the trumpet sounds and Jesus returns.

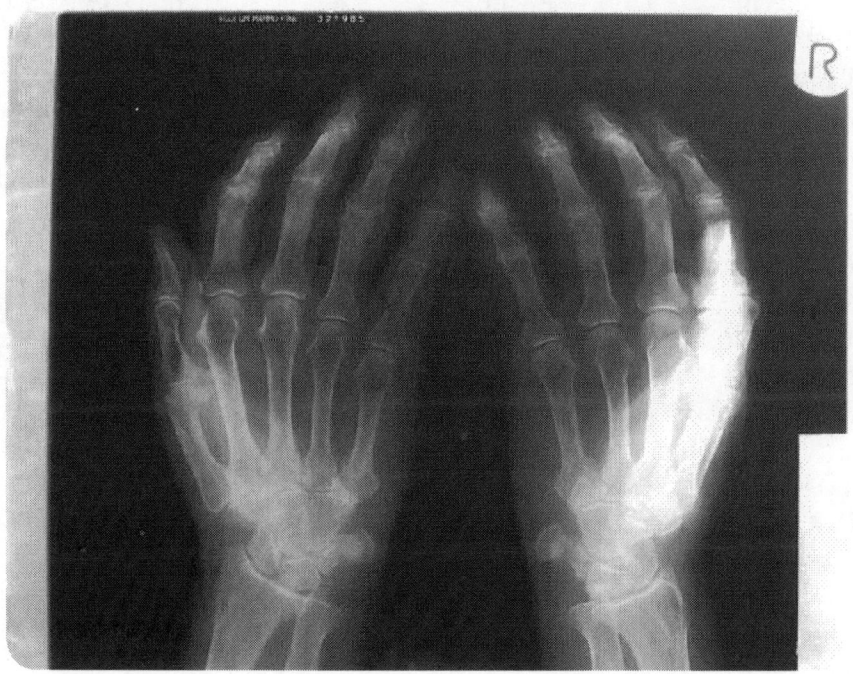

These are my mother's hands; they look angelic, don't they? Supplicating? Are they dancing? Covering her eyes? I wonder what she discussed with her doctor on the occasion of this X-ray. I wonder what was wrong with her that day.

After my mother died we found piles of X-rays just like these in large envelopes underneath her bed. You could piece her body together; there were scans for her head, her mouth and nasal passages, her chest and stomach, her pelvis, hands, knees, and feet. My little sister and I couldn't bear to throw them away, so we divided the pile between the two of us.

My mother was a book burner. Sometimes, she was so agitated about the books the teachers and librarians insisted I read at school, she was on fire; I could see smoke and flame coming out of her orifices, her ears, her mouth. Mind you, when I was young I didn't want to know any of this and I got into the habit of not listening and not taking any notice; it was safer that way. Otherwise, I thought, I would go up in smoke too, that she'd take me out to the backyard next to the chooks and the ducks and slip me into the incinerator as well, burn me along with the books, burn me for being naughty. I didn't dare read any of the 'wicked books' she was talking about; she had a list of them. But I tried to imagine what lay between their covers, what could be so bad.

Angel Rendle-Short was a morals crusader, an 'anti-smut' campaigner. An activist. She was on a mission from God to save the children of Queensland. She wasn't the only crusader in Queensland at this time; she wasn't in charge, there were others. But she would do anything to make her views known: agitate, protest and appeal to the highest authority she could find. So when I discovered a letter from my mother deep in the National Archives of Australia in Canberra, dated 7 August 1971 and written to the Governor General of Australia, His Excellency Sir Paul Hasluck, copied to the Prime Minister of Australia, The Right Honourable William McMahon, and to the Premier of Queensland, The Right Honourable Joh Bjelke-Petersen, it didn't really surprise. But what I read made my heart curdle with shame. She said the books we were reading in school were pornographic, 'lewd literature' and 'sex saturated', that teachers had betrayed parents' trust—'this is not EDUCATION; it is DEFILEMENT'—that her own children accepted her 'control' because they knew it was 'exercised in wisdom and love'. She pleaded with the Governor General to do something, to root 'this great evil out of our society'.

Introduction

35 Durham Street,
St. Lucia,
BRISBANE.
QUEENSLAND 4067.

7 August 1971.

To: His Excellency Sir Paul Hasluck K.C.M.G.
Copy to: His Excellency Sir Alan Mansfield K.C.M.G.
         The Prime Minister of Australia, the Rt. Hon. W. McMahon M.P.
         The Premier of Queensland, the Rt. Hon. J. Bjelke-Petersen M.P.

Your Excellency,
   We wish to bring to your notice a matter that is causing the gravest concern in the community. We refer to the type of book that is currently recommended by the school teachers and educational authorities for reading matter at the sub-senior and senior levels, that is grades 11 and 12, in the secondary schools of our land. We have in mind such titles as "The Group" by McCarthy, "Bring Larks and Heroes" by Keneally, "Catch 22", "Love Story", "The Wayward Bus" and "The Grapes of Wrath" by Steinbeck, "Kangaroo" by D.H. Lawrence, to mention but a few. More particularly we would draw your attention to the use of the book by Salinger, entitled "The Catcher in the Rye" which is currently being studied in Church and State secondary schools in Queensland.

   The young students are still minors, and they are being asked to make a detailed study, often in the class situation and with the implicit approval of their teachers, of these and other similar books which, whatever value they might seem by some to have, are strongly pornographic in content. To prevent misunderstanding we accept the Oxford English Dictionary meaning of that word, where it is defined as, "the description of manners of harlots; treatment of obscene subjects in Literature", and the O.E.D. definition of the word obscene is "repulsive, filthy, loathsome, indecent or lewd".
I quote a short extract from the book in question:-

> "If you want to know the truth I'm a virgin, I really am. I've had quite a few opportunities to lose my virginity and all, but I never got around to it yet. Something always happens. For instance-------- if you're in the back seat of somebody's car, there's always somebody's date in the front seat, some girl I mean, that always wants to know what's going on over the whole goddam car. I mean some girl in front keeps turning around to see what the hell is going on. Anyway, something always happens. I came quite close to doing it a couple of times, though. One time in particular I remember. Something went wrong though. I don't even remember what any more. The thing is, most of the time when you're coming pretty close to doing it with a girl, a girl that isn't a prostitute or anything I mean, she keeps telling you to stop. The trouble with me is I stop. Most guys don't. I can't help it. You never know whether they really want you tp stop or whether they're just scared as hell. Anyway, I

> keep stopping.———— After you neck girls for a while you really can watch them losing their brains. You take a girl when she really gets passionate, she just hasn't any brains.———— If you really want to know the truth, when I'm horsing around with a girl, I have a hell of a lot of trouble just finding what I'm looking for, for God's sake if you know what I mean. Take this girl that I just missed having sexual intercourse with, that I told you about, it took me a whole hour to take her goddam brassiere off. By that time she was about ready to spit in my face".

Your Excellency, up to this time we have trustfully committed the welfare and education of our children to the schools. But the schools have betrayed this trust. They have also betrayed the young lives and souls of our sons and daughters. This is not EDUCATION; it is DEFILEMENT.

We, the Mothers and Fathers, stand on the sure ground that in the final analysis it is the Parents who, before Almighty God, will have to answer for their child's moral and spiritual welfare and guidance. This is underlined by the wording of Paragraph 3 Article 26 of The Universal Declaration of Human Rights, " Parents have a prior right to choose the kind of education that shall be given to their children", and the text of the Declaration is to be "disseminated, displayed, read and expounded principally in schools and other educational institutions".

We are Parents who, within our families, give direction concerning the reading material for our sons and daughters, and particularly is this so in the case of minors. We actively discourage the presence in our homes of lewd literature and sex saturated books. This control is accepted by our children because they know it is exercised in wisdom and love.

We ask that the schools and the Educational authorities behind the schools will uphold these standards, and make a resolute stand against lust depravity and vice. We ask them to point the children to Literature, of which there is an abundance, that is edifying and of an uplifting and ennobling quality.

Having written to those in leadership in the Educational field in Queensland, we wish, humbly to inform Your Excellency on this matter, and we ask that wherever possible you will encourage and implement all action aimed at rooting this great evil out of our society.

I remain, Sir,
Your Loyal and Obedient Servant,

Angel Rendle-Short.

Mrs. Angel Rendle-Short M.B., B.Ch., B.A.O.

Introduction

Growing up, I knew about some things to do with her campaign because they involved me directly, other things I've uncovered in the archive. I found out for instance that there were a number of booklists, both long and short, that were circulated and published in different forms such as in pamphlets, in letters to the press and to 'concerned parents', in delegations to government. I discovered she was discussed at length in the Queensland parliament. Martin Hanson, for example, the Labor Party Member for Port Curtis in Gladstone (1963–1976), thought she was a 'very fine woman' and concurred with her views about the 'salacious' books '1000 per cent'. Bit by bit I've pieced together a picture.

Some stories are hard to tell, they bite back. To write this one, I've had to come at it obliquely, give myself over to the writing with my face half turned; give my story to someone else to tell. My chosen hero is a girl named Glory. She sits in the dictionary smack between *gloom / gloop / glop / gloppen / glore* on the topside of the column and *gloss / glossal / glossanthrax / glossary* on the bottom. Her mother, who I have named MotherJoy (written all one word), called her daughter Gloria at birth, Gloria when summonsed. Sometimes there was a soft alternative—Glory Girl, said with affection or Glorious Glory Girl, when singing God's praises.

Glory knows she can never tell her mother what it is she is writing, that she *is writing* at all—won't her tongue be cut out for doing such a thing? And she can't tell Onward, her father, either; he is as good as asleep.

But wait, she is jumping ahead. To tell this story Glory wants to take you back to when tongues and the eating of tongues were ticklish and innocent, first things first, back to when she liked to sing.

This is Glory's story.

It's a sin

1

GLORY WISHES SHE COULD remember her very first taste of tongue, the first mouthful, that first bite. It is like trying to remember her very first kiss.

You see tongue was Little Glory's favourite food. She asked for it as a special treat on her birthday, even though the Solider family had it served up to them by MotherJoy at least once a week. 'Ah well,' MotherJoy said, 'it is your birthday after all.' So they ate pressed tongue and boiled potatoes with the smoothest of white sauces served with the mushiest of pale-green peas from a tin. For pudding, the sweetest of white blancmanges upside down on the plate, in the shape of a star.

The two youngest Solider girls, known as the Little Girls, helped their mother prepare the tongue meat the night before, watched her peel off the grey skins, watched her curl the tongues in a kiss in the pudding basin as they did themselves with their eating mouths. At tea, Glory and Gracie had their mouths full but were still laughing, laughing because the tongue they were eating kissed and tickled their real tongue and their real cheeks.

'Keep quiet or leave the table.'

They blushed red for daring to make such a hullabaloo. Dashed to their rooms without looking back. Didn't they know from the Bible that the tongue was a fire, 'a world of iniquity?'

That night, you could hear them in their bedroom playing around on each other's bed. The Little Girls kissed each other, at first lips to lips, then Solider mouth to Solider mouth. 'Touch tongues,' they dared each other, to more great peals of laughter. Into the night their laughter became a ripple, then a purl, an improvised scat with the flying fruit bats outside chatting up the Brisbane breeze. Their giggles floated above the tall palm trees, high into the clouds. The girls swung about, upside down with the yellow fruit and the bunch of squealing mammals, and together they shed light like baubles and jewels swinging on a Christmas tree. Tongues hanging out. Lolly pink. Hearts racing with excitement.

Writing this now Glory can still feel the roughness of her sister's tongue on her own, the taste of warm saliva. Her first kiss. She smells her sister's perfume, Chanel 5, the one she wears today. A memory of forbidden desire swells within her. She feels the blood in her temples thudding on either side of her face, pulsing visibly like the gills of a fish. She wonders, privately: will writing this change things; change how she feels, change what happens?

2

GLORY RECKONS GOOD BOOKS shed light the way strips of skin peel off from around fruit, and this light—the colour, the smell, the juice—squeezes into the cracks of our hearts. You can feel it, taste it. Books seduce us. They make our hearts beat fast. The best of them can disrupt us, shift the axis of our universe, nudge us word by word into unchartered spaces. They allow us to swing about in the breeze. They change our feelings. That's why Glory loves working in a bookshop. To talk about books, to share them.

To read a really, *really* good book for the very first time—especially those books that were once strictly forbidden—it's sweeter than you could ever imagine. A good book can sometimes be better than a good kiss, a first book better than that first kiss. Reading can tickle and turn you upside down. Make your tongue hang loose. Books show us how to love, really love body to body between the pages. Love perhaps where we've never loved before, that's what Glory hopes.

Reading changes things.

3

GLORY DREAMS SHE IS A character in the books she reads, that the characters are people in her life, a transfiguration. The books come to life.

This one in her hand is tattered: Harper Lee's *To Kill a Mockingbird*, a 1960s edition. On the front cover she reads that it won the Pulitzer Prize for best novel in 1960, that it was on the American bestseller list for eighty-two weeks, that it sold over five million copies by 1973. Hard to believe MotherJoy wanted it banned, that it was on her 'death list' of books. People ask Glory, what's wrong with *Mockingbird*? What was your mother's objection? Did she really want to burn it?

Glory finds her own name on the inside cover in spidery black-ink lettering, there, under the yellow sticky tape holding the pages together—it's her handwriting for sure, only smaller, tidier than now. There are her annotations throughout the book, lists of key words, characters and page references, notes about how the narrative is told through a series of events with flashbacks, about the structure and its pleasing symmetry, about the centrality of the mockingbird and its song. How these birds sing their hearts out for us, they don't do any harm, and how it's a sin to kill them.

Glory wonders: did Onward ever think MotherJoy went too far?

She promises herself she will read the whole book again, this time cover to cover, word for word and very slowly. Like slow breathing. Without missing a beat. She wants to get stuck in the pages of this story, let Scout Finch tell it her way. See what's in it, for herself. Read, to patch her universe together. Like singing your heart out. No matter what.

4

Her mother's voice is on the answering machine, one day—just like that—greeting Glory when she comes home from work. The machine sits on the wooden pew in her kitchen and Glory presses the replay button to listen. 'Gloria is that you?' The voice is crackly, old, a wee bit warbly but unmistakeable. There's the way MotherJoy says her daughter's name, the emphasis she puts on the *Glor* in *Gloria*. And the formality; nobody calls Glory *Gloria* these days. She has to confess she rather likes it. She likes the attention.

It repeats itself—'Gloria, Glory is that you?' The upward inflection suggests disappointment, even annoyance that Glory is not there. There is a certain charm too in her mother's bewilderment, the voice that hints at being caught off guard. 'I'm going in for a little procedure,' she says, 'an investigation, no need to fuss.' There is a pregnant pause (MotherJoy knows how to play her voice) before she finishes with a benediction: 'And, and, blessings on you one hundred times.'

Oh! Glory feels a hitch in her throat. A lump. *Blessings on you:* her mouth goes dry. The machine blinks red, off and on. Glory watches it warily: it is an animal and she is in a trance.

She wants to put her mother's voice and message from her mind, but she can't because there it is, recorded, on tape: clear, resonant. And it's not that MotherJoy has a horrible voice. In fact she speaks with a lovely musicality, able to float words, full timbre, with character, *body*. People say they like her voice. People tell Glory, 'Your mother sounds so sweet, old-lady sweet.' No, it is the authority her mother attaches to that sometimes-confiding tone, before she cuts with the imperative. MotherJoy knows how to work it exactly to get results, results she wants.

It doesn't surprise Glory that her mother is going into hospital for 'a little procedure'. Her father had already rung a week or so before to say MotherJoy was sick, to say she had been in and out of the Prince Charles Hospital for a range of tests. Onward is always matter-of-fact, that's his way, gets straight to the point. He rattled off a surfeit of medical terms and jargon, multisyllabic words that don't mean a thing to a layperson, certainly not to Glory. The routine's enough to make her feel inadequate though, as if she *should* know what he means. As if he thinks that being in the Solider family means you understand medical procedures and terminology through some kind of Solider osmosis or genetic code.

She said: 'Doesn't sound too good then, does it?'

Onward and MotherJoy, both being doctors, love the medical world, it is their stomping ground—the Solider children know this. You haven't got a chance unless you're a part of it—talking diagnoses and prognoses, visiting surgeries and wards, writing out scripts from *MIMS*, getting second, even third opinions, fourth, seeking out the best medical minds Queensland has to offer, insisting on going 'to the top', as if to God. The story in the Solider family unfolds in this way (Glory knows it by heart): girls live through their husbands so the task is to find one of them, a good husband that is, preferably medical (that's best, obviously), clergy an excellent second, and an academic could squeeze in third if he worked in certain disciplines. Anything else is folly, sometimes a sin (sometimes it would be better to be dead). It's for life, so don't ever get divorced. None of the six Solider girls pass the test, by the way, but become the subject of much prayer.

There was a bit of a lilt in Onward's voice about these latest developments with MotherJoy. *Something was happening.* Something medical. Onward was in his element.

Glory finds out the detail about what's going on from her sisters. They tell her that all but one of MotherJoy's coronary arteries is blocked and she needs four heart-saving grafts, and soon too, if she's going to avoid an inevitable heart attack (hence the Prince Charles, the big heart hospital in Chermside on the north-east flank of Brisbane). It's very risky for a patient over eighty to have this kind of major operation, she's very nearly *too* old, the doctors say. But they go ahead anyway, on MotherJoy's insistence. All the girls agree this could be *it*, they'd been expecting *it* for sometime. Perhaps insisting on the surgery is the beginning of MotherJoy's exit plan—she knows where she is heading: hoping a major bypass operation ends in a stroke and MotherJoy is dead on the table and on her way to heaven.

Glory feels numb, helpless—*shamed*. None of the six girls live in the same state. If the Solider girls were part of an ordinary family each of them would make sure they were with their mother in her time of need even though they are so far away. Other families rally around, don't they? But the Soliders aren't used to being close to their mother. Even so, Glory makes a decision for herself. She decides that the news coming from Queensland this time is more significant than casual 'investigation'. She decides to go, not because she wants to but she thinks it's the right thing to do.

It is then, after Glory has decided to fly north from Melbourne and after telling Onward, but before she's spoken to MotherJoy, that she replays her mother's benediction: *And, and, blessings on you one hundred times*. When she gets to this part, MotherJoy's message warbles like a magpie chortling under a sprinkler on a dry lawn in high summer. Glory listens to the blinking machine again and then over and over and over. She replays it all through the evening, as if she needs to imprint those eight words and the precise carriage of their meaning in a song onto her heart, to carry them with her as a balm for what she knows comes next. Whatever happens, these words will carry them into the unknown. And she almost believes MotherJoy, almost believes her mother means what she says this time: *Blessings on you one hundred times*. Very nearly.

The thing is, you can never trust her. Not *really*.

5

So this is how she finds herself, a day later, in the Intensive Care Unit, sitting beside unconscious MotherJoy post-operation on an orange plastic chair with a red book in her lap.

She bought the fancy notebook at the airport, even though she has an old one in her bag, half empty. She has to do this whole thing right. Fresh. From the start. There'll be a lot of writing to do—so much is happening—but she won't be able to talk about it, not seriously, deeply, anything to do with her mother leaves her tongue-tied. The spunky new notebook glows like a jewel. It looks like a real book too, with its hard cardboard cover, buckram cloth and neat crossover corners, its red marbled endpapers and perfect case binding. There's a matching ribbon to mark her place.

'You can stay as long as you like,' a nurse tells Glory in a comforting voice, soft-shoe shuffle. 'You can stay here in ICU until she wakes up.'

Glory wants to say thanks—the nurse is so kind—but she can't get a word out, she's choked up. She manages only a little nod. 'I'll bring you a cup of tea if you like.' Another gesture. 'She's going to pull through this, you know.'

This is more difficult than Glory imagined it was going to be.

It's not the hospital *per se* that gets to Glory, she's accustomed to the smell of the place, the routine and order of things, and she rather likes the interesting machinery too, especially in intensive care. Nor is it the idea that her mother is in hospital, for this has happened before. No. What gets her is the smallness of MotherJoy. It is a shock to see her again. Her mother is a version of her former self, a carapace. Muscles now all but evaporated. Skin in folds over bones like brushed-cotton cloths for polishing the silver. Will she ever wake up? Everyone says the first twenty-four hours is the test after a procedure like this, and it looks like she'll come through, if the shuffle and purr of the nurses is anything to go by. You wouldn't be sipping slow cups of tea if this were an emergency, now would you?

Glory's knees press against the stainless steel bedstead to make white dints in her skin. She smells crisp cotton sheets. She's close enough to touch the cardigan the nurses have wrapped around MotherJoy's shoulders and arms to keep her temperature up. Like a baby in a matinee jacket. The cardigan is one of MotherJoy's re-made creations, Glory can tell, with its bold pattern of colours and black satin trim around the edges. It has a black crocheted collar that looks like something MotherJoy has made as an extra—she is good with her hands. It sits comfortably, cradling MotherJoy's neck and throat. She looks snug, warm. Glory reaches out and runs a forefinger along the ribbon satin smoothness, traces a line of stitching along one edge, and wonders about her mother's heart, hidden from view underneath the wool. *Thunk-thunk-thunk.* A heart that has been kickstarted on the operating table to keep MotherJoy alive. A heart protected by surgical stitching. For what? For how long?

Glory stands up suddenly. She leans over her mother to tie the cardigan ribbon that lies across the bandaged chest into a small pretty bow. MotherJoy would appreciate this gesture, Glory is certain; her mother has particular taste. She always insisted on presenting herself with care and attention, she was a professor's wife after all, if a little zany; had a reputation to uphold. Glory wants to kiss her too; she's close enough now to her mother's body and it would be so easy to do this while she is asleep. For isn't this what families do at times like this—show affection, kiss one another in salutation, tell of love? She imagines bending to her mother's face, imagines touching her mother's soft cheek with trembling lips, her mother's soft cheek like the finest underwater sea sponge in which to get lost. She could kiss her mother quickly in this moment of reprieve. There's time. Nobody would know.

Glory pauses, suspended there in a long shadow over her mother's body. She listens to her own wavy breath going in, going out, hears it instead of the clink-clink of the machines. She's daring herself to do it, egging herself on—go on, kiss her. Kiss Her. The cardigan's colours dance in the artificial light, all whirly, a blur, like a rainbow paddle-pop melted in the Brisbane heat. She's so close to doing it now she smells the nearness of MotherJoy's body. They are the only two who exist in the entire world—just her, just her mother. Go on, Glory instructs herself, just kiss. A snatch. You'll regret it otherwise.

Glory steadies herself, her hands are shaking, her lips fizz.

But she can't.

6

EVERY NOW AND AGAIN Glory disappears out of the unit to text Gracie and the others in the family on her mobile, to keep them up with the latest. To get some fresh air and nibble on an apple. The nurses reassure her that it's quite normal to have a break; her mother is in good hands. *So far so good,* Glory keys in, good at lying about things that matter.

They say I can stay here sit by her—
They say patients do best with family near—
Pleased I'm here, funny thought—
And yes quadruple.

Gracie has decided to come too, is on her way, crossing the oceans by plane from London to Brisbane. She replies to Glory's messages from Singapore on a stopover: *She doesn't do things by halves clearly never did!* And: *Boom. Boom.* Glory laughs out loud at this last message; it's so easy laughing with her little sister—even when they sense they shouldn't be doing such a thing at such a time. But it's such gorgeous relief. A moment that flies free of restraint, makes Glory's skin shimmer. She laughs at her own laughing then, and that makes her feel even better. She wishes Gracie was already with her, arm in arm, as she goes back in to her mother and the whispering machines.

What will happen when MotherJoy does wake up? Glory wipes tears from her eyes, wonders what she'll say then. She thinks: *You won't be able to admit to being pleased that you're here by her side.* No laughter now. *You'll fluff it. When it comes to it, your chin will fuse up, go all numb, and the words you think you hold in your mouth, the words you suck like small stones, will sink.* Glory has never been able to say what she means. *Your tongue will get in the way.*

Glory goes back over the anatomy of what has happened already, what she knows: her mother on the operating table in theatre; the sharpness of the surgical instruments, the prick and slice of a knife—that first incision through skin, bone, muscle, organ; her mother's ribs being cut open and peeled back like butterfly wings, the wide-open chest cavity for all to see; her heart muscle fully exposed, in pieces even; and her body on the heart-lung bypass machine four times over to replace four arteries harvested from veins in her leg. Gracie will say: 'It's scary; her heart is strong as it is.'

Later, MotherJoy will insist on going over these details with the surgeon. She will want to get it right in her head. She'll want to know what happened to her, what went where and in what order, who did what. She will boast that her wound is the height of a small child. MotherJoy likes to be in charge, she is a difficult patient. She will dress down doctors if she has to. Nurses who make any sort of slip up don't stand a chance.

Now, though, unconscious, she is so passive she's a stranger.

Now, MotherJoy lies on the cusp of it all, between her mortal life—a life lived vigorously—and very possible death. Heaven's pearly gates are visible on the horizon, beckoning, and something like a curl of the lip on MotherJoy's face suggests a promise. Her hope of being bestowed a crown of jewels when she arrives. 'I am bound for glory,' MotherJoy liked to pronounce.' Can't wait to get to glory, Glory.' And her voice would pause midway through the sentence, skip a beat with the comma between *glory* and *Glory*, the words buoyed up with a stray little laugh and a punctuating pillow of support with the capital *G*. 'Names are so precious aren't they? Glory for glory,' she liked to sing like a laugh. A mother's little song for her fifth daughter.

7

GLORY DOESN'T LIKE TO BE reminded of her name. Glory used to boast to Gracie that she was mentioned more than three hundred and fifteen times in the Bible according to *Cruden's Complete Concordance* not to mention phrases such as *give glory, glory of God, thy glory* and the use of *glory* as a verb. Her sister Gracie only had plain *grace, grace of God* and *grace of our Lord Jesus*, no verb to speak of, and her name was only mentioned one hundred and thirty-five times. Once, the Little Girls counted every verse in the Bible, but that's another story.

The real story goes that Glory was named after a duck, well two ducks, her and Gracie, the Little Girls at the bottom of the Solider family. MotherJoy liked to keep animals, she was good with animals; she had grown up with a menagerie. She was particularly fond she said, of her very first mallards, the ones she had as a girl in Northern Ireland, Glory and Gracie. Pet ducks, mark you, not to be dressed for the table, not to eat; there was a difference. And then she would laugh.

MotherJoy's laughter was infectious. She could tumble turn her family with surprise. Sometimes it would come out unexpectedly; sometimes it gave Glory a fright. Glory reckoned that when her mother laughed she forgot where she was, *who* she was. MotherJoy out of control, if that were possible. Quite the spectacle. Hearing her laugh, Glory nearly forgot what had gone on before too and could almost put aside what might be on its way.

There is no sound of laughter in this place.

The machines surrounding the bed in headstone formation blink blankly at Glory, flickering candles at a vigil. She watches the graphs squiggle like snakes across the screen. The machines are veiled in high tech and medical secrecy. She waits like a sentinel on the orange plastic chair beside the bed, as if waiting with her mother at heaven's gates, fingers crossed. *Can't wait to get to glory, Glory,* she hears her mother whisper even though her lips are shut tight. Oh for a little laughter now, the sort Glory knows off by heart. Oh for a squeeze of hands. To have her live.

8

GLORY TRIES TO REMEMBER whether it was one hundred or a thousand times she has been blessed. Does it matter if you get these kinds of things wrong? What difference does a factor of ten make?

She fingers the black satin on the cardigan draped around her mother again for comfort. MotherJoy probably bought it at St Vincent's, Vinnies, a favourite place to shop. She must have split the front up the middle with a pair of scissors, from the belly button to the throat, as though she were her own heart surgeon. 'Look, I crocheted a pretty collar too,' MotherJoy will offer later. 'Nothing is worse than hospital fare, don't you agree? I'll never get into one of those backless gowns … I don't think that will be necessary, do you?' At times MotherJoy faces her daughter with such openness, her expression an open book—Glory has to laugh and her heart returns to its place.

Glory promises herself then, that when she gets back home she will keep saving MotherJoy's phone messages—*Glory Girl is that you?* No matter what MotherJoy says—*blessings on you*—no matter what happens next. It will be her way of remembering. There must be a special word for this—a particular word for the way a body reacts to a voice it recognises. A medical term even. *Blessings on you.* Glory hears the voice resonate in her own body now, as though their hearts have been switched, cavity to cavity: a voice to make Glory jumpy, then freeze up all lumpy.

All lumpy. Jumpy. The singsong of the blinking-red warble on the answering machine back at home on the wooden pew in the kitchen; the song in tune with the beep and tickle and roll of boxy heart machines in intensive care. The thought of it lumping down her tight throat like hot porridge.

Don't do anything you'll regret. Glory sits up to attention on the hard orange plastic. It feels like she is breathing through a tube too. Can you choose your own way of dying, Glory wonders? She waits. She makes shapes on the white paper on her lap. It could be writing, it could be drawing. Even breath. Glory moves the feeling embodied in the lines around the page as if she is dislodging and relocating old river rocks in a newly-landscaped garden. The lines and shapes swim in and out of focus, impossible to read. Her throat hurts, her lungs are tight, her heart feels one hundred times its usual size—what difference does *this* factor of ten make when it's to do with things of the heart? She writes a single, coherent sentence: *Everything will be okay.*

A nurse brings Glory another cup of tea. 'It won't be much longer now. She's on the mend.' Glory writes this down—*on the mend*—to the *bleat, bleat* of the machines, the *clink, clink* of china crockery. Her notebook presses its bookly shape into her thighs in a red square, *I'm writing in the dark, this doesn't make sense, what's going to happen, is she going to die?* Words fall onto the page now in a rush. But what if MotherJoy hears the scratch of her pen?

It's not going to end here—not like this. She promised one hundred times too—so what if I really believe her? Multiply that by ten—blessings on you one thousand times.

9

ONCE, MOTHERJOY TOLD GLORY: 'You think too much. Thinking is dangerous.' Glory can't remember what they were talking about at the time; she was younger, at university. It could have been about all sorts of things: about heresy in the church, about women praying out loud in public, about censorship and limitations to the freedom of expression, about how things used to be better in the old days, the generation gap and evils of rock music and playing the turntable backwards to find out what was being said subliminally (Onward really did do this), about the politics of health and sickness. Such was the usual talk in the Solider family. Glory was always biting her tongue.

Still, she can hear her mother's voice: the choice of words and syntax. *You think too much, Gloria.* And she remembers how her body reacted: heels pressed into shoes so that they ached, cheeks blushed scarlet, and her chest tight with rubber bands. All familiar. And she remembers what she was wearing: a vintage red crêpe dress and diamantes, with sharp-pointed, zipped-up, punk boots. Did MotherJoy object to what her daughter was wearing on that occasion too?

'Thinking is dangerous.'

Did her mother pause when she said it? She was a shrewd woman; she did like to foster dramatic airs. She had a way with words, an ear for balance and rhetoric; she listened in to her own declaration to test its economy, its display. There was always a garnish with everything MotherJoy said: the world sat up, it listened. On this occasion, the combination was like cut crystal, a skin chill: a nasty taste on her daughter's tongue. There was no going back. Not then, not now.

Glory decides writing is a way of thinking: to think, to write, is dangerous. Transgressive. It is no small thing for Glory to tell this story in Glory's way, to put into words things that until now have been left unspoken, to pin her heart to the page. Writing changes things, changes everything. It's a risky business.

10

AT MIDNIGHT, Glory slips out of the Prince Charles, whispering some pleasantries to the night-duty staff. It's late, time to go.

'You won't recognise her when you see her next,' they tell her. 'You'll be able to talk to her then. She'll love that.'

Glory trundles north up the highway in Onward's Falcon to her parents' retirement villa in Buderim, ginger country. It's not far. He's asleep when she gets there, in his own room. She settles herself into her mother's room, because it's the obvious place to bed down in this tiny two-bedroom villa. She's never slept in this place before, let alone this room. In fact, she's never been in this room *on her own*, only ever at her mother's invitation and in her company.

Instead of falling into MotherJoy's bed exhausted, she finds herself rummaging in the floor-to-ceiling bookcase hidden behind the velvet curtain. She's looking for something she knows must be there. Mind you, Glory is in two minds about doing this—*just leave it, will you*—about daring to look in forbidden places—*you'd hate someone going through your belongings*. But she insists on being reckless. She knows MotherJoy finds it hard to throw things out. Knows she will find shoeboxes of precious things, revelations, maybe even her mother's booklists.

Somewhere.

She remembers the scrapbooks, the pages and pages of cuttings. *Let things be.* She's not sure what there is to find, but feels sure she will locate something. *Don't dig.* She wants to make sense of things back then, even if only in a small way—there's no harm in that, is there? *It's my story too*, she retorts.

The curtain burns the rub of her hand.

11

GLORY DOESN'T GET MUCH SLEEP that night. She can't get MotherJoy out of her head. The musty smell of the room mixes unkindly with MotherJoy's perfume of choice, 4711. She imagines her mother lying in this very bed. She lies awake, tosses and turns. It feels like the walls and ceiling of the room are closing in, the vegetation outside is growing so fast it's coming in through the cracks and under the door to choke Glory. She feels the tickle of her mother's hair on her cheek. The smell of hairspray now. Her oh-so-close proximity. Glory's own heart is pounding. It's hard to breathe. There's not enough space for them both. She feels the roughness of her mother's hand, holding her tight, holding on so that neither of them falls out. Glory struggles under the covers to set herself free.

Glory hadn't found anything of substance behind the red curtain, only an old stethoscope in a chocolate-coloured bakelite box, an instrument that knocks knees to check reflexes—complete with perished blue rubber stopper—and plastic bags full of skeins of wool and old dress material. But there is that sixties white hat with polyester flowers covering its crown that MotherJoy loved to wear going to church every Sunday. Glory remembers it well, the tickle of flowers in her eyes when she tried it on for dress-ups (it was far too big), the rush of butterfly wings.

12

I<small>N MY FAMILY</small>, we also went to church every Sunday.
There is a photograph my father took of my mother and me dressed and ready, Francesca and Angel *going to church*. I know that's where we're off to because my mother's handwriting is on the reverse side, her signature across the yellowing photographic paper.

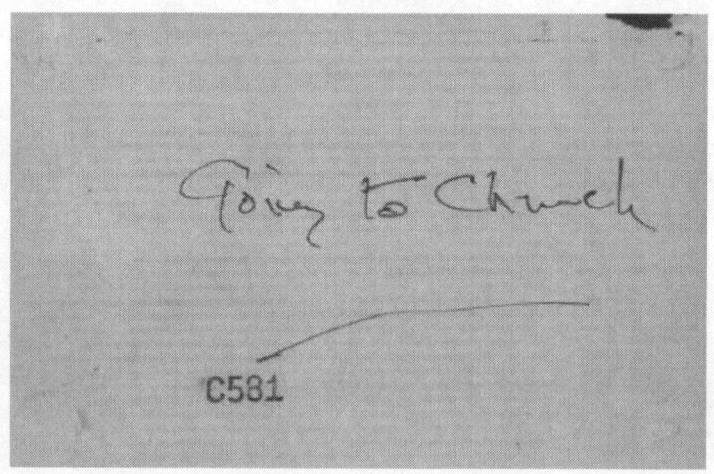

When my mother wrote, her hand moved in a slow dance. She perfected a deliberate, queenly way of writing: she knew where to start, when to press in as one of the letters turned a sharp corner, when to lift the nib off the paper, and how to stop. She knew when to allow the mark she was making trail away, when to curl the letters so that they turned nicely, such as on the tail of the last letter *g* in the first word *Going*. Contrast this to the strength of the crossed *t*, bang in the middle. She took pride in her handwriting; she knew exactly what it was she was doing—there was no mistaking her intentions. It is impossible not to feel the scrape and speed of the final stroke as a bottom line, to conclude, her writing hand swift across my foxed skin. Impossible not to feel her touch.

It's a sin

I imagine I am that close to her body I can feel her spelling out Bible verses across my tender years. Close enough to her body to feel her breath writing hymns of praise over my pale and freckled skin. How I loved to trace heat on other people's bodies in church, the sweat marks drawn on their clothes in all the secret places. Very hot days enlivened my attention, my imagination. I would watch patterns take shape in dark patches and lines down the centre of backs and in concentric circles under arms. Sometimes, I would see two half moons emerge from under some women's breasts if their dresses were hug-fitting, sometimes wet patches around the crotch of the pale-coloured shorts some men wore tightly, in the 1970s style. How the congregation breathed as one.

My mother looks the part, doesn't she? Happy, in a staged sort of way. We look like we are from the same family, don't we? No mistaking! With the same bone structure around the nose and mouth?

My father must have taken this photograph from a lower-down step. We are standing just off the verandah before it was remodelled with an iron railing. We look as though we've been planted to grow out of the rockery. I remember there were small frangipanis on both sides of the steps, a big one off to one side and out of the picture. And crucifix orchids.

I recall, too, the grip of her handhold. She didn't want to let me go.

My mother's hat, made of feathers, or is it tulle? In any case, a crown of butterflies in white polyester wings ready to fly off. In those days, everybody wore hats to church; women were not allowed to betray their sex, their heads had to be covered as a symbol of submission to God and their husbands. But my mother continued to dress up in hats well beyond the time when it was thought to be culturally and religiously necessary. She even wore pretty hats on her final trip to hospital. Sometimes I think we should have dressed her in a hat that day she was laid out for the mortuary, ready to be buried. She had plenty to choose from. And my father would have laughed at how funny she looked; it would have cheered him up.

One of her favourites near the time of her death was a straw hat with a wreath of pretend vine leaves around its crown and bunches of purple faux grapes—one of the removalists wore it into the nursing home when they moved her there. When she went shopping up the road astride her red duco buggy with her shoulders back, head high, full throttle, you could almost fancy those grapes in a jet stream behind her as a star-trail of brilliant colour, the purple jewels catching the light. 'Look at her go,' the elderly residents chorused, 'surely it must be illegal to speed like that,' they cautioned. 'She's going to knock someone over!' Wouldn't feathers fly then? 'She'll be arrested!' I can hear my father calling out too: 'Angel! Do be careful!'

13

Back in the sixties, Brisbane was asleep, asleep in the sunshine, before things became reactionary, before Little Glory lost her tongue. Brisbane was a big, fat, country town tucked up in bed, cushion-safe in the south-east corner of the state of Queensland—when everybody did go to church in hats, when they wore gloves. It was before the swinging sixties took a hold in the rest of Australia. Before Queensland dug its heels in, and said no, '…we're different, we're not like those people down south'. We're talking late winter (there are only two seasons in Brisbane), 1967.

It was well before the idea of censorship had taken hold of ordinary people in Queensland. In a couple of years Germaine Greer's *The Female Eunuch* would be published. (And yes, this book was on MotherJoy's list, just like Harper Lee's *To Kill a Mockingbird*.) Books such as *Lady Chatterley's Lover* (another on the death list) and the furore over its contravention of obscenity laws were stories belonging to other places in the world. Talkback radio was only beginning to take off, metropolitan radio stations embracing this clever and inexpensive way to fill dead spots on air. The protest group MotherJoy belonged to, STOP and CARE, hadn't yet got going: STOP, Society to Outlaw Pornography and CARE, Campaign Against Regressive Education.

Queensland was innocent. As was the Solider family. They little suspected something almighty was around the corner. There was no reason to: in the early to mid-1960s after a mild winter in the Sunshine State where winters were always mild at the best of times, in the pointy state of Australia—Australia's crown, Queensland people liked to say— in the home of the Solider family in the leafy, university suburb of St Lucia, the going was pineapple-sweet.

14

THEN CAME THE BLAST: STUDENTS IN CLASHES WITH POLICE. The headline caught Little Glory's attention. Front page, large font—the largest font of all the headings on all the pages—right across the very top of the broadsheet left to right next to the masthead. 114 ARRESTED. It was impossible to miss. This was Brisbane's *Courier Mail* speaking.

But what did this newspaper story have to do with the Solider family? Theirs was a very private world, an inward-looking family of routine and order. What the world did on the streets of Brisbane had nothing to do with the Solider family gathered around the table for lunch about to say grace. God himself had instructed: *Set yourselves apart.*

Glory sneaked a peak at the bowed heads across the plastic tablecloth, lots of closed eyes. Blank faces for everyone, empty as dinner plates, except perhaps for her oldest sister Elsie. Glory wondered if Elsie's face might have changed colour with the hullabaloo, changed to match the hue of the warm pink tongue they were about to eat. 'For what we are about to eat may the Lord make us truly grateful.' Glory wanted to catch Gracie's eye, to laugh.

Onward had brought the Saturday paper home at lunch after his ward round at the children's hospital. He brought the paper home and with it the beginnings of MotherJoy's story, and a very particular story it turned out to be. The mounting of a morals campaign in a strangely responsive social and cultural environment, the only state in Australia it could happen, (so it is told) at the only time in history (so the story goes). He brought home a bomb wrapped up in that particular Saturday edition, a bomb which exploded around the table that lunchtime—ricocheting out into the community and back into the family while the warmed tongue, mashed potato and peas went cold.

MotherJoy lost her footing. MotherJoy reacted.

Perhaps she had been itching for a fight for a while. Did it take her by surprise? Or maybe, the responsibility of those six children was too much, was eating her up, those six girls now seated around the plastic folds, their heads bowed in prayer. They were growing up fast too, ready to leave MotherJoy's kitchen one by one to swim into the world. The skin of all those girls was becoming slippery with sunbaking oil. They were sliding downstream—Elsie was already almost nineteen years old. Fear of her downfall became the trigger for doing something, doing *anything* for God. Putting a stop to it—whatever 'it' was. MotherJoy's own salvation was at stake no less, a salvation that depended on her children, her girls—the jewels in her crown—getting it right. As simple as that.

There they all were, around the table in order. You could trace MotherJoy's spiritual journey through the names of her children, from the top to the bottom. Elsie first on MotherJoy's right represented non-belief; the middle three, Mary, Ruthy and Eve stood for repentance, being born again, belief; the Little Girls to her left, Glory and Gracie, spoke of hope for her arrival at the pearly gates—Glory for rejoicing, Gracie for grace.

You could trace them in other ways too, something Glory likes to do in this story, to keep her sisters close by, to keep them from drifting away. There was Elsie, the one with the now pinkly face, who was an organ player studying music and maths at university. She was a brilliant sight-reader, everybody said. Next came Mary, who liked to clean her teeth after every meal as white as goodness she said; who once persuaded Little Glory to kneel down and pray in a ferry in the middle of a river-crossing in order to stop a barge on its way down to the river hitting the ferry; who laughed then at the near miss and said it was funny, which it was. When the ferryman mumbled thanks for saving them all, as he helped them step out of the boat onto the pontoon, Mary's face was so open, inviting, the ferryman didn't know where to look. Then Ruthy, the third daughter, who would learn to think for herself on the conveyor belt at the Golden Circle cannery in Northgate, yet at the same time be able to fly so close as to almost clasp MotherJoy's heart—how did she do that? And Eve, the fourth of the big girls, the reserved one, the one named after her great conversion MotherJoy said, the one who liked dissections—she brought home a dead rat once—who insisted that if you dissect things enough, into lots of pieces, you begin to understand. Eve understood MotherJoy, Glory reckons, the way she understood the circulatory and nervous systems of the body. She was terribly clever like that.

Finally, at the bottom of the family, the two Little Girls, Glory and Gracie, like twins Onward said, born less than a year apart. Gracie was the baby, who liked to be tucked in under her sister's wing. Glory felt stronger with Gracie in the world; Gracie gave Glory courage *to be*. With Gracie holding her hand, almost from the beginning, Glory thought she would be safe.

The family, tucked into the dining room table, waited to say grace. They were starving, eager to get eating. But Onward and MotherJoy weren't in their places. No: MotherJoy and Onward exploded out through the bedroom door where they'd been arguing, as if *one flesh*, to stand before their children and the lunchtime spread.

Bang! With the *Courier Mail* in her right hand MotherJoy slammed the front page with her left fist. *Bang, bang, bang.* Time stood still, all hunger forgotten, the whole family suspended. What was wrong? How hot they were. Shouldn't someone shut the blinds on the verandah to keep the sun off the floorboards? Glory suddenly wanted to go to the toilet to do a poo. But nobody moved, nobody said a word. Not even MotherJoy. *Bang, bang.*

Onward cowered in her wake, while trying to look tall. He kept licking his hand to smooth his hair across his bald patch. The other hand fiddled with loose coins in his pocket. Perhaps he wished he had never shown her the front page; perhaps he wished he had forgotten to pick up the paper that Saturday morning at the bottom of the road on his way to work.

Bang.

The whole family knew that something terrible was happening before their very eyes. If only they could stop it, whatever it was, go back to before. None of them wanted to hear what MotherJoy had to say.

MotherJoy had been happy earlier, playing the piano for morning tea, hands and fingers all over the keys in trills and arpeggios. 'Playing,' she said, 'not practising, no, this is music to sup on.' She liked to tease them all with it, fill the house with warm, homemade runny jam: 'O Danny Boy' to loosen the throat, J. S. Bach's 'Erster Teil Praeludium 1' with which to enter God's presence. She spoke of heavenly things. Her fingers thumped away and she smiled this way in that enticing way of hers. Everyone forgot themselves when she played. That morning was no different. Just before this altercation, with the trill of the piano for a treat, she was oh-so-close to doing that, to letting go: *completely*.

How quickly things change.

Once the banging stopped, once the newspaper was relatively still, the sisters could read the words POLICE, CLASHES, STUDENTS, the headline print bolded, black and upright. They read: '1500 sit in street: Mob protests over new laws'. And then they saw MotherJoy pointing at the photograph under the headline and looking Elsie's way.

Elsie was over the far side of the table, next to Onward's empty chair and furthermost from MotherJoy. (She must have guessed what the newspaper was reporting, surely? Although it was impossible to tell who it was in the newsprint the photograph was grainy, the picture small.) She knew where she had been the previous day. There had been scuffles and arrests at the sit-down demonstration in Roma Street in the city and later, in King George Square. She must have recalled how a policeman bailed her up—but she hadn't seen the camera in all the confusion, not by the look of innocence now on her face.

'I am ashamed of you!'

Kaboom! MotherJoy spat out the ordinary words as expletives.

Those five words sprayed across the room, across the lunchtime spread of cold meat. Elsie sat frozen, dead straight in her chair, jaw locked, unblinking. Those five words—*I am ashamed of you*—grafted together the bodies of the six daughters and entered their mouths and throats to circulate with their blood, settled in a skin around their lungs, a crust on their hearts; to congeal in all their hidden and not so hidden places, inside and out.

15

MotherJoy went into shock; she boiled with outrage. She suddenly became interested in politics, she read newspapers; she questioned everything. Things began to be different.

Three or so decades later, just before MotherJoy had her heart operation, Big Glory went on an excursion to the National Library of Australia, to find the photo and master the newspaper room and microfiche and photocopying machines. She decided to see for herself if what she remembered was true—Elsie had given her a tip off about the date, boasted about it once being her first foray into the news. Glory found the place where they kept the *Courier Mail* in great big grey filing drawers. She found the year she wanted and spread of months. She worked out how to thread the reels on the sprockets and how to position the pages on the screen. She found the exact paper, the actual day.

There it is—*Courier Mail*, 1967, early September—first report of the day, front-page news, leader in a string of further exposés all about the growing civil disobedience and unrest in Brisbane, a melee with three thousand students.

And there *she* is, Glory's big sister, Elsie Solider, plumb in the middle of the front page, smack bang amongst forced lifts and throttle holds. 'A girl student' it reads, being questioned by a policeman in uniform, another policeman nearby ready to take a swing. Glory can't quite believe it—it's Elsie all right. It was true. Her blood rattles with the fan. The figure in the picture is in profile with her torso set in Elsie's characteristic way, her shoulders, her chin, her hand, just so. Glory is transfixed by the face.

Look! That is her! Glory wants to exclaim, pointing at her sister's cheek, a cheek turned away from the camera. But she swallows her words, consumes her excitement at what she finds, cornered as she is in the library with its hum of silence and the quiet of research. You can turn and rustle pages in libraries, whisper questions to the librarians on shift, clunk coins into photocopying machines, but you can't burst out with joy, *protest* at what you find—little kiss curls around the ears, black-rimmed glasses, a cap-sleeved polyester number with a ruffle across the princess line. Glory fancies her sister's dress is the colour of lemon with off-white details; she remembered she wanted it as a hand-me-down. And that left hand resting against her cheek in a gestural and characteristic pose, suggesting: *Who me?*

Glory clamps her hand over her open mouth. She can just about feel words exploding on her tongue. Still, true to nature, she doesn't speak a word—practised at obeying rules—but writes, furiously, in her notebook, the scratch of the pencil barely keeping up with the tumble of what she is thinking. She writes: *It really is her. This really did happen.*

Glory pays for a full-size copy of the tear-page: purple ink on gloss paper. She hides the evidence away, not telling the others about it, not even Elsie. She doesn't want to remind her big sister, bring it up. If she tells Elsie she's been hunting for evidence, she might have to tell her about what it is she's beginning to write.

When Elsie talked about this protest, she confessed she didn't know what it was about really, politics weren't her thing at university. She simply went on the march for a boy named Brett. 'I thought he was terribly smart,' she said, 'terribly committed.' Brett was learning to be a vet and he wore a nylon shirt and tie and long white socks. 'How funny.' Glory loved the way Elsie then started to laugh at this footnote to her history. In trills and purls. 'And afterwards we went to the Belle Vue Hotel for a drink, you know, the beautiful old one that Joh knocked down. Opposite parliament. ' That was their only date.

16

Nobody ate very much for lunch. Onward tried to slice the pressed tongue but it fell apart all chunky. He sat clasping the knife and fork on either side of the plate, his lungs heaving for air. He was left in charge of the meal table, the eating, while MotherJoy dressed down Elsie in the big bedroom. Elsie had to pick her way across the floor on tiptoe, careful not to step on the newspaper that MotherJoy had shredded. The three big girls left behind ran sweaty palms over their skirts, smoothed the material down the length of their legs to pull the bottom edge over their knees. Glory could see the tops of their arms disappear under the table as they felt for their hems. She squeezed Gracie's hand more tightly, hooked up their little fingers. Under other circumstances they'd call this finger-hold 'a finger kiss' but not on this occasion. Afterwards Onward disappeared into his study, buried himself in his Christian books.

That evening MotherJoy took to her bed. Onward said: 'Don't disturb her, she needs to rest.' The next day, the big girls prepared the Sunday roast pork and potatoes for lunch in the morning as usual, turned on the oven, and the Solider family went to church without MotherJoy.

The minister and elders asked after her in their kindly pastoral way as they pressed hands with Onward and the rest of the congregation in the breezeway of the vestibule door. They said special prayers that morning to keep everybody safe in this time of civil unrest (did they recognise the paper's cover-girl?). Onward muttered excuses to everybody—MotherJoy had *never* missed church before. Glory shook the minister's hand too. Glory loved the clasp of warm, praying flesh—the pressing of godliness in this way, the incalculable hold of sweaty rightness. She made sure she shook hands each Sunday, morning and evening, as a seal of approval. She liked the way the minister looked at her, liked his smile from on high. But she did wish MotherJoy hadn't stayed home. It didn't seem right to miss a Sunday. Not to be with God.

This Sunday morning, the Solider family sang the hymns louder and with more insistence than ever before, as if by singing beautifully and in harmony with each other and the congregation they could drown out the unruly crowd of private feelings—mob protest even, headlocks and half-Nelsons. They barricaded themselves against the world and this illegal demonstration with gusto: 'Onward Christian soldiers / marching as to war'. Glory loved singing hymns. She loved the feel of the sounds rising out of her throat across the soft palate and down her tongue like a slippery dip. The words huddled there in her mouth before pouring out in what seemed at first an unsettling gush, only to become warm liquid song, sweet honey. Notes and words floated, suspended in soft clouds. 'How Great Thou Art'. 'What a Friend We Have in Jesus'. Glory sang her heart out and imagined she was someone else. It was a way of forgetting that she had to go back home after this. She was learning to read music too and sing alto. Elsie smiled at Glory along the pew, made a point of saying Glory had quite a nice voice, that it might even turn into something if she looked after it.

Later, over Sunday lunch—still no MotherJoy—crackling and all, and sweet apple sauce, there was a discussion about exactly that: about the instruments everyone was playing and singing teachers for Glory. Onward said, as if in apology: 'I'm no musician, but I do like to listen to you all play.' The Solider family was like a little orchestra—organ, piano, clarinet, violin, viola, flute and xylophone. Everyone was pleased for the distraction, relieved.

Glory volunteered to take a tray into MotherJoy, still ensconced in bed. In preparation, she laid the tray with a pretty doily and napkin, set the cutlery and arranged the roast pork and potato on the plate, a dollop of sauce, just so. A little salt and pepper. A glass of water. She even went out to the front porch and snipped off a crucifix orchid growing wildly in the rockery up the front steps, a burnt orange and yellow one, the colour of fire, and put it in a peanut paste jar with a little water. MotherJoy would like that she thought, a little reminder of beauty, of paradise—especially given it was a Sunday. Glory knocked gingerly on the bedroom door.

'Ah Glorious Glory Girl, there's a dear, just what I wanted.'

What a comfort these words were after everything that had happened. How Glory loved their sweetness, and the way the room lit up all golden in this cloudburst, as though the sun was out after summer rain. She had called her *Glorious Glory Girl* too; she said: *There's a dear.* Her mother's voice was soft and beguiling, beckoning. MotherJoy patted the bed to draw Glory close. How everything smelt good. How proud Glory was that she'd thought of the orchid too. Something was going right.

Later, after everyone had finished eating, Glory volunteered to fetch MotherJoy's tray. This time she called out in a strong voice: 'Are you finished yet?'

'Yes I'm done.' Glory skipped in. 'You can take it now.' MotherJoy patted the bed a second time. Glory wanted to ask about the orchid, the jar on the tray was empty. MotherJoy must have guessed her thoughts: 'I've pressed your orchid into my Bible. For safekeeping. Such a pretty flower too.'

Glory felt really blessed now, and she decided then to take it upon herself to always make things better. She'd find a way to protect and save her mother from any sickness of the world; help keep her eyes on the prize of heaven. She'd be one of the good ones. As Glory decided all this, she realised it might suggest Elsie was bad, and far be it for Glory to separate the sheep from the goats, that was God's job. Oh how it hurt her head to sort these things out! Because all she wanted to do was simply to keep this shiny light in front of her, all yellow and burnt orange. She'd find a way to *shed light*, whatever it took. She kept this cross-your-heart promise to herself, a promise the shape of a crucifix orchid pressed between the pages of her mother's Bible.

17

GLORY KEEPS QUIET about the Glory-story she now writes in earnest—the habit of writing like the habit of praying pressed between the pages of her red notebook. The words fall out in their tens and hundreds, even thousands: *blessings on you*. She can't tell anyone what she is doing, not even Gracie. That this is more serious, more revealing than anything she's written before—she wants to find out what happens next, no question.

She lies to herself too—it takes less courage this way. She doesn't admit to the direction these words are taking. How they bunch together, swirl and form eddies. The way the current picks up in strength with each new thought, each new memory. She's afloat in the middle of a big brown river, perhaps the Brisbane River, like flotsam, and the li-lo she's floating on begins to move with the flow, glide downstream towards the mouth—one thing leads to another. Memories are being dredged up in scoops from the muddy bottom in gloops, such suction.

After MotherJoy's heart operation Glory stays in Queensland for only a couple of days. The nurses tell her the patient is recovering well. The doctors think she'll enjoy a few more years. 'Her heart is strong,' they say. 'These are the best years of her life.' Gracie is staying on—she has a few weeks before she has to return to England. That's why it's good being part of a big family, a tag team.

Glory packs up MotherJoy's clothes in their assortment of plastic freezer bags, the ones MotherJoy bought especially for this task. She arranges the suitcases the way MotherJoy would like them to be arranged, clothes in one, everything else in another—papers and writing materials, sewing gear, hymnbooks and Bibles. It is Gracie who accompanies MotherJoy up the Sunshine Highway in an ambulance to Buderim Hospital and a new lot of staff, new nursing care—much closer to home, nearly there now. This will be some convalescence. 'You'll pull through,' the doctors say, 'we fixed your heart.'

The other girls rally around as much as they can. Things are different now for MotherJoy and Onward. For a start, Onward needs to stop driving: he's too dangerous now that he's losing his memory because of the onset of Alzheimer's. They shop around for a new-fangled motorised wheelchair for MotherJoy, fresh off the production line, the sales of which are booming in Buderim, the retirement Mecca of the Sunshine Coast. Everyone is retiring to Australia's ginger country, near the Big Pineapple, the business of Old People is a roaring trade. The sisters talk to the minister from the church about different ways their parents can get there each Sunday. They cook up two-course meals for Onward (his talk softens with good food, especially with sweet things, and delicatessen cheeses—stilton and brie). They discover the complex where the retirement villa is, that it serves meals in a communal dining room (with cake and cream); they arrange Meals on Wheels in case of emergency. They firm up a weekly appointment with the cleaner, and start to investigate *the next big step*—a nursing home.

18

Historians say 1967 was the year things changed in Brisbane for good. They say the turning point was that civil liberties march in September along Coronation Drive and the banks of the river from the University of Queensland in St Lucia to the heart of the city—Elsie's march. And it wasn't only in the Solider household that there was disturbance. Brisbanites felt unsafe. This kind of unrest and fervour was new to Brisbane, to Queensland. Across Australia in other states, there were protests, mostly to do with the Vietnam War, but not in the Sunshine State, not *here*. Protesting was illegal in Queensland. Elsie's march was all about establishing *the right to protest*, before the next step of protesting something larger like Vietnam. It would have been a farce if it weren't so real.

If the letters to the editor over the following weeks and months were anything to go by, the September march divided public opinion. Ordinary Queenslanders were shocked by what this turn of events might mean. Demonstrators were dismissed as soft-mouthed ratbags. The university was criticised for brainwashing impressionable students. 'If university students can waste time and spend days wandering the streets in protest with their long hair and unruliness, shouting and carrying on and disturbing the peace for normal citizens going about their ordinary, private business,' people said, 'then something is terribly wrong with what they are being taught.' Or something like that. It was as simple as two plus two.

Thankfully, for those Queenslanders who were alarmed at what was happening, the evangelist Billy Graham was coming to town. The whole grubby affair could become the subject of prayer. The Billy Graham Crusade set up its massive open-air meetings at the Brisbane Exhibition Grounds. Many more thousands than the protesters marching along Coronation Drive could ever boast of, squeezed in to hear the Word of God, to confess their sin, to pray and to be saved, not that MotherJoy would have gone, she didn't like these mass services. Glory was too young to go, but the four oldest Soliders went, dressed in pale-coloured muu-muus and white stockings, their hair pulled back in plaits held with bobby pins. Before patting their hands to say goodbye, MotherJoy stood them up on the table, turned her head upside down to check the length of their hems. 'You can't show your knees, now can you?'

19

THE MORAL RIGHT started a war; only this kind of activism and protest was legal. 'We have to gird our loins like real soldiers,' MotherJoy said, 'it is our calling.' She told the Little Girls to put on the armour of God, to gather up swords of truth, don breastplates of righteousness. Once, MotherJoy dressed the Little Girls in their Sunday best even though it was a Saturday afternoon and took them with her in the car, deep into the heart of the city, to the Brisbane Festival Hall on the corner of Charlotte and Albert Street. 'Come along now,' she said, 'we've got a job of work to do. Soliders for Christ, remember.'

Glory and Gracie had no idea what was going on, nor what MotherJoy had in store for them. But they trusted her. Glory liked her puffed sleeves, patent leather shoes. They took with them bundles of STOP and CARE pamphlets as well as other Christian tracts, *Jesus to the Communist World*.

When they got to Festival Hall, it was so crowded they couldn't find a car park nearby and they had a way to walk. MotherJoy wore her white polyester hat, with the flowers, and carried white gloves. The city air blew warm and MotherJoy fluttered along with her hat perched on her head like a nest of a thousand butterflies, the Little Girls in her slipstream. Glory thought her mother might fly to the moon that afternoon. The three of them stopped outside one of the many side doors to the hall on the hard pavement. Glory had never seen so many streams of people in the one place, all off to see the latest thing, *Jesus Christ Superstar*, the posters said, a matinee performance. It didn't look like a church thing.

'Blasphemy! Blasphemy!' MotherJoy began calling out, for all to hear.

She thrust neatly folded pamphlets into the hands of all the people around her, slapped the milling bodies with them if they turned their backs. She used her theatrical voice, the one full of projection, timbre. She was quite good too, Glory thought, how she rolled the first set of consonants in *blasphemy*—a not inconsiderable gift of the tongue. Her voice carried well in the open air—down the pavement and across the street like a mini whirlwind, you could see it swirl above everybody's head, mess with their hair. They'd believe her for sure. Perhaps some lost soul might be saved.

There was a deep simplicity to MotherJoy's beliefs, yet they were unashamedly hearty. She knew what was right and what was wrong, where others erred, and considered she had *the right* to lecture them, the right to protest their fallen, heathen ways. She could make a difference, she told her Little Girls, and that's why they dressed up, in their Sunday best. Glory liked wearing the black shoes in particular because they were only brought out for special occasions—like the saving of waywards—but for all that, they did pinch a bit on the heel. Later that evening, MotherJoy popped the blisters with a needle that she heated in a flame on the gas stove and soaked Glory's sore feet in a warm Physohex bath. Glory loved her mother's gentle hands on her feet as she wrapped them up in a towel.

On the streets nobody listened. This ungodly audience just laughed and leered at the three of them. They waved extravagantly at the Little Girls.

Glory and Gracie handed things out too, with smiles all around, just as they did at the barbecues on Saturday nights under the grapevine at the back of the house, when they took around trays of piled-up fresh pineapple and gob-sized meringues. The Soliders liked to entertain, they put their best foot forward, they had a reputation to feed whether it was with Christian Medical Fellowship, Scripture Union, Youth Group or the Evangelical Union—groups they always referred to by their initials. The tongs came out with the barbecue apron for Onward to cook in (it was the only cooking he did apart from bucket-loads of mango chutneys and cumquat marmalade once a year). Trays of sausages were pulled out of the freezer the night before. Ruthy was in charge of cutting up the pineapple until she got a job at the cannery *doing pineapples,* as she liked to put it, over the summer holidays before university. After that she left the cutting up to the Little Girls. Glory loved the smell the pineapples gave off especially when they were very nearly overripe, loved serving people lots of it, until everyone said they were bursting! But nobody was interested in her offerings out here on the streets of Brisbane. Glory wished she could swap the pamphlets in her hand for trays of fresh fruit, or at least have something spectacular and irresistible to give away.

The following Monday, the newspaper reported there were as many as ten thousand people present at the show, a record number. Onward said as much, at tea. The paper also talked about protesters making a fuss—*Jesus is the way, the truth and the light; the righteous shall inherit the earth*—that sort of thing. Onward kept reading. Glory could see the agitation on her mother's face, the horizontal line of her mouth stretched into place. He said: 'You shouldn't have taken the Little Girls. They're too impressionable, Joy dear, for this kind of thing. We want to keep them young.'

The two of them had a small argument about it. They argued in a constrained, almost constipated way. It was so hush-hush you almost couldn't tell that the argument had transpired. Glory would have been hard pressed to know what it was all about, if she weren't so interested in the shape of her mother's mouth, the line it made. Onward repeated the 'shouldn't' part again: 'It *shouldn't* have happened this way.' And MotherJoy pursed her lips even more tightly together. Then, after a long pause, MotherJoy let out a puff of air, her forehead creased like the skin of an old mango. She turned to Glory and Gracie, her face hot now like a rising sun in the morning, and said: 'Run along now, you two.' Dismissed, but not before she gave them each one of Ruthy's rock cakes as a treat.

After that, Onward never said anything more again. Unless there was a private arrangement between the two of them to have discussions pillow to pillow while the girls slept. He certainly didn't mention these things again at the table, in the girls' presence, not that Glory can remember. He let MotherJoy have her way while Glory and Gracie concocted a plan to make things at home better. They became Little Soliders of Christ 'marching as to war / with the cross of Jesus / going on before'.

20

That's how it came about that the Little Girls helped MotherJoy cook tongue: Anatomy for Beginners. Gracie needed some persuading. Glory had to insist that it wasn't *so yuck*, that the tongue they ate for tea was different from the tongues that they heard about being cut out by Communists. In return for helping, Gracie made Glory make a promise and cross her heart, that the next time they went marching with MotherJoy in an anti-Communist march through Queen Street on a Sunday afternoon (for unknown reasons these marches were permissible), *Glory* would be the one to hold the placard that read 'The Communists Want Your Children'. Soon, though, MotherJoy would make a new one for Gracie to hold up: 'Burn a Book a Day for Jesus'.

Glory, on the other hand, rather liked touching and playing with raw meat. Always did. Later, in high school, her friend Lisa thought she was strange about this. Glory tried to explain, said she couldn't help herself, she loved the days MotherJoy came home with different cuts. Great stacks of it too. MotherJoy carried the meat into the house as if it were Christmas, triumphantly, the assortments tucked up in a large blue plastic crate like presents. Then Glory helped MotherJoy sort the meat, all red, soft and squishy, sometimes dribbly—put it into clear plastic bags ready to freeze: piles of mince, ox tail, whole chickens, joints of lamb and pork, and ox tongues for pressing.

Onward was particularly proud of MotherJoy's ability to press tongue. How clever she was, he boasted, how Irish. He said she was pretty good at anatomy too, not like him, he failed anatomy when he was a student.

'Let me show you how to do it,' MotherJoy announced one day, 'it might come in handy, you never know. And you are both growing up so fast.' This last thought seemed to excite and unsettle her at the same time: Glory and Gracie, two halves of a circle around the kitchen table with the ceiling fan whirring in its place overhead.

'We'll begin simply, get onto more complicated procedures as time goes on,' and, with that, she looked knowingly over her tortoiseshell reading glasses at the two of them perched there to make up a tight threesome. 'I'll demonstrate a bit of anatomy while I'm at it.' The Little Girls giggled and MotherJoy smiled. MotherJoy was fun when she was in this kind of mood. They liked these times, winked knowingly at each other; squeezed each other's arm in glee. What more could you want: doing something special on a summer's Saturday afternoon? Learning how to make tongue? Their skins were cool with the fanned air. They were in for a treat.

MotherJoy invited the Little Girls as if into a medical laboratory, to scrub their hands clean, don white coats and safety glasses, and they floated in the wake of her enthusiasm. They fancied they could hear the knives being sharpened just like Onward sharpened them with a swish-swash to carve the meat for dinner, could hear the clink of scalpels and tweezers and grips. For the occasion, MotherJoy went to Onward's study especially to get the surgical kit given out by the hospital as a standard issue. 'You never know when it might come in handy with a growing family,' Glory could hear MotherJoy telling Onward.

MotherJoy liked anatomy. And judging by the way she waved the scalpel about, she was good at dissecting too. Here she was then, a university graduate from Queen's Belfast in Northern Ireland, a practising doctor once—in the early years before she had children. Now in her fifties, a mother of six children, wife to a head-of-department professor-man, busy here with cooking pots and seasonings and the making of tongue to eat, giving undivided attention, to the smallest two of her offspring. She was on a mission from God. It was as though she'd given up on the others already, good as gone. It wouldn't be long before the four big girls disappeared anyway—already cooked. The roads south across the border into other places and beyond flickered in the dark, beckoning. They were ready to fly away, but that's another story.

First the knives were lined up in rows like soldiers on parade. The two tongues placed *splat splat* onto the wooden bread boards. The Little Girls lunged, took a tongue each.

'No squabbling,' MotherJoy intervened. 'Irish Granny said, always cook tongue with two, curled together—.'

'In a kiss,' Gracie said.

'All right then, let's say a kiss, just this once, that's nice.'

With the sharp point of her knife MotherJoy poked at Gracie's tongue first, lying on the table in front of her, wobbling all grey-pink and lumpy. Gracie jumped back, startled. Then MotherJoy got serious, with a wishful tone to her voice, declaratory too, as if instructing a group of medical students around the bed. 'Now listen up. The tongue is a sensory organ. Muscular.' She paused, mid-performance. 'This is where it attaches itself to the back of the throat,' and with a flourish she poked the woolly bit at one end, the raggy bit Glory didn't like to look at. Then she opened her own mouth wide as though she was at a dentist, to show the Little Girls where it came from, 'in situ'.

'Careful!' The Little Girls chorused. 'Don't slip!'

She nearly poked the back of her throat with the point of her knife.

'It's a muscle,' MotherJoy ran on without a beat. 'This is the root, the bit we have to clean up later. Dorsum, filiform papillae, fungiform papillae, vallate papillae, palatopharyngeal, epiglottis.'

The words rattled out of her mouth—wonderful. Unexpected too. They swallow-dived off her tongue the syllables waving about in the air on the point of the knife. It was impressive. How clever she was! Glory tried to repeat the last sentence with its list of terms, mimic its musicality, but the imitation fell out of her mouth all gobbledegook and Gracie fell about laughing.

What with Glory trying to say the words over and over in a repeated singsong—*dor-sum-fili-form-papi-llae-fungi-form-papi-llae-val-late-papill-ae-palat-ophar-yngeal-epi-glotti-epi-glotti*—and Gracie doubling up in laughter, the Little Girls nearly knocked the tongues off their slippery perch. And what was that story about MotherJoy not being very good at anatomy at Queen's? Who said that? Whoever it was must have got her mixed up with Onward. This small exhibition suggested she knew lots of things. Even the tongues seemed to nod with approval, wag their weathered tips in agreement, and dance a jig atop the boards in celebration of the butchery they were being subjected to.

Glory was so tipsy with enjoyment she waltzed around to the other side of the table and threw her arms about MotherJoy. Glory buried her head in her mother's bosom, her arms circled around her waist. 'Careful, I've got a knife!' For a second Glory didn't seem bothered by this, squeezed even harder—'but this is such fun,' Glory said. From the outside, it really looked like this small family gathering didn't have a care in the world. Glory made little popping noises with her mouth, showered MotherJoy with pretend kisses.

'Now then, what's this? Let's get cooking.' MotherJoy raised her arms to flay off her daughter, she'd had enough: 'We haven't got all day.' She was suddenly razor sharp in tone. 'Glory dear, you like looking things up, read the instructions will you?' It was as if Glory had bitten on a stray peppercorn accidentally at the back of the mouth. A turning. Flare of heat. 'Big voice now. There's a girl.' Glory wished she could pop those kisses back down her throat, swallow them whole back into the safety of her tummy. 'Get going.'

Glory-dear read from MotherJoy's 1951 *Good Housekeeping's Home Encyclopaedia*—'T for Tongue: To Pickle a Tongue' and 'Boiled Tongue'— and the girls followed the instructions, step by step.

1 Choose a tongue with as smooth a skin as possible—Glory and Gracie ran their hands over the tongues on the boards, as if to imprint the likeness of each onto their own skin, iron out unseemly bumps.

2 Wash the tongue very thoroughly—the tongues sat curled across the Little Girls' upturned palms awash under the cold running tap, one, then the other, taking turns.

3 Cut off any gristle at the root end—this was MotherJoy's job. She wielded the knife, and spritely too. Chop. Chop.

4 Soak the tongue in water overnight—and they did. The Little Girls slid the tongues into the big grey crock of a pot with a *slurp* and *slop* and watched them bob around, pushed them up and down with their fingers. MotherJoy slapped their hands and water went everywhere. 'Will you stop that!' Peppercorns jumped.

'Read what's next, Gloria. In a loud voice. You're a big girl now.'

5 Then simmer gently with root vegetables, peppercorns.

6 Cook an ox tongue for five to six hours. When cooked, plunge the tongue into cold water, so that the grey skin comes off more easily.

'You don't want to leave the skin on,' MotherJoy warned, and with that she left abruptly, to lie down. Left Glory to tidy up.

21

THE TONGUES DID SOAK overnight and throughout Sunday. There was to be no extra cooking on Sundays, apart from putting the roast on in the morning before church, that was the Solider law: Sunday was strictly a rest day. From time to time during the afternoon however, when no one was looking, Glory lifted the lid on the saucepan at the back of the stove, to watch the tongues bobbing about and to poke at them. She talked to them in whispers, like friends, blew bubbles their way. *Softens them up nicely,* she remembered MotherJoy saying.

Come Monday, MotherJoy cooked the tongues in the giant crock. And in the afternoon, after school—six hours later—Glory watched MotherJoy plunge the tongues into a sink full of cold water as instructed. MotherJoy peeled off the softened outer skin in long strips like a banana skin. Glory wished she could help, but didn't dare ask. MotherJoy was agitated again, keen to have the job done, wash-up, lie down—'just for forty winks now'—before the rush of teatime.

To finish off, with a flick and a push, MotherJoy laid the tongues in a pudding basin—her lips just about disappeared with concentration—first Gracie's tongue then Glory's, although they'd be hard pressed to tell which was which. *Flip flap.* The tongues curled around each other in an imagined kiss before MotherJoy covered them over with a saucer, pressing them down with a brick on top. If you listened closely you could hear little popping noises as the meat squeezed tight. As if the tongues were letting out air bubbles. *Pop, pop* overnight. To be tipped out when set. To swim in clear jelly, with green peppercorn speckles. Lolly pink when carved. Onward sliced thinly neat circles for everyone, which they ate heartily. Glory's favourite meat. And MotherJoy promised to bequeath the *Home Encyclopaedia* to Glory. On the title page she wrote Glory's name in large letters and the words 'T is for Tongue' for quick reference, so she wouldn't forget to give it to her when she left home.

That wasn't the only thing Glory had to remember from the anatomy lesson. Not the only thing she couldn't forget.

It's a sin

For unaccountably—and almost undetectable at first—as they were preparing the tongue, MotherJoy was crying. Glory watched her surreptitiously. At one point a single tear dropped onto the silver of the knife, splashed onto the skin of the tongue as if in slow motion. Glory saw Gracie's mouth open just at this point as if about to say something only to close on second thoughts. Was that when MotherJoy took a phone call? Got distracted? Things had been going so well too, MotherJoy was happy, she was laughing, and Glory felt sure MotherJoy leaned her way when she squeezed a hug. Only for it all to end abruptly. *Flip flop*. How was it that MotherJoy could turn like this? What had they done wrong?

Glory could only make guesses.

One minute MotherJoy was all heart, aglow in the light, the next she shut down, contracted into herself. Like being saved by being born again, except in an opposite but equal motion. Not to soar into the clouds, buoyed up by the Spirit's wings and by the momentum of flight and the promise of a jewelled and heavenly crown, but to plummet, crash, become darkness itself. Glory wished it wasn't so. Wondered what she could do now to help her mother to keep her equilibrium. If only she could divert MotherJoy before whatever it was that got her took root. If only Glory was old enough to cook the family tongue for everyone.

22

It was Lisa, her new friend at school, who would tell Glory she must never eat tongue again.

'You have to stop, Glory. Even on sandwiches. Eating tongue is bad for you.'

When Lisa said this to Glory, they were both in grade eight in the quadrangle eating big lunch together, as the two of them were in the habit of doing before English.

Lisa said: 'Mum says if you keep eating tongue something bad will happen to you.' She said her mother said you should never eat anything that has done an important job in a previous life.

'Even when it's your favourite?' Glory asked, 'because I really like it.'

'Even more so,' Lisa said, and that was that. There was no arguing. 'Just because you like the taste of something doesn't mean you have to eat it.'

At home, Glory could eat more tongue than her fair share, if none of the others around the table wanted their portion. But at school, at big lunch with all the other schoolgirls, when Lisa told her to stop scoffing the leftover tongue that sat between slices of white bread, she did, she threw it into the scraps bin. From then on Glory had a crunchy peanut paste and homemade marmalade sandwich for lunch. Lisa sometimes had a bite. They'd giggle and pull each other's hair and wrestle and hug each other as they rolled on the concrete floor of the school quadrangle in the sun, their uniforms all over the place, careful to avoid the teachers and Sisters on lunch patrol.

Glory loved being this close to Lisa; she loved the idea of being liked, of discovering how you could be friends. She'd do anything to agree with Lisa in order to bring them closer and for a time they were inseparable. The two imagined the quadrangle was a bank of green grass down by the river and pretended they knew what it was like to be in love. Separately, mind you. But surely tongues must have wagged.

Glory never spoke of these things to anyone. She kept the anatomies of home and school apart. At home she didn't talk about pressed bodies, about giggling and playing or making friends. At school she never mentioned God and sin. These opposite tastes never once curled in a kiss.

The most secret of all places

23

Angel was an activist. She appointed herself as moral guardian to the children of Queensland. She railed against what she called permissive educationalists, teachers who promoted alternative lifestyles, unabashed sex education, the spread of venereal disease, moral corruption, homosexual marriage and lesbianism—she liked to list it in this way. People thought her mad. In the press she was called a crazy reactionary, irrational, a ratbag.

Her regular letters to the editor appeared in the *Courier Mail*, often as the lead letter. She circulated pamphlets and was a regular on talkback radio. She called out *Shame! Shame!* in public meetings. She wrote letters to politicians and lawmakers pleading with them to do something. She was mentioned in the Senate's *Hansard* in federal parliament as well as Queensland's *Hansard*, applauded by the conservative leaders of the time—Premier Joh Bjelke-Petersen and his mates. As well as being an active member of STOP and CARE, set up to 'protect children and teenagers from all forms of moral corruption, and whatever else would tend to contribute to their delinquency and moral harm', she became a member of the Queensland League for National Welfare and Decency, and the Festival of Light. She was on a mission to save children's lives by controlling the books they read, always believing, *believing* she could rid this world of sin, that it was within her powers to save souls, that she was God's 'right-hand man' on earth. And that is how the death list came into being.

My mother, Dr Angel Rendle-Short, was unafraid of making her views known.

In one Letter to the Editor published in the *Courier Mail* she poses the question: 'Who are these so-called educators who are spooning this garbage to our children? I will tell you,' she writes:

> They are manipulating and twisting these young minds, and they are deliberately tearing apart the God-given institution of the family which is part of the very warp and woof of our nation.

In a typed foolscap pamphlet buried in the National Archives of Australia in Canberra, entitled 'Sowing the Wind, Reaping the Whirlwind', she insists:

> At last we begin to understand why so many of our fine young people, often children from upright Christian homes, are going off the rails, and around the age of thirteen when they start High School, before our very eyes, are sucked into the whirlpool of sex, revolt against their parents, drugs, violence, vice and crime ... They are being carefully instructed in these things; and being instructed they become hooked!

In the opening paragraph of this pamphlet underneath the masthead, Angel quotes from the libel case against D. H. Lawrence's book *Lady Chatterley's Lover*—my mother always liked anything to do with the judiciary.

Her love of legal matters had something to do with her belief in God as judge; it also had to do with her fondness for her brothers, in particular one brother who was a judge in Northern Ireland. She sometimes took my sister and me to sit in the public gallery of the law courts in George Street, Brisbane to hear criminal cases, so riveted was my mother by the goings on.

On another occasion in the National Library of Australia I tripped over a photograph of my mother in the Brisbane *Sunday Mail*. I tell you, when I saw her, rockets went off. She jumped out of the newsprint. It was in an article about the future of a new women's FM radio station in Brisbane, 4BW the first of its kind in Queensland. 'WOMEN AMONG

WOMEN!', The caption roared. 'That's my mother,' I blurted out to the librarian, who was looking casually over my shoulder, checking I had everything I needed. I'm not sure she believed me. 'It's really her,' I insisted, surprised by the loudness of my voice. You can find the article in the archive and see her for yourself—*Sunday Mail*, 9 November 1975, page sixteen. *It's really her.*

I would have been fifteen at the time though I knew nothing about this particular event. On the occasion of the 4BW starting committee being elected, a meeting of more than nine hundred women was held. Angel managed to stop proceedings in ten minutes flat. She was concerned that if a majority of 'radical women' were elected to the committee, family values wouldn't be upheld, rather, there would be advancement of abortion on demand, the placing of contraception vending machines in schools, the support of alternative lifestyles such as lesbianism and homosexuality.

'I want to put a motion, I want to put a motion,' Angel cried out from the floor. Angel and her followers had stacked the meeting.

'Switch her off, switch her off,' the paper reported the 4BW supporters yelled out. It was too late, it was explosive. It would take another four year before 4BW went to air.

I do remember the fake costume jewellery she was wearing that day, the off-lime spotted suit I see in the photo—I rather liked her in this outfit. Angel liked wearing this suit to church and I liked to lay my head across her lap so I could imagine the cream spots were cream-cake kisses pressing against my willing cheek. I remember smoothing my tears across the twin ridge of her thighs because my mother made the love of Jesus so enticing.

Who knows what else Angel brought to a halt, at least temporarily? I wish I had a list of all the confrontations. I recall finding her dress-ups in the small dressing room off the main bedroom: different hats and scarves, oversized purple tinted sunglasses, jewellery to fancy up her attire. She often put on disguises when trying to stop film screenings and storm meetings. It didn't work; organsiers soon knew it was her. I loved to hide in my mother's dressing room, away from everybody, in amongst Angel's blouses and dresses and fox furs, her hairbrushes and powders. It was a magic place, a place of change and possibility. When playing hide-and-seek with my little sister—playing Squashed Sardines—I'd always end up there, and she always knew where to find me.

24

WHEN I WAS SMALL, on some Saturday nights when my family wasn't entertaining people from church with barbecues, the kids would beg to have a slide night. We'd crowd into the lounge, close the curtains and *ooh and aah* at my father's pictures of us, his family.

In my family we made our own entertainment. We didn't have television. A television was a thing of the devil, like rock music, like long hair. Instead, bunched up along green vinyl lounge chairs, we hummed along to the slide projector with exclamations and sighs punctuated by the *click-yer, click-yer* of the forwards button, and my father's voice, saying: 'Next!'

'Look! There's Francesca in the backyard, playing outside with the pink bath.' Those plastic sandals are very sophisticated, aren't they?

The most secret of all places

One of my sisters tells me it looks like it's before we moved to St Lucia because I am so young.

I like the recall of warm skin from those Saturday nights, the feeling of body against body. The way we shunted in close to each other, squeezed ourselves together without any sense we might be encroaching, without any consideration of private space. There was a stuffiness too because of the closed curtains, the way the air hung heavy and smelly like old wallpaper, an always-smell of sweaty skin joining us up together, mustiness from our unwashed hair underscoring that we were from the same family. Each time we viewed our slides, no matter what order they were put into the carousels, we would laugh at exactly the same ones.

In my family my father took all the photographs. He hung his beloved Kodak Retina in its brown leather case around his neck; he framed and sized up his children through the lens, guessing at distances; he liked the science of the art in those pre-digital days. I can see him now getting a measure of the light with the handheld selenium meter, how he stretched his extended arm up to the sun, how he made adjustments with his eye, paused, considered. 'Now then,' he would say, clearing his throat to begin. He took his time. He concentrated hard.

The funny thing is I can't remember him telling us what to look at, when to turn, who he wanted and didn't want in the frame. He did like to cough to clear his throat, though—*herch-haugh, herch-humm*. He would puncture our lives with other small conjunctive phrases too, such as: 'What's the score?' 'What's the plan?' 'Let's press on, shall we?' Sometimes he even dared ask my mother questions—we thought him very bold.

Looking at photographs is a bit like reading books; they invite acute feeling. You reveal yourself in the most intimate of moments. They elicit desire; *illicit* desire. Because in my family desire was illicit, like alcohol, like dancing. If you pay enough attention to small things, there is a chance for connection, a chance for transformation and transfiguration to occur. Writing grows skin, grows bones, a new heart. Just watch. D. H. Lawrence knew this. He attests that *Lady Chatterley's Lover* was a beautiful book, that it was tender like a naked body.

25

Little Glory's mother said *Lady Chatterley's Lover* was a filthy book. Dirty. Smut. It was wicked MotherJoy said and didn't deserve to be read. She said it should go on a dung heap, although she wouldn't want to contaminate her own compost with pages of this kind. Oh no. Writing about it like this makes the older Glory think of the wet smell and hot steam of green dung sploshing in the chookyard—MotherJoy was at home cleaning out the pens—of the squirt out from behind the ducks. The acrid smell of fresh urine. MotherJoy slipping and sliding on her feet.

You think too much, Gloria; thinking is dangerous.

Big Glory takes a closer look at her salvaged copy of Lawrence's book. She found it in a garage sale, the book wet through, soggy from sitting in a box underneath a downpipe. The book is one of the small library she's building of all the books MotherJoy wanted to ban. She dries the pages out carefully with a blow heater.

This *Lady Chatterley* cost Glory ten cents. It is an old copy in the classic Penguin colours of orange and white. It has a Pocket Library stamp on it, and a stranger's name scrawled in pencil on the title page: 'Cody Blair, December 1965', the same year the ban on *Lady Chatterley's Lover* was lifted in most states in Australia. This edition is complete, unexpurgated, published in 1960 in England with a special publisher's dedication to the twelve jurors, three women and nine men, who returned a verdict of Not Guilty in the Old Bailey trial.

Glory asks around: 'Do you remember when *Lady Chatterley's Lover* was banned and when the ban was lifted? Did you own a copy? Do you recall the fuss?'

'Who could forget it?' a dinner-party friend says.

'Didn't a publisher in Australia arrange for the copy to be sent to them from England, page by page, as a way to circumvent Australian Customs?' Grace's husband asks.

The most secret of all places

'Oh yes, *Lady Chatterley's Lover* and then *Portnoy's Complaint*, the other naughty book,' Glory's girlfriend pipes up. 'My parents had a copy of *Portnoy's Complaint*. They'd have parties, do readings, but were careful about who they invited, because they didn't want to get busted. All very underground. Hilarious when you think about it.'

Glory forces herself to read the book, every word, and *forces* is the word, for with each syllable she hears MotherJoy's voice reciting the words that her daughter is reading. MotherJoy is in Glory's head. This book is such a difficult one to love, a difficult one through which to find a *new way* to love. Glory wants to get out, to escape, instead she's stuck between these pages. As she reads, even to herself in silence, even late at night in bed when completely on her own, when she reads for *herself* (even in one of those orange, Penguin-cover T-shirts, the *Lady Chatterley's Lover* version she was given as a joke by an ex-lover), it's impossible not to hear her mother's inflection, her diction, the pitch, the protest in her recitation. Impossible for Glory not to feel dirty herself. To be honest, Glory doesn't even understand why MotherJoy fixated on this book. It wouldn't have been on the secondary school booklists in Queensland, in the early 1970s. If it were around at all, it would have only been on the university's reading list for English literature, not part of MotherJoy's domain at the time. She was concentrating on saving the young.

Reading it is painful, but Glory persists. She experiments. Glory tries reading *Lady Chatterley's Lover* in different places, in a noisy room, in the foyer of the National Library, a gallery, in an airport with great multitudes of ordinary voices in a thrum around her as a method to drown out that single, characteristic voice of her mother's. But all she can hear, all these years later in whatever place she puts herself, are the words, the register, the phrasing, just as she once heard them being said. A voice to make her lumpy and jumpy. A recitation to make her skin soiled. Even if she is now forty-three years of age.

26

GLORY IS RETURNING to Queensland for the first time since MotherJoy's quadruple heart operation. Preparing for it is a physical challenge, much as taking a body to the gym to get into shape. She wants to give her body the best chance in MotherJoy and Onward's presence. She wants to learn to stand solid in the family, without melting to jelly or dissolving to vapour.

Her friends and workmates tell her how good it will be, they're jealous of her going north even if it's for a short time. 'Queensland is gorgeous at this time of year,' they say. 'How lucky for you to have a break there. If everything else fails, you'll be able to have a swim in the surf, walk along the beach.' They don't understand what Glory is worried about, not really. To look at her, she seems so strong, so independent—fiery even—Glory strikes quite a pose. She looks at home in the art circles she and her friends inhabit. They cannot imagine her being afraid: they don't believe her, actually. They certainly can't understand why she has to take Valium just to get there (she only admits this to a few). 'What can your mother really do? What's the worst that can happen?'

Glory arrives in Buderim to find MotherJoy on the verandah of the retirement villa, reading. She's reading history, reading about the potato famine in Ireland and the Ascendency. 'Such an interesting book,' are MotherJoy's first words, 'the women in the mobile library are wonderful. Onward and I are so blessed.'

MotherJoy's hands rest across the open book as she peers at Glory, intently. Glory reminds herself of how she'll have to slow her breathing here, get used to this weighted silence again, let her lungs fill with humidity. She'll have to find nuances in the weather once more to talk about, is thankful there is *a lot* of weather about in Queensland (she arranges different cloud formations in her head in preparation). It's easy to forget how much of a thing silence is in the Solider family, how it can be such an interrogation. Each time Glory returns she has to learn about it again, from scratch. Silence is always a call to answer—the right way, mind. Glory can never find her tongue. Certainly not about things that matter.

'So, how are you?' Glory asks, trying her hand at taking the initiative.

'Oh, we're all right. Thank you. Not so poorly of late.' And MotherJoy does seem not so poorly, even strong. With her rejuvenated heart. 'Let's have a cup of tea, shall we?'

Yes, a cup of tea, something to do, an activity to breach the gap. What a good idea. MotherJoy can be so attentive when she wants to be; it's almost touching.

'Onward dear,' MotherJoy calls out, 'do you want a cup of tea too? Glory is here now.'

Onward must be in his room, amongst his books where he feels he belongs. He loves it in there. MotherJoy says he's preparing his very last manuscript for publication online, a manuscript on the authority of the Bible, the authorised version, King James. But he's slow, forgetful, gets frustrated. She says he should have been better advised. 'At his age, after all his books, publishing like this doesn't do him justice.' They are both in their middle to late eighties. MotherJoy doesn't think she'll ever have time to read it, but she agrees it's good that he's kept busy.

'Onward does better with regularity,' MotherJoy says, confidingly. 'Things rotate here around food. How do you have your tea, Gloria? Onward!' She shouts.

'A drop of milk, no sugar, thanks.'

'I can't drink proper tea any more, not like I used to. Burns my throat,' and she holds her hand below her chin as if to protect her whole neck. 'What's to be done?'

When she gets up to put on the kettle with those few steps across the lounge room to the small kitchen, Glory watches. MotherJoy seems to want to defy life itself—defy that *onwards* strike of the clock on the hour. It's the way she swings across the room; her arms, her body, skin and bones swish back and forth in tiny dance steps so that Glory imagines her mother as a small girl. All jiggly with the boiling water too, bouncing atoms in the heat. Glory imagines a clap of hands from Irish Granny, MotherJoy's mother, followed by lemonade for afternoon tea. There's something ticklish and innocent about MotherJoy when she's like this. Mesmerising to watch. It reminds Glory of how she loves to hear her mother play the piano, hands all over the keys in trills and arpeggios. There is an indefatigable air about her, Glory thinks: perhaps MotherJoy believes she actually is invincible and will always *go on*. The dance of her bones seems to suggest just such a thing—a dance of a mended heart to defy ageing, stop death.

'You know Glory dear,' MotherJoy says then, as if she can read Glory's thoughts, 'last Sunday at church I was able to stand up for all four hymns. I don't play hymns anymore, I've left the piano behind.' She flounces back into the armchair with a puff of air. Smiles.

What Glory wants to know is how will it happen? How do we die? Right now, MotherJoy looks like she could go on forever even though she gets tired, while her daughter marvels at the distance she's flown that morning to see this particular show: pleased to be here. Glory wonders if she might not be able to kiss her mother this time, she feels full of promise. Perhaps she'll try it later on, when it's time to go.

She's wondering how she might find a way to summon courage, lulled into a false sense of security, when everything changes. It comes out of nowhere. Nothing in the visit up until this point suggested this turnabout was on its way. Glory should know better.

It happens as Onward walks in to sit down at the table for that nice cup of tea MotherJoy promised. He's barely touched the orange flower cushion with his bottom when MotherJoy whips round to Glory and says, sharply: 'You shouldn't wear a cleavage like that. That blouse is disgusting. In front of Father too. Cover yourself up, girl! I am ashamed of you.' It's not just the way she says it, although this is bad enough—she's not joking, this strike of hers is a question of morality—but it's how she reaches across the table with her hand, her hand is cold, and she squashes together the two sides of Glory's shirt, pulls and slaps at her daughter's skin.

She says: 'You know what I think. I think I can smell the dung of Jezebel. Isn't that what happens to whores?'

Onward doesn't know where to look, what to say. He opens and shuts his mouth. Glory is paralysed. She blushes deep red to her hairline and wishes she had put on that other shirt that morning, the one without buttons; the one up to the throat. What was she thinking? The shirt she has on is buttoned through to *nearly* the top, a short V-neck is the current fashion, and she is pretty flat chested anyway. Did MotherJoy really say *Jezebel's* name—did Glory hear right? Did her mother mean it? A whore? Why did it always come down to this, to how Glory chose to live her life? Thankfully, her mother didn't know half of it, Glory was careful to make sure things about her life didn't slip out.

The most secret of all places

Glory tries to steady her breath without showing it, sips her cup of tea, and is pleased she took a whole Valium now, not just half as she thought she should. She tries to swallow a way through to the other side of this scene. Reminds herself that this too will pass.

But not before Onward breaks up the silence by reciting grace. He has the habit of saying it now before any food or drink, before even a sip from a glass of water passes his lips. His prayer comes to the rescue. 'For what we are about to receive may the Lord make us truly grateful.' He repeats grace three times, slowing the pace as if to a full stop, as if his words can wipe out—possibly *forgive*—MotherJoy's words. While Glory pretends she's deaf, to everything.

And then another awful silence falls on the small party. It is always like this. Glory is glad she'll be in Queensland for only a night and a day. You never know what else is on its way.

27

IT IS ALWAYS like this.
Glory remembers once when she was in primary school by the Brisbane River with some friends, when she was allowed to stay over at her new friend's place. Sandra stopped being her friend the next day, because MotherJoy was weird. The only way Little Glory could comfort herself, was to keep on insisting that Jesus was still her best friend at Quiet Time.

The day it happened, Sandra had on her pink wings, a birthday present from her mother, pink feather wings with plastic elastics for her arms to go through. And it had been going along swimmingly too. Sandra danced the whole day through with the wings in place, danced around the desks in the classroom, in and out of the tuckshop, across the oval—as trippingly as her rather galumphing footfall would allow—she really looked like she could fly to the stars. Everyone wanted to follow her. She was the most popular girl at primary school and everyone wanted to be her friend. The reward came when Sandra invited a group of girls home to stay—for a coven, Sandra said, to tease—thirteen of them, including Glory, to sleep over. The only reason MotherJoy agreed was because Sandra's father was in the church.

Early on in the evening, Glory taught the girls a new card game: Shoot the Moon, the game Ruthy had taught her and Gracie during the holidays, downstairs underneath the house. Glory showed the girls how to deal the pack of playing cards, how to bid, score, and how trumps worked to advantage—always hearts. How to bid. Score. Glory felt very worldly, dangerous, on the cusp of something. It was like a grand opening act to a big piece of theatre, her Glory-character centre stage. Much later, a breath away from midnight, the schoolgirls taught *her* about séances and black magic. This, Sandra declared, was the point of the sleepover and Glory wished now she'd never come.

'We're only playing,' Sandra declared, but Glory wanted to slink backstage. 'It's not real,' Sandra added reassuringly, perhaps to guard against what might unfold.

The girls had the séance down by the Brisbane River at the bottom of a big rambling garden in Indooroopilly (miles away from home, Glory kept reassuring herself), in a garden that you could easily get lost in. They spun the bottle first as a way to get into the spirit of things (Sandra still had on her pink wings, she loved them that much), and girls kissed girls (Glory was never chosen). Then, they tried to lift the bottle that twinkled like a single star in the evening sky in the middle of the circle using magic. They held hands, chanted special spells, but the bottle didn't budge. So they put the littlest and lightest of all the girls in the centre.

Joanne lay obligingly, stretched across the diameter of the circle. Joanne closed her eyes and Glory wondered if Joanne was as nervous as she was. Still, they were only *playing*, weren't they?

Everyone tittered out of synch. The evening breeze ruffled Joanne's frilled, ever-so-short skirt so that it looked like lapping water across her thighs. Her legs were bare, bare feet too, and her loose hair swirled around her head in a whirligig so that her face was like a small creature floating mouth-up in the shallows, her lips in a posy of kisses and her small breasts looked suspended and disembodied as if across shimmering water, like iced cupcakes. Glory felt nauseous with the motion sickness of it all.

And then the girls chanted in unison—*ooh-aah-om, ooh-aah-om*—except that it wasn't in tune and they weren't in time with each other so it sounded rather odd. Not wrong enough, Glory thought, to be impossible. Her heart thumped in her chest and she felt sure everyone could hear it. The moon flickered in the heavens just as Sandra had planned: 'it only ever works on a full moon,' she insisted. The girls waited and watched. Still nothing. They couldn't make Joanne move.

They stayed on in the circle like that, past midnight, nobody game enough to break the spell, huddled together, skin touching for support. Nobody wanted to be blamed; they didn't want to get on the wrong side of their new best friend. Their bare crossed legs ached a bit. Joanne was moaning audibly and the kisses were spent. But still nobody said anything. Nobody even laughed; this was dead serious. All they could hear apart from Joanne, who they thought was helping, was the lap of the Brisbane River beside them in the egg-warm darkness. The fairy lights of the house twinkled on the rise a long way off.

Glory shut her eyes tight and tried to forget where she was, what she was doing. Her eyes ached for the squeezing and the crying like sandpaper. She tried to be invisible, tried arranging herself as vapour, droplets suspended in the dark; hoping, *praying* it really was just a game, for kicks, not for keeps. *Please God*, she mouthed, the two words hitched involuntarily to her breath in a piggyback and projected up into the dark canopy of trees above them and on, into the void. *Please God*, as if it could make a difference, as if God could rescue her, rescue them all. And that's when it happened. That's when MotherJoy turned up.

Suddenly Glory's mother was there, right in the middle of the circle—Little Glory didn't know how.

MotherJoy seemed to materialise in a great cloudburst of noise as if to challenge the night, to rail against *the principalities* of this very darkness. She was so angry it was truly frightening. She was fighting a fight not of this world. The girls fell apart, knocked flat. They cowered before her. Joanne leapt up, ran away in a fit, making a terrible screeching sound. She crashed into a tree.

'Stop it,' MotherJoy was saying, her voice leaping about like flames. But she wasn't addressing Joanne in particular nor the paralysed girls, not even her daughter. She spoke as if to something else. 'Leave them alone,' she said. 'They know not what they do. Get thee behind me, Satan.' Then with a yank she pulled Glory up, singled her out. 'Come with me, Gloria. You're in mortal danger.' There was no stopping to say goodbye. Glory was sent straight to bed when they got home.

The next morning, MotherJoy prayed harder and longer at breakfast, squeezing Glory's hand as she repeated the words till it hurt. There were fingernail marks in her palm afterwards. Glory scrunched her eyes shut while silently whispering the words *I'm sorry*, praying for forgiveness, whatever it took. She was scared; she couldn't eat her cornflakes. *The end of the world is nigh. Are you ready? We must prepare for the Second Coming.*

On Sunday, MotherJoy put in a word to the Minister and he prayed especially for *those amongst us who are tempted beyond all measure* that God would give them strength to fight. MotherJoy told Glory she was going to have a word with Sandra's father. Glory knew that in this church, sinners were excommunicated when they fell into temptation. The elders made them stand at the front in church. Not that she understood what the word *excommunication* meant exactly. It sounded like the worst of possible diseases. To make your limbs fall off, one by one.

The following Monday at school, all Sandra said, as if to conclude the matter, was the one line: 'Hate to have a mother like that.' The other girls took their cue and gave Glory the flick too. Glory may as well have been as weird as MotherJoy. The girls simply stopped talking to her. As if Glory wasn't there. Had really turned into vapour.

29

To make matters worse, that was about the same time she first got her period, not that Glory ever disclosed this event to her primary school friends. She made other excuses at swimming or for sport on the oval so nobody laughed at her and sometimes she stayed away from school altogether. When it happened, Glory was eleven years old. 'So young, but such is our way,' MotherJoy said, as if to boast. The becoming of Solider women had its own brand of forthrightness, of *way*ness, so the story goes. Glory felt her body catapulted into more dangerous territory with this betrayal—her capacity to do wrong multiplied tenfold. MotherJoy didn't let her forget either, saying: 'You're not a girl-child anymore. The seed of the woman shall bruise the serpent's head. It is our lot. Now you know.'

It must have been a big sister who prepped Glory about the coming of blood, the Big P—maybe it was Mary. 'It comes like a bomb Glory Girl when you least expect it, comes out of nowhere. And you can't keep your legs together after that, you'll see, with that hold-all between to catch the blood.' Mary liked talking about clothes, about dressing up, about being pretty as a girl. In any case, she was right. It *was* a bomb when it turned up. It dripped onto the lino in the pink bathroom from the most secret of all places. The colour red was startling when you didn't expect it. Her favourite pair of blue nylon panties had to be thrown into the bin. And she felt bad, dirty: 'Told you,' Mary said.

That same night Glory flooded the bed and MotherJoy burned the sheets holus-bolus in the incinerator. Glory had never seen so much blood in the one place. They had to turn the mattress over. Outside, MotherJoy made Glory stand and watch the flannelette stripes turn into ash. 'Nobody need know,' she said, her face puffy with effort. 'We Solider girls never do things by halves, do we?'

Mary was right too about walking like a duck, the stiff pads stuck between Glory's legs like mini surfboards making her waddle when she moved. She didn't want to go anywhere, ever again. All she could think about was that thing between her legs and the danger of leaks. MotherJoy sent Glory down to a wooden trunk underneath the house where supplies of sanitary belts were hidden, belts with elastic bits and metal claws along with bras of all sizes for occasions such as this. 'Get yourself sorted,' she said. 'Everything you need is in the glory box, Glory Girl. You're not a girl-child anymore,' MotherJoy declared, knitting together her brow with words. The trunk. The Solider glory box. The shape of a coffin really, if Glory thought about it too much. Full of white things for good girls with a wooden lid that went clunk when you opened it (Glory had peeped in before this for dress-ups) and its hinges quite broken so that it was hard to put back together again the way you found it. Glory stitched herself up, top and bottom, with cotton padding in both cases: pads between her legs and a bra to cover her breasts. The bra had a fancy circular design and an adjustable strap over the shoulders with an end that waved in the air if you didn't secure it tightly in a fancy knot. This was the moment Glory had been waiting for, to be bathed in heavenly light all radiant, splendid. 'Due preparation for marriage,' MotherJoy said—a girl's destiny—to be welcomed into the gathering of women. It just took some getting used to.

Now at least she really knew what the red plastic bucket in the pink bathroom was all about with its strange crusty smell. She'd ignored it until now. She learnt how to empty it into the incinerator out the back for burning at the end of the week, throw in the match. This was her new job; she had graduated. The best bit was watching the flames gobble up the packages in a slow feast, how they ate into the centre. The way the paper smouldered red and sparkled. How the newsprint the pads were wrapped in disappeared, turned orange then black. How the whirl of a breeze kicked up charcoal pieces and blew them in wafts above. How the cinders ascended on the breeze like feathers into heaven. And how fire put things right—until it was all but the finest of ash, everything spent. She liked doing this fire job.

There would come a time when she took notice of how she wrapped the parcels for the burning. She took her time, there, sitting on the toilet with her period, as if she really did have all the time in the world and there wasn't someone else waiting to use the bathroom—*hurry up, Glory!*— impatient rattles of the door. She would pull at the torn newspaper on the hook above the toilet roll where someone (was it MotherJoy?) had hung the pieces in a bunch. Glory marvelled how this loop of string was always full, even when all the girls were bleeding at once. She could do the wrapping of the period-parcel oh so neatly, tucks and pleats, the evenness and perfection of folds. She loved to feel the coolness of the newspaper against her skin.

There would also come a time when she took notice of the newsprint itself, took her time reading it. Her sisters would shout though the door: 'Hurry up, Glory! I'm busting.' But she'd just shout back, 'I'm busy,' sometimes confessing, 'I've got my period.' She read all sorts of things this way, mostly from the public notices, real estate pages, marriages and deaths. This was how Glory found out more about the disastrous Australia Day flood in 1974, how the Brisbane River rose to nearly a record of six metres, how seventeen thousand homes were washed up (the Soliders were relieved that it only came to the bottom of their street), how people at the University of Queensland were 'pleased' they only lost the rowing sheds and playing fields, and how the Regatta Pub on Coronation Drive 'went under' to the first floor, but that they still served beer. Onward said something about little children nearly drowning in the flood and ending up in hospital—but she couldn't find that particular story.

On the day Glory got her first period, MotherJoy read to her daughter from Genesis, not to rejoice, but to mark the seriousness of the moment. You could hear a note of triumph in her voice, the tension of her knitted brow quite noticeable. 'And the seed shall bruise the serpent's head.' With all this bleeding after Glory flooded the bed, MotherJoy allowed Glory to stay home sick without asking.

She gave her a promise box to mark the occasion. The box was decorated with tiny pale brown-speckled cowrie shells and lined with scarlet satin, shiny side up. It was filled with a bed of Bible verses, Precious Promises, each rolled into a tight scroll so that the whole thing looked like a hundred mouths in the shape of perfect O's looking up at Glory, a tiny pair of tweezers lying on top. MotherJoy and Glory picked out a gaggle of promises, each printed on yellow paper, in blue courier typeface, to read to each other:

> The hoary head is a crown of glory, if it be found in the way of righteousness.
>
> For our God is a consuming fire.
>
> And the righteous men, they shall judge them after the manner of adulteresses, and after the manner of women that shed blood; because they are adulteresses and blood is in their hands.

The most secret of all places

```
Wilt thou now commit whoredoms with her, and she with them?

Yet they went in unto her, as they in unto a woman that playeth
the harlot.
```

What kind of scary promise was this last one, Little Glory wondered; what does a harlot's blood smell like?

29

Big Glory can't help but recall these promises from her childhood. She smells the 'consuming fire' up her nose. Her face is burning: *lewd women, women that shed blood.*

Here in Buderim, casually visiting her mother and father *out of the goodness of her heart* (perhaps this casualness is her mistake), Glory crosses her arms across her chest. Her mother has had a turn and Glory must hide any possible cleavage from view, wishing she could cross her arms to erase her whole body, wishing too she'd packed a change of clothes. Oh to turn back the clock, to when she first arrived in Buderim, to MotherJoy offering cups of tea, to the welcoming-gambolling MotherJoy with her childlike choreographed steps. To the evergreen MotherJoy.

What about when MotherJoy played the piano, played those beautiful hymns? To spin a way out of anywhere with a multitude of crotchets and quavers? Her mother came alive then, without tears, Glory remembers. Everything MotherJoy had to say about the world, the burdens of emotion, the weight she felt against wicked forces, poured out instead through her fingers. Big Glory recalls how her mother's spirit lifted with each major chord. It was a way to give thanks. Rejoice. The music took her away to a place somewhere else altogether, a place where she forgot herself, the burden of being who she was, being mother to her own children and caretaker guardian of all the other children in Queensland. She went to a place where she became an angel whose job it was—the only thing in the whole world she must do—was to play music.

Sometimes Little Glory sang hymns with her. Sometimes MotherJoy smiled back. It was a miracle, the joy of this music task written all over MotherJoy's face, written on her body too, as she thumped the keys with her hands and pedals with her feet, as she moved her bottom this way and that on the piano stool, her head switching in time with the rhythm such as it was, as she made sense of the music of hymns written by geniuses, she said, all those years ago. 'Beneath the Cross of Jesus', 'Abide with Me', 'There is a Green Hill Faraway'.

The most secret of all places

'Play the piano Mum. Play a hymn. Please play for us.'

'Just this once then,' she'd say. She smiled as if present, but she was off, away.

The Little Girls persuaded MotherJoy to play again and again and again. For even though she insisted 'just this once then', they knew she wanted more too. Her playing was a kind of salvation on earth. For Glory, it was a way of getting as close as she could get to her mother. To kneel down beside the piano with her head key-high, see MotherJoy's fingers thumping away, close range—she had such fat, strong fingers—and to sometimes sing along with her in what always turned out to be a thin little voice next to her mother's big fat vibrato. Glory sang along as if to burst her heart out of its ribcage, to soar and loop the loop like an albatross. Occasionally, MotherJoy glanced down as if suddenly remembering the children were there.

But nearly always there was a far-off expression on her face, as if looking over the horizon. MotherJoy could have gone to the moon she was that far away. She was in a place where nobody else belonged where no one else could follow. Glory and Gracie made sure it didn't matter: as far as they were concerned she thumped the chords and they sang sweetly and everyone was happy. For the length of a hymn and then, perhaps, another hymn after that.

'There is a green hill far away / outside a city wall / where the dear Lord was crucified / He died to save us all /'

Gracie always cried singing this one.

Sundays like this made you whole, Glory decided, when everything else, everything that puzzled was forgotten. MotherJoy played the piano and her Little Girls put angel wings on in their hearts, as if they really did have cut-out paper wings stretched with coat-hanger wire and elastic just like the other children at primary school. Glory felt set apart like real Christians were and it didn't matter how much there was to forgive. That was then. Now—offering forgiveness didn't last.

30

When it comes to leaving Buderim the day after the Jezebel incident, Glory can't kiss her mother goodbye; MotherJoy decides she won't get up from the armchair either. Glory gives her a slow wave from across the room. It's a strain for both of them. Onward sees his disgraced daughter out the door. Nor does Glory say when, or if, she'll be back. Any blessing Glory was promised is breaking up, falling apart. Soon there'll be nothing left.

Back at home her boss asks: 'So how did it go, Glory?'

'I forgot to pack the right clothes!'

'What do you mean?'

'She called me a whore.' Glory knows she can tell her this; her boss is a great friend.

'Really? Oh well, all mothers call their daughter a tart at one time or another.' She was good at brushing things off, just what Glory needed. 'I wouldn't worry about it.'

If only it were that simple.

'You're beautiful, you know,' another close friend reassures. 'And your mother is a bitch!' She laughs. If only Glory could believe this too.

Why does she take her mother so seriously? A slip of the tongue, that's all it was—isn't that what her friends are saying? Glory feels a new weight of shame, the shame of not being able to shrug it off. She tries writing the words *it has to be different now* in her imagination, tries to weave a way out of her body. *She's a good person too*, she whispers, writing herself in the third person. If only we could write our own stories in the way we preferred them to be told, wish stories. *We all just do our best*. Round and round in circles Glory goes.

That night she almost persuades herself to stop writing this Glory-story. The knot she is trying to unravel just makes the string tighter with each found word. She folds her arms between her legs and curls herself into a ball. Her skin feels like it's been shrink-wrapped, a vacuum seal around her bones without any space for her lungs to breathe. Is this the way someone dies? When they die of shame? She makes herself comfy and dreams herself to sleep.

31

MotherJoy must have been both unsettled and excited with the thought of her fifth daughter growing up, about to start high school; especially given she was climbing to the heights of her campaign. The timing couldn't be better. The three older Solider girls had left home to pursue their dreams (or at least that's how Little Glory liked to think of it). Eve was in senior destined to study medicine—she was almost there. Little Gracie was still protected by being the youngest, still in primary school. That left Little Glory Girl: she who was about to become MotherJoy's star recruit. MotherJoy's aim was to keep this daughter from being morally (mortally) corrupted. And finally, seriously, publicly, MotherJoy had a single book to focus on—*The Little Red School Book*—that controversial book that everyone was afraid of, everyone was talking about: it was full of 'gutter words'. With the help of *The Little Red School Book* MotherJoy became a *bona fide* morals crusader; the newspaper said as much. The press championed her cause; she was getting results. People started to take notice.

This latest crusade had started like this: one evening, over tea Onward was discussing the theological distinction between predestination and free will in that unhurried, learned way of his. The air itself, each molecule, was saturated with theology. On and on it went. You didn't dare contradict him, unless you were able to mount a very convincing exegetical argument. He spoke without any space between any of his words; you'd have to be very quick to interrupt. In any case, Glory didn't understand his argument. How could she ever be certain of her own salvation? Being saved—being 'the one'—was predicated on those who were not saved—'the others' who were never going to be saved. In other words, the saved ones *actually needed* unsaved ones to be saved.

MotherJoy wasn't listening, she was rocking back and forth in her chair, muttering.

Onward hesitated: 'Joy dear, are you okay?' To which Joy dear crackled, like lightning: 'We're onto something, Onward. I'll get this book banned, mark my word.'

And thus ended Onward's dissertation.

The Solider children scurried about after that, did the washing-up in record time without squabbling, found they didn't even have to spin the knife for the divvying up of jobs. It was as if the small family was being chased around the kitchen at high speed, couldn't get back to their bedrooms quick enough to get on with homework and music practice.

From the safety of her room Glory heard the sound of her mother's voice, the triumphal ring in the ears like the echo of the gong that called them all to the table in the first place. All about books spilling out everywhere in disgrace, as though her mother's guts spilled out of her body, all over the place. 'We're onto something, Onward. I know we are.' A visceral madness—open-body surgery.

32

*T*HE *LITTLE RED SCHOOL BOOK* was first published in Denmark. It was an instruction manual on teachers and homework, sexuality, pornography, corporal punishment, drugs, adolescence and abortion. The Queensland Literature Board of Review banned it in April 1972, making Queensland the first state to ban it in Australia. Technically speaking, it was banned with a prohibition order against its distribution in Queensland under the Objectionable Literature Act. Everyone wanted a copy. The *Australian* reported that Premier Joh Bjelke-Petersen set up a triple-0 hotline to try to stop anyone distributing the banned book. It was reported that illegal, reproduced copies of the book printed up as small newspapers were being circulated by throwing them into gardens over fences.

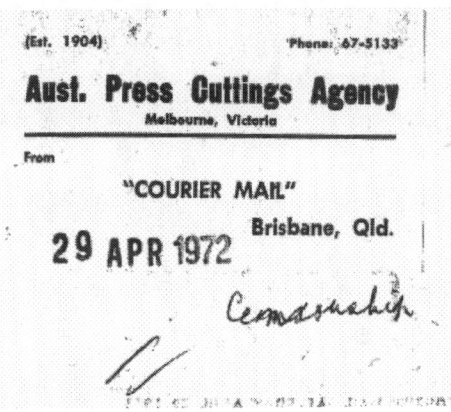

The arrival of *The Little Red School Book* and the furore around its publication started my mother's pro-censorship protest, although Angel had been building her moral muscles in preparation for a while before its publication. In the search for material on her campaign in the National Library in Canberra, in a file of clippings tucked away downstairs and catalogued under the single word 'censorship'—this was when libraries and press agencies did this kind of cutting and pasting under key subjects—I read that *The Little Red School Book* was 'pornographic', that it taught anarchy.

In this particular article, published in the *Courier Mail*, Angel Rendle-Short argued her case. This time, her rival was the university librarian, who said that to ban the book would deny adults 'the right to make their own decisions', and the treasurer of the university's anti-censorship committee, a committee set up in response to police raids, who said a total ban was 'lumping children's judgment together with adults'. Angel countered: 'It's a strong warning to parents that they must be vigilant concerning all the reading material available to their children.'

This is the file where I found Angel referred to as an 'anti-smut campaigner'.

33

Little Glory was worried that that *bad book* could turn up anywhere, in her street, at her house. That *The Little Red School Book* really was a plague, just like the swarms of flies and locusts, cane toads and hail that rained down on the Egyptians in Exodus in the Bible. What if, Glory worried, the Soliders woke up one morning and found a huge pile of books on the concrete driveway out the front under the Poinciana tree? A pesky neighbour deciding to play a practical joke, perhaps. What would MotherJoy do then? Would MotherJoy go to gaol? Would she want to burn the books—as a lesson? Get rid of the evidence in a victorious bonfire with a great whoosh of paper and flame and cinders. MotherJoy and this banned book, this now-illegal book, as a performance.

For it was the way MotherJoy did things that shocked.

34

It wasn't only *The Little Red School Book* MotherJoy wanted to ban. She had a long list of objectionable books. MotherJoy said, 'If I could get my hands on all of them Glory, all these dreadful books, I'd burn the lot. Burn them all. I'm bound for glory, Glory Girl; I'll get my reward in heaven. Nothing will stand in my way.' Glory, certainly, had no intention of standing in MotherJoy's way.

The two of them were at the kitchen table, packing the family's meat supplies into plastic bags for the freezer. Glory was leaning over the laminex, yellow starpoint on red. MotherJoy was distracted, planning her next move. 'Parents must be vigilant,' MotherJoy said, her cheeks trembling. She said she had a duty to perform because no one else was going to. It was that important—her service to God. Glory watched her mother's cheeks reverberate as she talked, especially around the collective noun *parents*, to punch the sentence out, then *vigilant* to hammer it home. She wasn't sure what her mother meant at first by *all those dreadful books*. How could you get hold of all the books in the world, living in Queensland too? How could one person do this kind of thing, to imagine it was even possible? MotherJoy must be joking. And what kind of bonfire would she have to build? It would have to be the very biggest of fires in the very biggest of backyards. Glory couldn't imagine it happening in the Solider backyard. In suburbia. Not in St Lucia. Down the back was certainly big and spacious, Glory loved getting lost out there playing with Gracie, but it wasn't big enough for this kind of demonstration surely. How could it accommodate all the books on the list MotherJoy was talking about, and not just single copies, but whole school sets? Her mother couldn't possibly mean what she said.

Mind you, Glory was only half hearted in wondering this. She was distracted too by the job at hand, the table lumped up with meat for the freezer. Any consideration of MotherJoy's growing agitation—her tremor of cheeks—was like opening the freezer door to be hit by a blast of cold air; maybe it could be avoided if Glory decided not to take notice.

For what a game these days were: this slurping of meat. The dribble of blood.

The meat assortment was piled up high: legs of lamb, sausages, globs of mince, some liver, ox tongues. How Glory loved to slap the meat down hard onto the table. *Ker-plonk*! How she liked to cradle the portions, squash them flat in their plastic pockets, poke the little stomachs, tickle the cheeks. She smoothed her hand over the skin of plastic holding the redness and the juice in place. How she imagined this meat was a body like hers and she could see through her own skin to the muscle and sinew in a concerto around her bones.

When MotherJoy started to talk then, about her specific list, about all the books she wanted to get rid of—one hundred books—Glory was somewhere else. But on hearing the big number she thumped back in her chair, as if rocketed back to earth. *Ker-plat*!

A death list, Glory thought, could it be? To kill books? One hundred of them?

The day was hot now. Heatwave temperatures even for Queenslanders. Glory was hoping for a cool drink of ice, but the air grew thick with what MotherJoy had to say, with her proclamation, and the fan overhead thwacked like Glory's heartbeat. *Blat! Blat! Blat!*

'I'm bound for glory, Glory Girl. I'll get my reward.'

This time, there was a sharp intake of breath in the sentence; her carefully chosen words had the knack of multiplying exponentially. Just as the two of them squashed out all the air in the plastic bags from around the family's meat, ready to pack the freezer full, MotherJoy sucked the air out of the kitchen with her words so there wasn't any breathing space left.

'You must help,' MotherJoy insisted, interrupting, passing Glory a lot of nails. 'We're the Luthers of today you know.'

With that, the two of them marched to the front porch to nail up the list on the front door. MotherJoy hammered the big silver nails with vigour into the wood, more nails than it needed. Sparks flew, metal against metal. The foolscap page looked like a skin, like one of Eve's laboratory rats stretched out taut, pinned flat to dry in the sun. Glory saw MotherJoy meant business all right. Saw her triceps flap with each blow *blat, blat*.

DR JOY'S DEATH LIST, the notice read. BURN A BOOK A DAY.

Below this heading, written out in thick red texta and underlined in black to make no mistake, was a list of one hundred book titles and their authors. Glory counted them later book-by-book. One hundred books condemned to burn in as many days.

What could Glory say?

She didn't say anything, of course. She was good at watching, though. Great at standing guard. Mesmerised. She watched MotherJoy strike up a rhythm, a seesaw action with the *blat, blat* of her arm. And Glory got caught up in the back and forth action with the swing of the hammer, the swivel for each nail. Her mother must have known what she was doing having this daughter by her side. For Glory believed her mother, she was a good Covenant child, her mother said. If MotherJoy thought that the books were wicked, then Glory thought so too, they must be. And tongues were cut out for such a thing, for wickedness that is, as well as for non-belief. It paid to be on the side of righteousness.

The Communists wanted to *get in first*, MotherJoy said, to 'cut out tongues'. That's why, she elaborated, the Communists behind the bamboo curtain cut out the tongues of 'brave Christians'. The Communists knew what they were up against with these Christian people, with the Bible foretelling things and all. Wicked people were terribly clever like that. And the punishment for Communists? 'A tongue for a tongue.' The price of sin was 'this precious organ of speech'. As her words sucked up the warmth of the day, her eye on Glory continued its steady gaze. MotherJoy said men that worship the beast would gnaw on their own tongues for punishment. That was what they ate in hell. It was a most horrible thought. It didn't bear thinking about—what it must be like—to eat your own tongue.

MotherJoy said: 'The lesson for us, Glory Girl, is always to be careful about what we say. With tongues like ours,' she said, waving the hammerhead close to Glory's mouth, 'we're a kiss away from hell. That's why Jesus must save us.'

Little Glory reckoned if MotherJoy really had her way with her morals campaign, her anti-smut ways, she'd not only burn all the books in the world, but she'd cut out the tongues of all the writers of all the wicked books in all the world. That would stop their jabbering. What a big job, though. MotherJoy would need help with this. To stand up against these people who worshipped the beast. Those who'd gnaw on their own *vital flesh* for as long as they burned in hell, and that would be forever. That would teach them to write stories down.

'Remember whose side you are on, Glory Girl.'

The most secret of all places

Glory paused before following MotherJoy back inside, to straighten the elastic waist of the red rickrack skirt, Elsie's hand-me-down, Glory deciding the pinkly tongue set for tea on the pretty blue serving plate in front of Onward wasn't the same thing at all. It would be a shame to see it go to waste. It was far too delicious. So too the tongue before it was cooked in their funny curling way. This wasn't the same either. This was a fun thing to do—pushing them around so that they wobbled as if they were talking. But no matter, no more playing now. It was time to put the meat away in the freezer—*slur-lop, slurp-blat*—finish the job they'd started, shut the lid. 'You know it's a sin Glory to leave a job half done.'

Still, whenever Glory left for school through the front door and saw the death list hammered on the door, she ran her tongue around her mouth and across her teeth, curled it over itself and poked it out to get a good look at the tip of it. Just to make sure her tongue was still there.

35

THE OTHER THING GLORY made very sure of was being saved—going forward for Jesus. This too made her heart beat faster.
Whose side are you on, Glory Girl?

Being saved once was never enough; Glory did it over and over, lots of times. To be certain. She kept thinking the same thing: What if they're really right and I'm wrong? What if God is as judgemental as they say? She made sure she belonged to Jesus, thoroughly, just in case. Still, if anyone were to ask Glory about being saved, to say honestly why she *went forward* for Jesus, she would have to confess it was the music, it was irresistible .

Glory liked the mournful slide of hymns—'Just as I am'—the move to the end of the phrase—'without one plea'—the length you could insert into every vowel—'O Lamb of God / I come to Thee'. She liked the commotion in her throat as she squeezed the notes out past her vocal chords, the harmonies she was learning to sight-read, and the sense of anticipation secretly embroidered into the waiting, into the singing. She particularly liked the way she could forget her peculiar pubescent body, forget about the big pimple growing fat and red and hot on her chin. Its angry white head and how MotherJoy would want to lance it.

Singing hymns, things came into focus.

The pace slowed right down, the congregation repeated chorus after verse, expanded and contracted the music with each phrase, sang the ebb and flow of the line, each note, breathed themselves into the meaning of every syllable. Everyone made their way through the multiple renditions of the hymn so that they shone the colour of golden syrup. The church filled with the sound of heavens, and everyone there was able to lounge about, buoyed up and supported by fat cushions, melody and rhythm, swim even, to the rise and fall of the bass notes. It was most wondrous. Intoxicating.

The most secret of all places

So how many times did the organist repeat the hymn that night in the gospel service before someone came forward? Did he almost give up? Did his salvation depend on how well he played?

Glory loved to *go forward*. She played the game of *going forwards* in different churches, at various conventions and evangelistic crusades; she was well practised. Too many times to count, too many times to remember: to do it more than once was naughty, perhaps even a sin but she didn't want to think about that. She knew the unwritten rule was that the church had to *get someone*. That was the point of these special gospel services. That was why they were popular; there was always a spectacle. Think of the legacy of the Billy Graham Crusades: every Queenslander of a certain age has a story. The measure of a congregation's faith depended on a regular trickle of saved souls. And Little Glory Solider had a sixth sense when it came to it too, as if she didn't know she existed until that moment, that it was the very birth of her, the bringing of herself into existence, the defining of her shape, her corporeality.

The hymn number on the board shone in white lettering. Hymn number 121: 'Just as I am Without One Plea'. She looked it up in the hymnal, kept its place with a lolly wrapper she found between the pages. Fingers trembling. Couldn't wait, but wanting to wait too. It made her ache with anticipation. Ache in the thinking—the thought, the *very idea*—that just before there was the chance to fill the void, to rise up and move forward, she might shatter into a million pieces, explode shards of shooting stars up to the steep wooden rafters and back again to fall over the congregation like summer rain. That her thumping heart would fly out her mouth in a swallow-dive divine to behold.

More than that, she ached because she knew they waited for her. There was a secret power in restraint as she bided her time. Any triumph came after the third, fourth, fifth chorus. This evangelical service would be incomplete that night without a Little Girl going forward, without a Solider soul being saved, without Glory Being Born. No matter that she was already saved, that this had all been done before. Some nights, it was excruciating; you could taste the Godly exuberance, almost choke, and as far as Glory was concerned these were the best. There was no going back.

On this night, the particular one Big Glory remembers because she was off to high school the next day, the organist began but nobody moved. She was at the faraway Baptist church she sometimes went to with her sisters, Eve and Gracie, the one with the big white cross on its roof and the plastic flowers in pots that needed dusting next to the pulpit. Eve sometimes took them her sisters in her car, told MotherJoy: 'We'll be right.' It was another muggy one too. You could hear thunder roll over the horizon, getting closer. The rain would come but would clear by the morning—Brisbane was like that. Glory's thighs stuck to the wooden pew, sweat trickled down the back of her knee and into her sock. The aisle and communion table throbbed with emptiness, the organist overplayed the hymn like it was a broken record: five, six, seven, eight versions of the slowing-down-to-nearly-a-stop chorus. Still Glory kept them waiting; she held back, she didn't give in. She was not going to be seduced prematurely.

If someone were to take her temperature now, they could see the mercury soaring up the thermometer. They'd say she was very sick, swab her with damp cloths. She couldn't look Gracie's way or the spell would break. She sensed Eve's head was bowed. Soon, soon, it would be over. She could feel something like clinking chains holding her down to the pew. Little whispers of words peppered her insides nearly puncturing her skin. *Not yet*, said the voices, *not yet, not yet*. Oh, sweetness.

At last, an eternity washed and dried later, Glory did indeed go forward. She rose up out of her pew and into the aisle in a sweeping gesture like the cadence of a conductor's baton. Stately. Beautiful. *Glorious Glory*. As if she were time itself: personified, to infinity. Glory brushed her sisters' hands as she squeezed past. The whole congregation heaved a sigh, more a long gasp—*aarrrggghhhh*—punched out lungfuls of air into a conglomerate of prayers, as though, for that execution, the whole church was one body. As if, when Glory rose to stand, this whole body was resuscitated mouth-to-mouth, Glory its now-beating centre.

Glory Solider gave herself up, newly composed for that moment out of nothing: *ex nihilo*. She was nearly a teenager, and being saved was becoming addictive. She had a plan for eternity clear before her.

36

Wasn't that what Jesus promised? *It pays to be on the right side, Glory Girl*, she imagined him reminding her. *Forget that doubting mind. Doubt is a sin.* And Glory Girl hugged the idea close, squashed it flat against her ribcage. She made it all hers, threaded light into her throbbing heart through its valves. She must hold onto this. Because Glory was about to be tested. Would the acrobatic dives and swoops and hollers she performed in church be heavenly insurance enough to protect her, knowing her tongue was only *a kiss away from hell*? Always remember Glory, remember being born again, going forwards, giving up to Jesus. Hold on tight.

The night before Glory's first day of high school in 1973, MotherJoy called her to her side, called her to the big bedroom where she liked to hold court, to warn her fifth daughter about what she was going to have to do next. 'Glory dear, I have no choice, I must speak my mind.' It wasn't this bit that surprised, the MotherJoy-speaking-her-mind bit, she'd used these words before. It was how it might involve Glory that nicked the inside of her throat. It was no preparation for what eventuated.

Yet, perverse as it may sound, what happened the next day at school jump-started a new way of being, not that anyone would have noticed by looking at Glory, least of all Glory herself, all daggy there in her blue and white stripes down to below her knees. She was in the deep end, that was certain, but like all good Queensland children, she knew how to swim and a few different strokes at that. She'd passed her lifesaving exams at primary school: Intermediary Star, Bronze Medallion. She could proudly rescue a towel-covered brick from the bottom of the deepest diving pool, even when the water was sometimes cloudy above and full of chlorine and she had to be right on top of the brick, inches away, to know where it was. She was good at concentrating hard, good at keeping her mouth shut, good at keeping her eyes open even when it hurt. She held her breath until she could grab the brick in two hands and shoot to the surface splashing, triumphant, with help from a push-off from the floor. Her lungs rocketed her skywards, her cheeks like cricket balls.

37

MotherJoy liked to talk to Glory from the comfort of her bed, 'to put things in perspective', she said. She liked to lie there in the middle of the day, said it helped her sleep better at night. No one in the family was convinced about this, as they often heard her after midnight, distracted and padding around the house in slippers or in the kitchen preparing a little sweetener, marmalade toast and a cup of tea. Eating settled the nerves. Still, when she pleaded that her siestas helped her in all sorts of ways, they never questioned.

In any case, there she was in the double bed, dressed in her housecoat with the red ribbon, propped up against a bank of pillows, a deep, blood-red eiderdown pulled up over her cocked knees.

'Shut the door then, there's a dear,' MotherJoy said, and she drew Glory to her side. 'Glorious Glory.' She made a little room, shifted a bit. 'Why don't you sit here,' smoothing a small patch on the edge of the bed close by her, patting Glory's arm.

'Now then,' MotherJoy began, a little formally at first. Her voice had the tone that she kept especially for occasions like this. It had a faintly ominous ring to it, low register, foregrounding the things she wanted to say, important things, things Glory might not like. She had no intention of letting Glory go until she had disclosed what was on her mind. 'I want to talk to you about a few things.'

Strangely, and at first Glory couldn't put her finger on why, it was almost as if she welcomed the idea: Glory welcomed MotherJoy's tone, her presentation. For a start, Glory liked it when MotherJoy paid her this kind of attention, singled her out. It made Glory feel alive, special. When she overheard her mother corralling the older ones to speak in private, she wondered what it would take to create the same kind of situation to allow her the same privilege: one to one with her mother. And not just to carry in trays for tea and crucifix orchids in peanut paste jars. But asking Glory to close the door for privacy. The saying, *There's a dear*. The beckoning to *sit close*. The comfort of the ministration. The patting of the

The most secret of all places

bed. That warm patch MotherJoy created on Glory's arm. Mother and daughter—*just her, just me*—no one else. Lovely.

It was happening as Glory had dreamed it might. Glory could feel her bones growing large, growing strong, her ribcage expanding. MotherJoy had something significant to say. The all-important elements of this conversation were being mustered and the smoothed circle on the bed was just one of them. There was the clearing of the throat too; little conjunctive words as useful bridges (Glory liked the idea of parsing, from grammar lessons in year seven), the directness of her mother's gaze, eye to eye. MotherJoy was ready to articulate her meaning.

If, supposing for a minute, her mother had been in the theatre right now and about to speak her lines with Shakespeare in her mouth (not a hospital theatre, but the sort MotherJoy disapproved of, with a stage and props and actors), everything about her was in readiness. As if her future success, her career in voice projection, the carriage and interpretation of this passage of this important play in which she had a title role—the way she threw her voice forward across space, across time even—depended on this very moment, her performance. She claimed it as her own. Her daughter was so taken with the very act of being there in the bedroom beside such a theatrical mother, so mesmerised by what she was experiencing, its dimensions and physicality, that she forgot to listen to what MotherJoy was actually saying, what the words might mean.

'Now then, there are two things I want to discuss.' That pause for affect. 'Firstly, I understand a very special thing has happened to you.'

'Oh yes,' Glory burbled in reply, 'we went to the Baptist over the river. We went as a special treat.'

'And I hear you gave yourself to the Lord Jesus,' MotherJoy's voice tripped over a little joy. 'You asked the Lord Jesus into your heart. That's nice.'

'I did.' A stray air bubble surfaced somewhere, in rapture. Ah, being saved and now being praised. 'Praise the Lord.' And she didn't mind MotherJoy knowing either, Eve must have told. Glory blushed in spite of herself.

'There is another thing,' MotherJoy said in the same breath. She rested her hand on Glory's.

Glory didn't like the sound of turning in her mother's voice—the cogs gathering pace. A dirty taste of coarse sand appeared in her mouth. MotherJoy had shifted her weight in the bed, adjusted the eiderdown, and Glory decided she didn't like sitting on the edge of the bed anymore.

'I'm going to visit your new school,' MotherJoy was saying. 'Talk to the headmaster.' The dry air of that voice could desiccate sea sponges. 'You're growing up, Glory Girl.' The voice rose. 'I have no choice.'

No, Glory thought. Not my new school. She held her breath, her tongue felt sore and heavy. She blurted out: 'Talk to him about what?'

'I have no choice, Glory dear, you must understand,' another pause, 'I must speak my mind.'

Glory really did feel sick now. Hotter than the hottest hot water bottle. Any residual sense of victory from being saved had sloughed off and slipped to the floor. *Please don't make a scene,* she begged, noiselessly. She didn't know what the fuss was going to be about exactly but knew she didn't want MotherJoy to interfere, not on her first day at her new school. Glory was suddenly cold, shivery. Perhaps she really *was* sick— that would be easier. Being sick was a good way to get MotherJoy's attention. That way, she wouldn't have to go to school.

'Gird your loins,' MotherJoy was proclaiming as if more than one of her children were in the bedroom with them, as if she had an audience. Her voice was loud, the pitch just so, her inflection controlled. 'Remember, Glory, Soliders for Christ. Armour of God, don't forget.'

38

THE NEXT MORNING MotherJoy spread the table with a freshly cooked breakfast, with a pretty white lace tablecloth. It was like a Sunday. On Sundays MotherJoy didn't get into flaps. On Sundays MotherJoy's pulse slowed enough to play the piano. Glory found herself lulled into a feeling of safety. Didn't every other child starting secondary school that day in Brisbane feel the same way? On the cusp of something grand, something nameless and wonderful? Glory was leaving her small sister behind, chasing the big ones over the river and faraway, with a feeling at last of something happening to move her away from childhood. She was still only twelve years old, but her teenage years had very nearly arrived. She dismissed any thought of MotherJoy's agitation, pushed her stomach back down her throat. *Let's press on*, Onward would say.

And she did.

The morning had arrived with the crackle of crickets outside and the banging of saucepans in the kitchen, the heat of the sun hot through the window, late January. Onward left for work without even a goodbye. He took Eve with him early after she promised to practice her piano for longer than normal when she got home that evening. Like her father, Eve was good at making herself scarce. So MotherJoy sat with her two youngest daughters across the kitchen table and read from the large Bible open in her upturned hands. 'You must write the word of the Lord on your heart,' MotherJoy said. 'Glory, you must go into the world to abhor that which is evil, cleave to that which is good. Say after me,' and the Little Girls recited with her, 'Romans 12:9: Abhor that which is evil, cleave to that which is good.'

They read great slabs of the Book of Romans together. Set about to memorise chapter twelve, promised each other they could. The Word of the Lord spun soft cases around their hearts in a swill with the rounds of grilled tomatoes, thin breakfast sausages and the slosh of cornflakes. 'I beseech you therefore, brethren, by the mercies of God, that ye present your bodies a living sacrifice, holy, and acceptable unto God, which is your reasonable service.' The fan circled above them.

Afterwards MotherJoy kissed them both fondly, kisses that burned soft patches in their cheeks. She squeezed their shoulders and waved them goodbye from the verandah with a great cheerio. She gave them each a crucifix orchid each from the garden as a keepsake and the flame colours were perfect in the morning light. Gracie went up the hill to the primary school, Glory down the hill to catch a bus and then a train.

No one from St Lucia went to faraway high schools. When it was time to move up from primary to secondary, the grade sevens spilled out either to the local high school in the next suburb or to the Greater Public Schools, GPS. It was that kind of primary, that kind of suburb. So why would you take buses and ferries and trains to go to a public school? Why waste time like that?

Glory laughed it off—she was good at laughing about uncomfortable things, it put people off the scent. Whenever anyone at church asked her about school, which one she was going to, she said she had lots of sisters and they all went to different schools all over Brisbane. It didn't seem strange for Glory to be going to a school none of her sisters had been to. Glory didn't know what schools STOP and CARE were targeting. She was just pleased with how she looked. She had on her blue and white tunic with a stiff white blouse underneath, zipped up and belted in. On her feet, sensible, black leather Robin lace-ups and long white socks. All brand new.

Stations came and went; she didn't have to wait for long. The train had pulled in quickly the minute she arrived and she easily found a seat in a near-empty red rattler. It looked like no one from her new school travelled this way; it looked like she might be on her own. But as Glory neared her destination, counting and naming the ten or so memorised in-between stations so she would know which one to get off, the rattler ballooned. There was the blue and white and grey boys of her school mixed up with lots of other colours—grey and red, green, blue, maroon—some public, some private. Numbers built up, rowdy and flirty, and Glory listened to the easy words slipping out of the pretty mouths of girls with their short skirts and long legs. The way the boys lapped them up too, hungry for more, making plans for after school. This was their world, a world in which they knew the rules, loved to play hard, play for keeps.

MotherJoy's words of the morning across the breakfast table from Romans Twelve shone brightly around Glory like a galaxy of shiny stars—*cleave to that which is good*—but the closer she got to her destination, the more she squeezed her legs and her eyes shut to wish she were somewhere else, somewhere safe, holding Gracie's hand. Yes, being a little girl again. She felt herself sliding into unfamiliar territory, like going through the wardrobe into Narnia: would Aslan, like Jesus, be there on the other side to rescue her?

One minute she was persuading herself she was the happiest girl in the world, off to high school at last with a head full of orchids to take with her into the schoolyard. The next and not so far up the track, with this mob of worldliness pressing into her in a tight scrum—wayfulness MotherJoy would say—her mouth dried up, her skin stretched tight with such a familiar feeling: the one squeezing her body of oxygen.

39

THIS IS WHAT HAPPENED.

MotherJoy was somebody, people said, of whom you took notice. Ordinary citizens did. So too educators, department officials, academics, and politicians. Even governor-generals. Whenever she asked a question people felt compelled to answer. Under normal circumstances, these people would be able to give direct answers, sound responses, educationally responsible replies, pedagogic explanations. But when she demanded to know why something was as it was, they spluttered and slipped up—why for instance, should Queensland children read these dreadful books as *compulsory reading*? MotherJoy addressed meetings, peppered guest speakers with questions, wouldn't give up the microphone, heckled from the floor. Her notoriety fanned about her like a huff of turkey gobbler feathers. Teachers and headmasters knew who she was even before she rang the secretary for an appointment or crossed their threshold unannounced. News travelled fast in this kind of adversarial environment, in a small place like Brisbane. It was one thing to take MotherJoy on in public with the press watching to record the fight, take photographs, the audience as witness: the satisfaction of pure physical theatre. But it was a different case face to face. Then, MotherJoy came away victorious. She was a woman to be reckoned with, intimidating, and that was exactly how she liked it to be known.

The staff at Glory's new school must have suspected she would do something. There had been an increased coverage in the media that summer about the 'parlous state' of education, and government high schools in particular were in the firing line. The school phones probably ran hot with MotherJoy's questions about the intended booklists, prescribed texts, and curriculum policy for their new English classes. A Solider-child's name appeared on the grade-eight list (there could only be *one* Solider family). And then on the first day, Dr Solider turned up in her turquoise car to have it out with the headmaster.

The most secret of all places

MotherJoy drove everywhere in that Holden. It had elongated taillights at the back like grand plumage. The suspension wasn't terribly good, it bounced in and out of potholes, the Little Girls *oohing* and *aahing*. The three of them often did letter-drops with important pamphlets in that car; MotherJoy told 'concerned parents' they would recognise her immediately by its colour—emerald green, turquoise, 'the colour of the Irish Sea,' she said. 'God's work depends on the angle of the light.' Glory would help her mother collate the pamphlets from pages and pages of roneoed piles in a circle around the dining table (she was quick with her hands). She raced against herself to see how many sheets she could assemble and fold in record time. Then Glory, Gracie and MotherJoy would whistle out to the outer suburbs of Brisbane to fill up letterboxes with the stuff. Sunnybank, Inala, Rochedale, Wynnum.

Imagine for a moment, MotherJoy and her two youngest girls on one of these sprees: MotherJoy pert and attentive to the road at the wheel, dressed in something special for the occasion; Glory and Gracie along the bench seat in front with her with laps full of wads of pamphlets, neatly folded, stacked and bundled into piles of fifty, tied together with knotted string; the dogs, Honey and Pooh, in the back seat, their heads hanging out of the windows, tongues lolling. Together, the Soliders sang little snatches of hymns on their way. Their voices braided together with the breeze like breath itself, and any anxiety Glory might have had about what would come next blew out through the wound-down windows, away behind the Holden in a twist of exhaust fumes.

There was something almost magical in the way MotherJoy swanned about, circling Brisbane with this carload, on her mission. She was in her element, everything in its place. There was something earthy about her attachment to *getting things done*, to being different, and she had such energy for it. She was colossal. People, especially women, drew close to her for that. They sheltered beneath her wings. She made things possible, and they dared to believe in themselves. MotherJoy and her fearlessness showed them how they could do it. Not that any of the women who signed up to be part of the campaign wanted to circumnavigate Brisbane delivering materials, to put pamphlets into letterboxes, to pray with near strangers for salvation from 'perniciousness'. But—and this was the crunch—it was through MotherJoy that they saw for themselves they were party to an extraordinary movement, in the same way you *know* the value of preparing and serving your family three square meals each day. They firmly believed—MotherJoy promised them this—they could and would make a difference. 'Things are about to change,' MotherJoy declared, 'we'll see to that. We'll make the government sit up and take notice. We won't be silenced.' She lifted their spirits from the verandahs of their outer suburban existence. They grew feathers like her. She made them see things *at large*. MotherJoy opened the doors to a kind of conservative but radical heaven. These ordinary housewives were not afraid, not with MotherJoy in the lead. Her beliefs sustained them all.

So, when MotherJoy pulled up for a meeting with the headmaster, the staff peered out from behind the venetian blinds, blinking. But it was not quite what they expected. First she parked the car illegally, bang outside the front office, one wheel perched on the curb as if she'd landed like that with a screech, a bump of the brakes. Then she rose out of the car, as if up out of the sea, a surprisingly small woman they all thought, dressed to draw attention to herself for the occasion in blues and reds, brass buttons, adorned with a long, floral scarf. Her hat had ostrich feathers pinned on the side. Quite a picture, if a little unusual. *Do everything with a smile*. MotherJoy disarmed her opponents.

Little Glory knew full well that her mother was going to *do something*; she had been warned. If this were the case (and she had tried so much to put the horrible thought from her mind), surely it would be in private, a more or less civil conversation over the phone between a headmaster and concerned parent to allay any fears: that yes, the school *had* received the Secondary School Principals Memorandum by the Education Department, and yes, the school had taken action to remove all the offending books from the school library. Surely not in person. Not in public, a dressing down. And not on Glory's first day.

'Face it, Glory,' Elsie once said in passing, years later, 'Mother will always choose God over her children.'

40

MotherJoy's appearance on the parade ground nailed Glory to the hot bitumen. Hadn't she just kissed her goodbye? Yet here she was, with the headmaster, for all to see beneath the flagpole on a small stage. At the first bell. Loud voices and red faces into the sun. MotherJoy was saying: 'I thought you said you were a God-fearing man.'

He looked helpless: 'Look, I've really got to get going. First day.'

'Not before I have your assurance.'

'I've already given it.'

'God's word?'

Thanks to the new PA system, everyone could hear them. Word for word. Hear the tail end of what sounded like a very heated and personal altercation. 'Standing *at ease*' had been the instruction to the pupils, lined up in rows according to years, legs apart, hands clasped behind the back. The old hands knew the drill. All twelve hundred of them stood there in the sun astride the melting bitumen, a single line of teachers at the back. First day back, first parade, it always took a bit of getting used to. It was the first bump into routine, a longer parade than normal. They were waiting for their headmaster to make a speech, welcome them back after the long summer holidays. The school needed to watch the flag run up the flagpole, sing 'God Save the Queen' in unison.

Glory was there too in amongst the new grade eights. Glory Solider, the dag. Glory Solider in her long tunic, hemmed to well below her knees. Glory Solider amongst all the other girls with skirts barely covering their bottoms, skirts split up the side seam to reveal the pinks, yellows and whites of their panties. Glory thinking about the subjects she was going to take—Maths, English, Japanese—who her teachers might be. Thinking about anything else but this.

MotherJoy saying: 'I will not have my child subjected to this filth.'

Glory feeling the scratchy material of a new uniform against her bare legs, the trickle of sweat around her bottom and down the back of her thigh. She might pass out.

'They are old enough.'

'Can you look me in the eye, and tell me that *Lady Chatterley's Lover* is not filth? '

The teachers on the perimeter exchanged looks, raised eyebrows. They knew it shouldn't be on a school list, even at senior level; they knew the Department said it should only be read at university.

'Do our children need to read this abomination to be fulfilled?'

The headmaster waved his hands about now like an injured praying mantis. He looked defeated: not this, not now, not here.

'I don't think so.' She was answering for him. 'No, I've got whole list of books too. I'll be back, you can count on that.' His eyes boggled. 'Mark my word. This filth will be eradicated.'

At first, on the parade below these two figures, there was a hush, but soon whispering and snickering laughter broke out like wild fire. Was she for real? The school's amusement at this spectacle was contagious. Soon, the whole parade was trying not to laugh. They clasped their hands behind their backs more firmly to help them stand tall, to stop the muscles twitching. Everyone was involved, even the teachers. Poor Glory, stuck in the middle, found she had to look the part. She bit down on her lip with her teeth. Grimaced. Nobody must know that that 'mad lady' belonged to her—she wished this more than anything.

The headmaster was so flustered he didn't have the presence or the authority to hush the school, bring everybody to attention. He was losing control.

MotherJoy was on her way down the flight of stairs by now, about to leave, her court shoes clattering on the metal steps, but not before she swivelled smartly on her toes, went back to the edge of the balcony, and addressed the entire school body, sprawled out across the playground below her in their whites and blues and greys, smirking. This was her chance to make an impression. She had come to this place this morning *for this* opportunity, for the children of Queensland. Glory could see it written on her face. She would save them from a pernicious world, save them from themselves. She stood up to the microphone. She had about her an air of royalty. The feathers in her hat waved their part. What she had to say didn't sound rehearsed, it came from the heart, and the whole school stopped still, to listen. The schoolchildren responded, as she seemed to know they would.

'Children today,' she began, 'all you.' She stretched her arms out to form a very large imaginary circle encompassing everyone gathered

The most secret of all places

below. Her voice, modulated now to perfection, a lullaby. 'All you thirteen-year-olds, fourteen-year-olds, fifteen-year-olds, sixteen- and seventeen-year-olds,' she paused again to look at them all, as if to individually count each child gathered there. 'All of you shall be taught what is true … what is good … and what is honourable. This is my word.'

Might this performance be enough to save Glory?

MotherJoy threw her carefully chosen words like boomerangs—the *true, good, honourable* words—so that they circled to embrace the whole school, loaded, impressive, before coming back. Enough to silence everybody. It was only once she'd left that the tongues started. 'Isn't she that crazy reactionary everyone's talking about? She tied Sir up in knots,' they said, 'that was funny. But she's a bit weird, isn't she? Hate to have her as a mother. Imagine that!'

Glory couldn't think straight. She had to block her ears. Pull her hat down to her chin. She wanted to make herself scarce, disappear down cracks in the concrete slabs; she felt she was being squeezed through a sieve. But what could she do?

Lessons came and went in a first-day swell, Glory caught in the rip. After school, Glory took her time to get home. She dawdled behind the pack streaming out of the gate to the station. Took the long way round down the backstreets, kicking grey stones in the dust to bounce down gutters. She didn't mind scuffing her new Robins. She was in no hurry. She deliberately missed a couple of trains before getting on one and finding a seat in a near-empty carriage at the front. How cold was the glass she pressed her cheeks against. How the wheels rattled her teeth, rattled houses and trees whistling past to a blur. How she loved the familiar bridge swinging high above the Brisbane River (she decided to go home the long way), and the river coiled in slumber like a brown snake. What a drop too. This yawning space below her: a space in which to be alone without feeling guilty, not at school, not yet home. She sucked on a licorice lozenge to see if one could last the whole journey.

Up the final road from the bus, she tried to make herself invisible too, dashing in a fast walk from tree cover to tree cover—in under the peppermint and around past the palms and mango. Nobody must see her. She hid out in the backyard beyond the septic behind the incinerator, at the very far corner of the garden. There, between the mulberry and wild bamboo, right on the fence line, she sat on her port, hunched over, her body doubled up. She rocked herself like that back and forth, hands over her mouth, staring into her fringe to go cross-eyed.

She tried to vomit, too, like the girls at school said they did, not to look good like them, or to lose weight as they boasted, but as a way to lose the words, toss them away. *Hate to have her as a mother. Hate. Her.* She'd overheard some of the bigger girls at school boasting in the toilets about their preferred method of chucking. How they used two fingers. How it worked every time without fail. Glory wasn't sure how it would make her feel when she did it mind you, what the taste of tongue sandwiches she'd had for lunch might be like back up the throat the wrong way, but if the girls at school could do it—and *feel better*—then so could she. It couldn't make her feel worse than she already did.

It didn't work of course. She gagged, horribly, made such a noise. She was thankful for the garden around her as stuffing, a muffler. And for the quack of the ducks, they always enjoyed company.

She didn't tell Gracie about what had happened that day either. She tried to forget everything. Glory had to find a way to live through it, whatever it took, whatever *it* was. At teatime, MotherJoy insisted Glory eat up.

How funny the potato tasted that night. The peas needed double pinches of salt. What a clacking of jaws and teeth and tongues, the noise of chewing and swallowing. Glory was dizzy with the sound. She knew MotherJoy had more to say, she could feel it in her bones all through at tea. In the way MotherJoy straightened and restraightened her knife, never happy.

After, Glory took out the compost without being asked. To slosh and slurp into the chookyard. To ease her nausea.

It didn't feel like a normal sickness—sore throat, fever, aching legs, a rising temperature—this was a kind of sickness that made her ache in her mouth and neck, and in her chest. That burned. Her tongue felt double its size, swollen but dry and hard as a bone. She wanted to spit it out. Glory knew she couldn't say anything, what was there to say? But she could teach herself how to bury this thing that hurt like billyo, bury it alive. She was alone now and that was how it had to be. Not even Gracie could help.

The Little Girls sometimes ran away together out the back to the septic tank. They played there on the tank underneath the frangipani tree. It felt safe, their friendship watertight. They could make up the rules any which way—and stories. The stories always ended in a hug, whatever happened, in laughter. That was how it went. But not with this story.

The most secret of all places

Dear Gracie must have sensed something was up because she didn't ask Glory a thing.

Glory whooshed out the compost with a high swing of the bucket and the scraps of potato peel and pineapple skins went flying across the ducks. *Quack, quack.* The outside air seemed to huff a wayward note. The ducks fluffed up and scattered to the pond and the chooks and turkeys on their roosts cooed and murmured. One day, Glory promised herself, one day she'd learn how to vomit things up on command, just like the other girls. One day, she'd stop being squeamish, she'd shine, like that look of golden syrup everywhere when she was saved by Jesus: *going forwards.*

41

Later that night, Glory heard her mother in the big bedroom, pacing the floor. Normally, MotherJoy sat on the front porch last thing at night, sometimes with Onward. They sipped cups of sweet tea together in the cool of the evening, in the softened night-light. From there you could get a peppermint hint of the sea breeze blowing landwards. Watch thunderstorms. Hear the fruit bats squealing yellow. Glory would come and say goodnight to them there, kiss MotherJoy on her forehead, Onward on his rough cheek. They sometimes read a passage together from the Bible as insurance for sleep, said a small benediction to whoever was listening.

On this night, MotherJoy wasn't there. There was no blessing. Glory could only hear the pacing. The squeaky floor in the space between the bed and dressing table. Then there was a click of the bedroom door, a kerfuffle of slipper footsteps down the corridor, and the rattle of the sliding door into Glory's room. Glory's bedside lamp was off for the night but the light from the city beyond the vertical strip of louvres made the room bright enough. Perhaps there would be another storm later, at midnight, a thrum of rain on the iron roof. That would be nice.

Glory turned to see MotherJoy come through the door. She saw her open her mouth to say something only to shut it again. A change of mind, a quick movement: a trap door. Instead, MotherJoy put a finger across her closed lips to say *shush* to Glory: not yet a word of exchange. She came over to sit on the edge of the bed, Glory's high, narrow hospital bed (a bed rescued from dumping), and reached out as if to touch her daughter. Did her fingers tremble? Could Glory read what this gesture said? Glory longed for her to speak, for her to say something ordinary and mundane. Ask, for instance, how was your day? Did you make friends? What are your teachers like? Like any mother might do.

But it wasn't to be. The silence lapped between them. The light that had been helpful at first in seeing her mother's mouth, shifted, so that her face was now in shadow.

The most secret of all places

Before tea, Glory had written in her little daybook in a 2B pencil: 'Starting a new LDB today—yeah!—first day at high school—first day without Gracie—three pussy cats on my bed this afternoon—wanted to tell Gracie about the jelly tops ice-cream—missed the train—ages to get home—Mum didn't say anything—.' She didn't write about what happened at school. She didn't want to spoil things. There was a feeling of newness with her new daybook, the first page: its blankness. The way anything might be possible on these lines. She was careful to rub things out if she got too flustered with what was being said, if the words scrambled, became illegible. She made sure she didn't press too hard with the lead.

The writing started after Glory found an old exercise book in MotherJoy's bottom drawer: Reding *Universal*, ninety-six pages. She found it at the end of primary school, over the school holidays. MotherJoy had said she could have it, didn't ask for reasons. That was that. Imagine then folding back the first page ready to compose. Running your hand over smoothness, emptiness. The smell of this new paper too. Making it yours with your own words, stealing words from other people. Anything was possible. Glory didn't write in her daybook everyday like proper diarists. This was more ad hoc. And she definitely wasn't to know how long this habit was going to last, how she was growing herself a ribcage and lungs with writing. At the beginning, she only wrote about good things, things she was proud of. Then Onward happened to show her his father's little daybooks. It was a prize collection Onward said, one he treasured. He kept his father's things in boxes with the words *The Grace of God* spelt out in his distinctive sloped lettering. One time, as Glory leaned against the doorjamb to his study one time to say hello, to bring him a cup of tea on a prettily arranged tray, she asked him what they were, what it all meant. That day he was happy to oblige, to indulge her questions. He said: 'A pity you didn't know Bristol Grandpa, Glory, he was a great man of God. He had a way with words.' Onward wore his faraway look. He confessed there had been a time when he was ready to throw the daybooks out, along with his father's lecture notes and sermons. This was before he became interested in 'what Father had to say' about theories of evolution versus creation, and started writing about it himself. Did he think he was growing new muscle? 'Father didn't throw away a single word,' he announced proudly. 'He was a brilliant thinker.' When Glory found out she was descended from a line of little-daybook *Universal*-project people, dating back to her grandfather, she was so pleased that she named her growing collection of notebooks 'Little Daybooks', or LDBs.

At first Glory wrote notes to herself in soft 2B pencil. Added verses from her Precious Promises. Then she started collecting words from newspapers and pamphlets too, cutting them up and sticking them into her daybook with Clag. Scissors going *clip-yer-clip-yer*. What began as a primary school project on ACTIL cotton products (Australian Cotton Textiles Industry), developed into this, her *special project*. She would spread out the collection on her bed, words and phrases and sentences she'd found all over the place. She didn't throw anything away. She played with different patterns to make a sort of poetry, made choices as to how assortments might go together. It wasn't long before she cut up other things for sticking in too: dictionaries, recipe books, photographs, even old Bibles Onward and MotherJoy collected from second-hand bookshops (she was careful to rip out whole pages so no-one could tell). The arrangements and rearrangements floated like waterlilies across the pale blue chenille bedspread on her bed. Glory's very own water garden.

On the evening of Glory's first day at high school the waterlilies had opened their near-perfect flowers like the splash of a Monet painting. The scent had filled the room to make Glory, and Gracie who was watching, dizzy and tipsy, quite heady. Later, tucked up underneath that blue bedspread, Glory was wondering in the scrambled light, how would she ever find the words to describe what happened that day. She was ready to sleep, lulled by the closeness of rain perhaps, the feather-down comfort of night time, the softness of ebbing thought as the body and its physical needs took over sensible thinking, when suddenly, in a movement full of impulse and surprise, MotherJoy fell on Glory to hug her.

Glory gripped MotherJoy in return. She squashed handfuls of flesh, her mother's arms and shoulders, kneaded happiness into her bloodstream. Half-formed sentences corralled about in her mouth— *I love you ... love you I ... you love* (how many permutations of this set? If she were a mathematician like Elsie she could work it out in her head). Her tongue pushed the syllables forward and around, did its very best to order them about in different ways and combinations, like button-sized prayers, the words slipping and skating on saliva. *I love you. I. Love. You.* Three simple words. She could write this down. Three syllables that looked easy enough to say phonetically but nearly impossible to voice.

The most secret of all places

As Glory hugged her mother she felt sure she could feel MotherJoy's heartbeat through the flannel material of their nighties. She felt MotherJoy's breath on her neck. Egg warm. If only she could make it be like this forever, Glory was thinking, if she tried hard enough, squeezed the right way and sang in tune, she could love her mother properly from this exact moment on. No matter what. Amen.

MotherJoy interrupted: 'Don't forget to say your prayers now, will you?'

Glory purred. She had it in her now to sing all night. And the words were very nearly sung out loud so her mother could catch them. But MotherJoy was gone, with a swish of tail cloth, a bang of the door.

42

It would take two weeks for MotherJoy to make up her mind about what to do next. Little Glory was called to the headmaster's office late one morning after little lunch, between Japanese and Science. She perched in a corner on the orange plastic chair in the waiting room. She hated being singled out. Wanted to get away from this place as fast as she could, away from the shrill voice in the room next door. For MotherJoy was at her school again, reciting passages from one of those dreadful books—*the sensual flame ... her bowels and breast*. Glory sat all trembly. She wished she could press her ears flat till they hurt. She would do anything to make MotherJoy happy. Whatever it took. The chorus *I love you I love you* was still stamped on her tongue.

The secretary looked, with a friendly smile, out from across the top of her bifocals over the veneer counter every now and again to punctuate the heated exchange coming from the adjacent room. But her sympathy didn't alleviate the muscle pull of the quicksand Glory found herself sinking into. The young schoolgirl wanted to hide behind the patterns and orderliness of the repeated shapes and colours of the flower arrangement in the wallpaper that bloomed around the walls.

'I simply cannot sit back and do nothing, not with so much at such risk,' Glory heard her mother say.

If only Glory came from an *ordinary* family, she thought, from a family that had no pretensions with a mother who didn't take it upon herself to save the world. Didn't take on the burden of looking after *all* the children of Queensland. Glory wondered how she could float away out of this room. What would it take to rise up, fly windward, to dissipate into vapour?

Bifocals smiled, encouragingly, to cheer her on.

'You will not stop me! Never, ever!'

From where the young Solider sat, all flesh stuck to the sticky plastic chair, she saw the paper walls rain down, the roof cave in. MotherJoy's voice, at a crescendo now, knotted her into a half Nelson.

43

IN THE SOLIDER FAMILY things could develop very fast, overnight if necessary, like growing tropical plants. There were no details to go on, none that Glory could track down, no mathematical equation to solve: x plus y equals z. Lots of voices, though, MotherJoy's and Onward's, behind closed doors and late into the night while the girls tried to practise their instruments. It was a great talking, an untidy whispering campaign. A jabbering like the best of speaking in tongues, if the Solider family believed the Lord's Spirit moved in such a way, which they didn't. And leakage: the duet of MotherJoy and Onward in all its multiplicities of accent and timbre and pitch coagulated into thickness and oozed between the cracks in the floorboards, slipped between the tongue-and-groove of the weatherboards. Not even Eve's vigorous playing of the 'Flight of the Bumblebee' on her flute could drown out their voices.

Glory buried her head into her pillowcase singing lines from a Christian chorus: 'And the rains came down / And the floods came up /'

Then, while the rest of the world slept, MotherJoy and Onward made a decision. The Soliders didn't stay on the cusp of change for long, teetering precariously. You always knew where you stood by sunrise.

44

WHEN GLORY CAME HOME from school the first Friday afternoon of her first week, a new school uniform greeted her, laid out in the shape of a girl down the length of the blue chenille. Thirteen pieces, ready and all. A doppelgänger. There had been no time for the usual fittings in town at McDonnell and East's. MotherJoy had guessed at Glory's size. It was a new grey dress with bright red trims, hat and gloves, and a red satin ribbon to be tied around her neck. And there was a grey sports tunic with red bloomers, and red and grey striped togs folded neatly in a flat rectangle beside the head.

Glory knew exactly where she was going next. She'd seen these colours on the train. She recognised the uniform's associated smell—the perfume, liniments and deodorants. She heard them show off, the flirty girls and their sometimes-coarse mouths. She really wished she could send her double instead of herself, so that on Monday, newly enrolled and dressed in grey instead of blue, instead of turning right at the top of the gangway to go to the high school, Glory's doppelgänger would turn left, as per MotherJoy's instructions. 'Let God punish the wicked,' as MotherJoy liked to say. That was that.

That Friday night they ate hot pies from the Toowong bakery for tea. 'We need softening up, don't we?' MotherJoy snorted in a sort of laugh. For an extra treat Glory was allowed to lift the lid of her pie to fill the middle with squashy tinned peas, squeeze dollops of tomato sauce from a squidgy bottle, make faces on the pastry.

Over the weekend nothing was said about what happened. They mostly did chores like polishing the silver with Silvo and soft, smelly cloths before they went to church. By the end, the silver was so buffed and shiny Glory could see herself pulling faces in the reflection.

Late on Sunday night, MotherJoy suggested they memorise a new Bible chapter in the morning: 'We're living in the last days, Glory Girl,' she said, '"Blessed are they which are persecuted for righteousness' sake: for theirs is the kingdom of heaven". Matthew 5:10. Let's learn it this week. What do you say?'

The most secret of all places

Glory transcribed the verse into her LBD in her best copybook writing. She recited it out loud, punctuation and all: *Matthew five colon ten full stop Blessed are they which are persecuted for righteousness' sake colon for theirs is the kingdom of heaven.* The bit that fascinated Glory was the colon buried mid sentence. The word *persecuted* had such a ring to it too. Glory thought about Jesus dying on the cross, the Spanish Inquisition and witches being burned at the stake, martyrs being stoned and tortured and executed with sharp blades. *Persecute*—such a forthright word. According to *A Modern Classroom Dictionary* it meant 'to torment; to oppress, to cause someone to suffer because of his beliefs'. It sat between the words *perplex* and *persevere*. It wasn't far away from the ridiculous-sounding word *pernicious*, which, whenever Glory tried to say she would almost say *delicious* by mistake. *Remember we live in a delicious world!*

Glory loved looking up words in Onward's dictionary. She had to be sneaky in his study though, quick as a spark plug so he didn't know she'd been there. Besides, it smelt all funny, got up the nose, books and papers, a musty odour of him and his skin, or was it his wispy hair? She never wanted to stay there long.

There was something grand and exotic about chasing words. She wasn't very good at remembering them afterwards, or how to use them, but what Glory liked, in the first flush, was the way the eye ran over the collision of words and meanings, columns and columns of them in the dictionary, how you couldn't possibly know them all, and then the delight in sounding them out with her tongue. Mastering the movement, getting control. How they floated off on their own, quite perfect.

But what of this word *persecuted*? How, if you are persecuted are you also blessed? She'd read the tracts that piled up under a layer of dust on the windowsill in MotherJoy's bedroom: *Jesus to the Communist World*. Cut out different bits for her daybook: stories of Christians being tortured in Russia and China behind the Iron and Bamboo Curtains, Christians having their tongues cut out as punishment for what they believed. And the stories of rescue by *brave Christians* from the West who took boxes of the Good Book across borders. They disguised the Bibles by putting them between covers of other books, ones with different colours and titles and hiding them in the lining of cars, under bonnets, strapped to metal underbellies. You wouldn't want a Bible to come unstuck and fall out on the road by mistake, its Indian paper pages flapping white in the breeze like a flag, a magnet for the border police. Glory wondered how these Christians did it, how they got through? How did they make their tongues say the right things to the Communist guards, knowing full well that what they were smuggling was no more than a leg away? Would they be forgiven later for telling lies, Glory wanted to know? At the last trumpet?

Glory thought about all the tongues the Solider family cooked and ate, the numbers of them if they were stacked in a pile, their anatomy before the dissection, the grey raggy bits she could barely look at where the tongues were torn from the animal's body. Would a human tongue look the same? What would human tongues taste like?

45

Richo, the King of the Talkback Radio must have given MotherJoy the idea about sex education, not that Glory knew who Richo was back then. Because that Saturday, on a dreamy Brisbane afternoon and after the chores were done, MotherJoy made the announcement: 'We're going to make brawn. I'm going to teach you a thing or two.' With that, she plonked a pig's head down on a cutting board in the middle of the kitchen table. The sockets for the eyes glowered back at the Little Girls. It was another startling beginning. Sometimes Glory didn't know where to look.

Sex education was a family thing, MotherJoy insisted. Any teaching of this sort must happen within the privacy of the four walls of the home. It was sacred. At least that's what MotherJoy told King Richo. If you let teachers teach the ins and outs of sex and reproduction, if you left it to books to do the talking, who knew where it would end? 'I'll tell you,' MotherJoy exhorted, on air. 'Heartbroken and in the gutter with venereal disease and homosexuals running rife, teenagers rebelling against their parents.'

'I am the proud mother of six,' she told Richo. 'I have the God-given responsibility to teach my children. If I don't, who knows where they will end up?'

After that very public announcement, MotherJoy became nibbled with worry. A seed of doubt had been sown. Perhaps she should say something to the two smallest of her daughters, the two who were still in her direct care. Should arm them with breastplates and swords? Glory in particular needed God's precepts. She was in the lion's den of secondary school now. So just like that, for this very special weekend of transition from one school to the next, for this moment of coming of age, MotherJoy said: 'Gather round. I'm going to teach you a lesson or two.'

Like old times, like the lesson of tongue—*it might come in handy one day*—Glory and Gracie sat around the kitchen table ready for their cooking lesson, a cooking lesson that developed quickly into an anatomy lesson: not just the anatomy of the meat in front of them, but also that of the female body. 'I asked the Toowong butcher most politely,' she said. 'Had to order it in.' The pig stared back with vacant eyes. MotherJoy radiated pleasure. 'Let's begin.' So there they were, open vessels, pig and all.

First, the pig's head was cooked, holus-bolus, in the biggest pot MotherJoy could find. It took three hours to soften, gurgling away in a swim of water, awash with a handful of peppercorns thrown in and a branch of bay leaves for seasoning; MotherJoy never did things by half. 'To soften but not fall apart,' she explained. When ready, when the timer went *ping* just so, she lifted the whole head up out of the saucepan with a whoosh and a great splash of fatty water across the stove and plonked it down on the spiked board. Then she swished across the room to the table with a flourish, a near dance in the doing with the head of the pig leading, snout out in front. Glory wishes MotherJoy could have gone on dancing like that around the kitchen all day with her Little Girls in tow, dancing together the Piggy Jig. She sometimes did like to kick up her heels as if nothing troubled her, clack about on the linoleum floor, sing a little ditty in her own Irish way: 'And when the saints / go marching in.'

Today, as MotherJoy prepared the meat she looked humbled by the task ahead, humbled by the delicacy of the job, by the part she was playing as midwife to her daughters. Perhaps all along she really did want to be a surgeon like her father-in-law—medicine was close to the priesthood, the breath of God, and surgery was at the top of the tree. She responded so enthusiastically to the high level of concentration necessary, aware of being a master of transformation. This was a perfect activity for such an afternoon as this—and what a lovely long time it would take with all MotherJoy's talk.

Silence fell, as MotherJoy held up the knife ready to make her first cut. It was such a large, sharp knife too. The silver blade flashed in the sunlight. Glory and Gracie held their breath, they leaned into the dissection. The three of them formed a ring, they were together now on an island with any sea of trouble quite forgotten, with the fan whizzing around in the heat overhead as a constant, its sound a measure of their joint heartbeat: *thwack-thwack.*

At first, MotherJoy barely scraped the surface of skin even though she was *that* close—Glory got goosebumps. Instead of making an incision, she pointed at sections and parts of the pig. She pointed out the obvious features: eyes, ears, snout, cheeks. The knife hovered above the parts of the pig she was interested in as if it were floating. It was as if MotherJoy floated there too, to test the water, hovering and testing her daughters.

The most secret of all places

As if she didn't want to go in too far, too deep, not yet. But there was no mistaking her intentions.

'You've got that?' MotherJoy asked, drawing breath to pause and going to the sink to drink two whole tumblers of water. 'My, what thirsty work.' Glory poked and prodded a bit of the pig's cheek herself while her mother's back was turned, careful not to dislodge any part prematurely, careful not to leave a trace. For this was when it got serious, concentration ratcheting up a notch, if that were possible. This lesson, this anatomy, this movement of the knife was all that mattered. Then MotherJoy began to match up the parts of the pig's head in front of her with an imaginary map of the female anatomy: the cheeks, the eyes and snout, represented the annotated diagrams of the female reproduction system remembered from first-year medicine at Queen's. She worked with assurance, a deft touch, cleverly, opening up the flesh a sinew at a time. Everything else from around that kitchen table fell away, didn't exist, and Glory swallowed the word *ouch*; she was transfixed.

The pig's eyes became ovaries, left and right. The sinus passages became fallopian tubes (the scale wasn't quite right, MotherJoy conceded), the nasal passage the uterus. The uvula—the bit that bobs up and down—became the cervix (it's the wrong shape she noted, but it will do) and the pig's mouth—ah, the *pièce de résistance*—was the 'birth canal' as she liked to call it. 'And the teeth?' Gracie dared to ask, trying not to smile. But MotherJoy didn't have anything to say for the teeth. 'It's a bit rough,' she conceded, 'but close enough.' This pig didn't have a tongue either but that seemed to fit her method. 'We have to allow space for a small child here,' and as she said this, her knife bounced in the cavity where the tongue once belonged.

'Say it all again,' Glory said, liking this lesson a lot. 'Go over the different bits once more.'

In the same way the Little Girls persuaded MotherJoy to play the piano over and over again—*we love you playing*—she obliged this time too, and went back over all the different parts again: ovaries, fallopian tubes, uterus, uvula, cervix. Like her daughters, she seemed to like this form of replay.

Then MotherJoy said, to neither of them in particular: 'We women really are remarkable creatures, don't you think?' They smiled together, lassoed by the emotion they were all feeling. 'We're special, you understand,' MotherJoy puffed up her chest, 'not like this pig here.' Glory was hypnotised. 'We're made in the image of God, to wonder at.

Beautiful.' Glory wanted to agree, didn't want to contemplate what the girls at her new school might think, what they would make of the lesson.

But the warmth of the day and the comfort this Solider family cocooned themselves in soothed nerves, pushed away the hows and whys of explaining any of this afternoon's activity, if ever asked. Together these three Soliders existed for each other, on a grotesque planet of their own making, deep in the safety of their kitchen. MotherJoy hummed a snatch of the hymn 'How Great Thou Art' while she set aside the good meat from the pig's head into a large mixing bowl. She set the fat and gristle aside for the chooks in the backyard. Then she pressed the bits and pieces into a glass pudding bowl, poured in a warm gelatine mix spiked with a little salt for seasoning to just below the surface of meat, and covered the top with a saucer weighted down by a brick. She slipped it into the fridge for the night. They would have the pudding on Sunday night for high tea, MotherJoy promised, where it would sit, shiny and glittery in amongst the bowls of peeled hardboiled eggs, racks of toast, and plates of boiled pineapple cake. How Onward, would be pleased! How Onward did love to eat brawn, carve it up too. He liked to sharpen the blade of the knife at the table with a decisive swish.

But for all that, all Glory could see in the pig made up now for the table and ready, were different bits of her own body eddying about in the glistening jelly—ovaries, fallopians, uterus, uvula—the anatomical terms tacked into her skin. Very distinctly too, with all the funny syllables and sounds: *ut-ter-us- fall-op-pi-an-uv-ul-a*. The unfamiliar syllables stirred in her gut. Something didn't seem quite right. Indignity scrambled her organs. As her father sliced up the brawn in beautiful rounds—he was very good at his part—she wanted to turn away. 'Be careful of foreign bodies,' Onward volunteered in his medical way, not suspecting a thing.

But then Gracie came to the rescue. Glory felt her sister's warm foot slide over hers underneath the table bringing her back to the present. Gracie rested it there, skin-enveloping skin, and smiled at her big sister across the table. This was better, this was normal. Glory felt breath return and swell up in waves from her belly: a steady quarter time. She sensed herself returning slowly to shore with every mouthful.

Later, in front of the mirror, the Little Girls laughed so much their bellies ached. They were trying to talk without a tongue like the pig, with their mouths and cheeks and jaws going haywire. Jelly wobble. They laughed until their bellies had stitches zigzagged across them, as though they had eaten too much jelly and gone swimming like that, blocking their ears to Onward's warning: *You know that's how small children drown.*

Kill! Kill!

46

THE DAY I FOUND MY MOTHER in the Queensland archives—really found her there, her voice and all—was a very ordinary Brisbane afternoon, unremarkable for the season. I knew it would only be a matter of time. I'd been making good progress tracking down references to do with her campaign, but when I saw this new material, my heart caved in. It felt personal; I could hear her voice speaking to me directly, accusing, protesting and pleading.

> I have gone back to general practice ... I am absolutely aghast at what is happening to our young women ... One thing is the disease. Our young women are rotten with disease. I am absolutely appalled at what I have found ... I have no doubt whatever that one of the factors has been the type of literature that has been promoted in the schools.

Dr Angel Rendle-Short was making an appearance at a Queensland inquiry into education known as the Ahern Inquiry. The inquiry received over three thousand written submissions from all sorts of organisations and from people from all around the state. Public hearings were held over seventeen days and 'the doctor' was invited to appear at one of these in Brisbane at Parliament House. This was different from any other public appearance my mother made; there was a formality to the proceedings—the Chair of the inquiry was in charge, he directed the interrogation. My mother was being questioned and she was on the back foot. There were six pages dedicated to her examination.

> I tried to interest my children in Shakespeare, in Milton—some of the really, really great men in the past—and they have already abandoned them; they are not interested...
>
> They have a room to study in, they have peace and quiet in the evening, they have everything, and parents who are interested, quite a big library of books—but in my view, coming out the other end, they are not educated at 17 or 18...
>
> Give a 13-year-old *Catcher in the Rye* and I think he is a goner...

At the time my mother was making these declarations, I was eighteen years old and in my final year of high school. 'I say this of my own children,' she said at one point. 'I hope nobody is listening or is going to take this down in writing.'

This is when it became personal, and not just because she was criticising her own children—which she was. But it was her naivety that brought me up short; suddenly I saw her fragility. Surely she knew that everything that was being said that day was being recorded. Didn't she hear the *clack-clack-clack* of the *Hansard* stenographers belting out her words onto foolscap, and the shuffle in and out of the room as a shift ended and another one started? The examination would have taken some time, a full session.

```
to my mind they are not educated.  ]
.  I hope nobody is listening or is
in writing, but a family which has ;
```

That day there was a group of primary schoolchildren from a Brisbane state school sitting in the gallery, watching proceedings. The Chair addressed them at the start, saying, all this was for them. I wonder what they made of what they heard. Did her voice rise in pitch at this point so that everybody stared? Did they detect the catch in her voice? Did she look a little bewildered? Did the audience laugh? Snigger?

There I was, some thirty years later in the quiet of the Fryer Library in a sandstone tower at the University of Queensland, reading everything that she said that day, hearing it in her tone, her particular way of putting things, her choice of vocabulary and inflection, the register and accent, her parenthetical syntax. It was as though I were present in parliament with her, in the flesh. I imagined her centre stage, with everybody watching her, including those small schoolchildren hanging over the wooden gallery railings trying not to giggle. I wondered what she wore that day. A new dress from Life Line? A fringed scarf? She would have been concentrating hard, her eyebrows knitted together. Did she have notes, a clipboard? Or had she memorised her lines the night before? Was her heart thumping in her chest like mine, thumping fit to burst?

I read this transcript in concert with the other thing I found in the archive that day, a report making fun of her and her manifesto, published in the University of Queensland student newspaper at the time of my mother's opposition to the women's radio 4BW: 'I stand against homosexuality, sodomy, bestiality and similar evils, all of which threaten to destroy our society.'

I could feel her warm breath protesting across my skin. I tried to remain calm. And I remembered the pig—the 'sex pig' from my childhood—the smell of meat boiling away on the stove, the feel of oily steam in the old kitchen, and the trill of my mother's voice as she catalogued our anatomy. The pig's eye sockets beamed back accusingly across the years and that idea of shame, implicit in every quavering word of my mother's response to the inquiry's questions, stuck in my hair, knotted my throat, infiltrated my imagination. Her timbre and cadence scrambled the words and pages of those manuscripts and reports I was now reading in the library.

But do you know what? Perhaps it was the ordinariness of that afternoon—dark thunderclouds over Mt Coot-tha and butcherbirds rollicking in the jacaranda waiting for the rain. Perhaps it was the pleasure of the find—I wasn't making up this story about a 'death list', after all. Or maybe it was the pleasure of writing Glory's story—finding language to shape a new self: like reading, writing changes everything. Because, as I left the sandstone tower that afternoon, I danced a merry jig all the way home through the rain. I was bursting. So very pleased to be alive.

When I left home as a nineteen-year-old to go to university travelling across the Queensland border by Greyhound bus, my mother warned me as she waved goodbye: 'Whatever you do, Francesca, don't do English literature, do something else, anything else.' It had taken decades for me to find the courage to read *Lord of the Flies* for myself, to *really* read it, to learn of Piggy and Simon, and to read about Simon's dead body and the cloud of tiny creatures looking after him, floating with him on a journey to the open sea.

I found out William Golding writes beautifully, he makes me weep. It is, as somebody once remarked in protest against my mother's war cry: 'a literary work on the side of angels'. I discovered this counterview on Golding's book buried in a report on a public meeting of 'religious extremists' held in a Presbyterian Church hall in Brisbane organised by the Queensland League for National Welfare and Decency. That was one of the meetings my mother stormed out of shouting *Shame! Shame!*

47

BIG GLORY WONDERS if she has the stomach to continue writing this story. It's closing in. The story is beginning to turn on the plate. She feels her body—all the different parts—there, on the dissection table for all to see. Floating in gelatine. Ready to eat. Is this how Piggy felt?

Lord of the Flies was first published by Faber and Faber in 1954. The copy Glory owns was published in 1975, the twenty-first impression. In 1983, when Glory was at university, William Golding was awarded the Nobel Prize for Literature. And there, in Glory's handwriting in the margins of her copy of the book and in 2B pencil, are annotations from her first year, things like *Appalling! Appalling!?? How can someone write this?* She must have been channelling her mother even though she thought she was being brave Doing Literature at university. *What horror! This is evil*. She won't ever tell her bookshop mates about this bit of her story. She feels too ashamed to admit it.

She reads the book now, rereads those difficult passages, the ones that once made her squirm. She insists on keeping an open mind. *Lord of the Flies* is a difficult book, sure. But she needs to discover what Golding's words do to her now. How they make her feel. How they turn something inside her that was hard and awkward and immutable to softness. He knows how to make reading compulsive. What it means to perform magic.

Glory starts to build her own library of books based on her mother's list from all those years ago. She calls it her 'death list library'. She imagines a reading group working their way through the list, reading all one hundred books. She wonders how long this would take. Wonders too what the group would say in conversation over chocolate brownies and fair-trade coffee, whether they would set themselves to working out what it is that might have secured the book's place on the list: what was so objectionable, why was it considered 'dirty' and 'salacious'? The idea might just take off.

Glory scrounges through second-hand bookshops, garage sales and market stalls whenever she can. She takes the list with her everywhere. She likes finding editions from that time, the ones published in the 1960s and early 1970s; copies she imagines her mother collected. She likes the smallness of these books, nearly all A-format paperbacks, the tiny typeface, the way the print jostles the edge of the paper. The lovely smell of these yellowing pages, like turned earth. The old-fashioned covers. Their simplicity, aesthetics.

She piles up the growing library on the floor against a wall of her bedroom so that they form two tall towers. Glory has to be careful the turrets don't fall, she's methodical about putting larger-sized books at the bottom. George Johnston's *Clean Straw for Nothing* in hardback underpins one tower, and Germaine Greer's *The Female Eunuch* the other. Both are first editions. She wonders about the original ordering of her mother's list, wonders what methodology was behind that taxonomy. The list is not alphabetical—by author or by title. Why does Lawlor's *Summer of the Seventeenth Doll* come first, for instance? Why do some books by the same author, like J. D. Salinger's *The Catcher in the Rye* and *Franny and Zooey* (Salinger spelt both times with a *B* as Ballinger), sit side by side, while D. H. Lawrence—the author with the greatest number of books—is included four times, but split up? If Glory can solve this little puzzle, then perhaps she might understand MotherJoy's thinking better.

She reorders the death list using her piano as a bookshelf, this version fitting across seven octaves from A to top C alphabetised by author from Edward Albee's *Who's Afraid of Virginia Woolf?* to Paul Zindel's *The Pigman*. Dr Joy's Death List—a piano of books. She can identify the gaps now: sixty-six books in total, thirty-four to go.

Glory has to remember to take the list with her everywhere, for she never knows when she might trip over missing titles. A friend says: 'You should write the lot in small print as a tattoo up and down your arms. That way you wouldn't need a list. That way you'd remember.'

When Glory is visiting the markets in Canberra, a bookseller wants to know about her interest in E. R. Braithwaite's *To Sir with Love*—'I'd just never think anyone would want to read that book today, such an old-fashioned book, amongst all these,' she confesses, gesturing at the collection she's selling off, 'why this one in particular?' At a seconds' bookshop in inner Melbourne, the shopkeeper asks what's the connection between the list and the ten books already in Glory's arms. 'Is it a booklist for an English class?' When Glory explains that she's looking for books

Queenslander campaigners wanted to ban, he laughs and says: 'That'd be right. Takes your breath away really. I remember the fuss with *Lady Chatterley's Lover*, even in Melbourne, we were all scurrying to borrow the book from friends! Some people tore it into chapters. You made a lot of money that way, selling it in bits.'

Of course she could always get the missing ones online. Type in an author and name and collectors from all over the world pop up. Lists of books with notes about the condition of the edition, whether there are pages missing, annotations and varying costs. But it's not the same as going into a bookshop in person, expectant and hopeful, with a list with crossings out in red—the musty, bookish smell of these quirky places, the time it takes, these anonymous conversations about her project and her purchases, her excitement.

48

This is how Glory finds herself in a second-hand bookshop in Buderim, back in Queensland, when she's on an emergency visit. On this occasion, Glory gets a call from MotherJoy to say she and Onward are moving from the villa into a nursing home. They've been given twenty-four hours to make a decision and then seven days to take up occupancy in the new beds. MotherJoy needs help.

Not that she says this in so many words. She never asks. But Glory can't imagine how she and Onward will be able to do it themselves without help—move out of a two-bedroom villa with two bathrooms and a lounge room and kitchen and a laundry and garage into two small rooms separated by five corridors in a nursing home down the hill on the coast—with only two buggies, Onward on a walking stick and forgetful, and MotherJoy with feet that flare up with rheumatoid arthritis.

When she gets to their house, Glory finds MotherJoy making phone calls to all the missionary societies she and Onward donate to, to tell them they won't be able to do this anymore, because things have changed, for good. She's in a tizz. Her voice is high and squeaky but ever so polite. After each call, her hands move across the table settling and resetting the piles of paper in front of her, moving the rocks she uses to weight them down, to and fro. She doesn't look up. Onward sits on his bed in his room still in his pyjamas with his hand resting on the two books he has decided to take with him: his Bible and a book on paediatrics in Queensland. Nothing else is organised. Nothing has been packed. There are no cardboard boxes to be seen. No newspapers to wrap things up in. And although MotherJoy has booked a removalist van for the next morning, she doesn't know what time they will arrive and she can't remember the name of the company.

This is the last move they will make like this. The next one will be to a hospital with hand luggage; Glory can see the knowledge written into the lines across their brows. Already they are diminished. Statistics record that many new residents in nursing homes don't last more than four months; if they do, they last for years. Glory has never worked so hard, so fast. It will be a very long night.

The next day, when two boofy men turn up at sunrise, MotherJoy is still thinking about what to take with her. She fancies she might do some entertaining from the white wicker garden set with its floral cushions that she'll set up in the small walled courtyard off her room, put it amongst potted orchids. The other thing she has to choose is which hat she'll wear out of the villa to say goodbye, and which one she will wear into her new abode to make an impression. 'My lovely hats make me vain,' she confesses. 'Do you think they'll all fit in?'

Eventually, the removalists can get cracking—they don't mind sitting around as long as they get paid. They leave behind rooms full of detritus, suck on iced water, and take turns to wear MotherJoy's hats laughing all the way down the path and up into the truck. They sweat into folded newspapers, and smoke through the rainstorm as they unpack at the other end. Onward keeps asking: 'Where are we now?'

It takes seven full days to empty and clean the villa ready to hand over the keys. Ruthy and Eve help too. Together, they discover old passports and birth certificates astray in a filing cabinet they very nearly threw out before looking in; the Salvos take the kitchen stuff—holus-bolus. They divide up precious family memorabilia into little packages to send to the others and to the grandchildren. Glory asks to have the old dictionaries. They smash a couple of pretty blue and white dinner plates—the willow-pattern china, like new spring flowers—over the garden in celebration of the sheer effort, then they take ages picking up all the shards, laughing and crying to stitches. They eat fish and chips so many times the shop assistant asks what they're up to: *she's dying to know*, she says. And Glory rubs away the truth of all that she's feeling from around her sore heart, rubs it away with one of those damp cleaning cloths they've been using.

49

GLORY VOLUNTEERS TO TAKE a few boxes of books to the second-hand bookshop, to flog them there. Onward has a library wall to sort out—they've got to put it somewhere, give the books away if they have to.

The bookshop owner is very kind, but she doesn't want Onward's old books. She says: 'I think I know your father, surely it's the same name, I've already been to his home once before to have a look at his books. Christian books mostly, books about creationism.' She suggests Lifeline down the hill might be interested. 'They'll always take books, and it's surprising,' she adds, 'how many Christians there are up this way. I'm going down there this afternoon, I'll take this lot for you, if you like.'

Glory thanks her, then pulls out the grubby list that goes with her everywhere to ask about some of the missing titles on her growing piano of books. She can't bear to let this opportunity slip, even though it doesn't feel quite the thing to do. 'So you're the rebel of the family then?' The owner asks with a laugh. 'What would your father think of these?' Together they find twenty books for fewer than one hundred dollars the lot.

Glory doesn't know how to respond. It turns out the owner has read most of the books Glory purchases. 'Why would people want to ban them,' she asks, 'what's wrong with these? They're all good books. That's why I'm in this business.'

It's only at the end of the transaction, and when she's almost out the door with a different box of books under her arm to the one she came in with, that Glory turns. She blurts out: 'By the way, my parents don't know anything about this,' gesturing to her box, courage a pill under her tongue. 'If my mother comes in, and she might too, don't say anything, will you? She doesn't know I'm writing about this.' Glory is certain the woman can hear her noisy heart beating fast *blat! blat!* What if MotherJoy *does* find out what she is doing?

Out in the warm Queensland sunshine on the street, Glory tries to regain her composure, takes exaggerated breaths. Everything looks normal here she tells herself, everybody going about everyday tasks. With the sun on her back, she gives herself a pep talk, dawdling back to the villa: *Remember why you came.* She thinks of what MotherJoy and Onward must be going through, as they step closer to heaven's gates. MotherJoy's eyes are already like two empty holes; she's gazing right through Glory to the other side.

50

It's true—about MotherJoy climbing a ladder to heaven. Earlier, for instance, Glory suggested she help sort the wall of books in Onward's room. MotherJoy said they needed to do this, to have peace of mind, to know which books to take. 'You'll need more than two, Onward dear, even if you don't read them.' She says this in a moment of commiseration while touching Onward's arm gently. He looks towards her beseechingly. He really doesn't know what's going on.

'I'll help you,' Glory volunteers. Brightly.

The three of them sit in Onward's room together, Onward and MotherJoy on the bed, Glory kneeling on her haunches on the floor at their feet. MotherJoy and Onward take their time, what little time there is, develop a rhythm, move the books back and forth between them, build piles of favourites on the carpet, throw different books into different boxes to go to different places. They even discard some into the bin.

The three develop a system. First, Glory pulls the books down from the shelf in a caterpillar of a dozen or so at a time, the books squeezed between her hands to keep them from dropping. She blows away the thick coating of dust that has collected along the top and this cloud guides her to the floor. Then she passes the books to each of them, one at a time, asking the same questions: 'What do you think?' and 'Where will this book go?'

'I really like this one.'

'What a lot of books we have.'

'Throw that away, it's rubbish.'

MotherJoy and Onward begin to talk to each other as if Glory is invisible, as if they are alone, just the two of them. They form a private reading circle. Glory stops asking questions.

'What's so good about this one again?'

'Since when have you read that?'

'I want to take this one.'

'Listen to this…'

'Look, this must be my favourite.'
'Will you ever read it again, really?'
'I might read it now.'
'But you've never read it.'
'I really like Spurgeon, he's such a good writer, a good preacher too.'
'No, you can't read it now, do that later.'
'And J. C. Ryle.'
'Let me read you this bit.' MotherJoy's eyes glisten with delicate pleasure.

Glory listens and watches, quiet now so as not to disturb them. For with each line spoken something soft and beguiling begins to grow in the room. Is this the way they speak to each other everyday when no one is looking? Do they speak with books, through books, *because of* books? Imagine this is how they get close to one another: with the passing of favourites, the reciting of remembered passages, like the saying and exchange of prayers. A kind of reverence descends on the small room—stillness. Glory watches, witness here to a sacrament, the intimacy of sharing like the giving and receiving of Communion in church, the passing between them of bread and wine—the body and blood of Christ. These two people have been together for over half a century and now hold each other together at this crossroads with a saving grace they administer one to the other, with the pages of the books they've read and loved and cared for over the years. These books map out a story of their lives—no matter that they are mostly religious, Glory thinks—a biography of shared experience, a way to knit up 'the ravell'd sleave of care', to borrow from Macbeth, for isn't approaching death a kind of sleep? Not that Shakespeare gets a look in—MotherJoy is contradictory on Shakespeare—she drops an old collected volume of his plays into a bin bound for St Vinnies. 'I didn't know I had this. Must be from when the girls were at school.'

Glory wonders: might this be the last time they share Communion? She tries not to interrupt her parents' concentration, even though her legs are screaming pins and needles.

It is MotherJoy who breaks up the circle, but gently. She says: 'Onward dear, I think you and I need a cup of tea, don't you?' They all jolt back to earth. Then her eyes flick Glory's way to notice her momentarily. 'Let's leave it to Glory, shall we? She'll know what to do with these books.' As she says this, she takes one of Glory's hands into her own and slowly pats the back of it, just the way she used to do it when Glory was a little girl, with the faraway look on her face, just how Glory likes it done. Sunny side up. MotherJoy says: 'He will not let us suffer beyond that which we are able.' A tremulous reprieve before turning the page.

51

MOST OF THE GIRLS at Glory's new school were so self-absorbed they didn't notice her slip into their nest. Besides, she looked the part in her grey dress heavy down past her knee, red ribbons in her hair. MotherJoy had faith in this all-girls' Christian school and the Sisters who ran it, a belief that she and they would see eye to eye.

On Monday morning Grade 8a were in the Music Room, a large open-plan rehearsal room beneath the library, a room filled with music stands and soft-clothed brown instrument cases. Miss Babbage was in charge. Miss Babbage was trying to expand on the finer intricacies of symphony, the meaning of the word in musical parlance, how all the various instruments might fit together in harmonic combinations—sometimes dissonant ones too, if the work called for it—enabling the composer to explore the nuance of sound. Glory felt at home with music, a good beginning. Miss Babbage was explaining, but the other girls weren't listening. Her dulcet tones dissolved in their nattering like Disprins fizzing in water. These girls were more interested in catching up with what everyone had done on the weekend, which girl was going out with what boy. They had already established a pecking order. They surveyed Glory like you might a cut of meat at the butcher and then, with only a semiquaver rest, *allegro*, resumed their chatter. Two weeks at this new school and they were acting like old hands. Everyone except Lisa.

Lisa saw Glory before Glory was aware of Lisa, or so Lisa reckoned afterwards. When they reminded each other about it much later, Glory swore she noticed her in amongst the faces, saw Lisa smile; a wry smile from the percussion in the back corner, a grin from out of the timpani.

At lunchtime, Lisa sat beside Glory on a bench in the quadrangle. Even this small gesture made Glory blush. Not that Lisa said anything particular that first Monday, not that she struck up much of a conversation. It was more something born out of nonchalance, a peculiar character trait of Lisa's. Just enough words to ask Glory who she was, where she'd come from and why so late? Glory mumbled a tale about the caravan getting bogged on Bribie Island—her first lie—how her parents had only just decided which school to send Glory to. 'All very rushed, very last minute,' she offered. To her relief, her tongue didn't burn although she did have to turn her face to hide her cheeks as the words slid out unceremoniously, and there was some loose spittle at the corners of her mouth—she wasn't proud of it. It was enough though—enough of a story for the moment.

That was Day One. The taste of pineapple was still in Glory's mouth from the jelly-belly laughs with Gracie from the night before. Oh to live that first day over and over, too, Glory thought, to have that one roll into all the others: a repeated performance. That would be bearable. She could write the music for it by ear—with the music stave and treble clef and all, with the melody and minim and crotchet rests, repeat bars. Miss Babbage would give her good marks.

But it didn't happen like that, this abandonment to a good melody.

Going to school each day from then on was like walking on coals from one of Onward's open fires (he said they reminded him of the old country). It was a score Glory didn't fancy. Made her edgy. She was jumpy even though nothing was said out loud in those early days, nothing to Glory directly. But the girls soon let Glory know that she was different from them. One time, one of them tripped her up to see what would happen. They wanted to see how the new girl would react: get in quick and then everyone would know where they stood. The girl had crept up behind Glory after school on the way to the station. She'd waited for cracks and kinks in the concrete, unevenness, and then whipped out a hockey stick. Down went Glory all over the footpath. Everyone was cheering. Nobody looked back. Nobody helped her get up.

What Glory was to discover was this: being in between the covers of a Christian school wasn't going to be the end of the story. This school wouldn't save her. It didn't spell safety, *p-r-o-t-e-c-t-i-o-n*.

MotherJoy expected great things of this school. She was watching closely, its brand of teaching and Christianity was on trial. She was more than prepared to tell the Sisters that what they thought they were doing right, was *wrong*. The likelihood of strife rustled the pages of all the books in the school. It was as if the books themselves came alive with the whispering campaign, flung open their covers to talk, to garner support. If they were going to survive, they had to stick together. They would need the imaginations of their authors: Sylvia Plath, Dylan Thomas, Lawlor, Griffin and Steinbeck. Even the Bibles in the school rustled their

Indian silk pages together in support of English literature. The challenge in Queensland in 1973 was not only to keep the books alive, but also find a way to refute the claims of the campaigners.

And Lisa? Glory knew that Lisa knew something early on. For one, she had recognised Glory's name. She once said, offhandedly: 'There aren't many Soliders in the White Pages, are there, if you look them up? You're it.' The other thing she said was this: 'They say Joh Bjelke-Petersen trades with brown paper bags. Your mother knows the Missus, doesn't she?'

While the other girls talked about buying shoes at Myers and lipsticks and bangles from Sportsgirl, Lisa rustled around politics. She knew how Joh liked to do business (her dad worked in government, she said, in the 'law enforcement' section, so he should know). She knew all about the Springbok rugby tour and the anti-apartheid riots—Joh's declared State of Emergency. She wanted to march in the protests—she boasted about this in class discussion—get arrested by the police and be put into paddy wagons and into Boggo Road Gaol. Except her old man wouldn't let her, she said, he wouldn't want his only daughter dumped in a Queensland gaol—'it's no place for girls,' he told her. Lisa's family lived out west, her parents worked at the gaol, both of them Lisa said, as a team. They were in charge of the new inmates.

Sometime later Lisa would tell Glory about hearing MotherJoy on air on the new talkback program on radio, about the right-wing morals campaign on Open Line on 4BC (in the Solider family radio, like TV, was evil). 'It's got to be her'—Lisa said—'she's a member of STOP and CARE, isn't she?' She lent Glory a radio transistor to hear for herself, so she would know for sure. Glory clutched it to her heart, never gave it back.

Lisa was different from the other girls. She didn't mind what anyone thought of her; she did her own thing. Lisa was a scholarship pupil, not that she broadcast this particular fact. She was 'special', the Sisters said, needed looking after. Glory never went to her friend's place—just as Glory never invited Lisa home to St Lucia. Glory came from the other side of the river to Lisa. Hers was a suburb of wealth and prosperity, sandstone cloisters, flowering trees and riverside swimming pools. It was a suburb for professional people—it whispered comfort, privilege. How much did this word play its part in MotherJoy's unfolding campaign, her speaking up? Did she think she had immunity?

Not Lisa.

Kill! Kill!

'Ooh, that Lisa, she has a tongue on her, doesn't she?' The Sisters complained. That's why she was often seen outside the Sister-in-Charge's office. She'd sit there all perky on a stool, poking her tongue out at any of the other pupils passing by, as if to dare them. She knew the Sisters wouldn't throw her out, no matter what she did. She knew they were afraid.

Once, when Lisa had been hauled up to see Sister, she produced a matchbox squashed full with baby mice, quite dead and beyond rigor mortis, rubbery soft. She had already shown them off in geography. The other girls screamed when she shoved the babies under their noses. One girl tittle-tattled so then Lisa nearly lost them to the science teacher who came to the defence of the geography teacher. Lisa had to glue together a few lies to buy time and keep the mice from being confiscated. The bell saved her. Mind you, if she did land in Sister's hands, when the teachers ran out of ideas, Lisa knew she could do no wrong.

Glory liked Lisa. Her brazenness. She liked how she rescued the mice from the scalpel. How, if it was a matter of dignity, Lisa dived in, no matter what the consequences. It was one thing to cut up fully-grown mice, pin them taut to the dissection table, another thing altogether to cut up their babies. That's what Lisa said, anyhow. That's why she rescued them from being slit open down their tummies from the throat to the anus, from being pinned to a board with dressmaker's pins. Glory was touched; she liked the thought of these babies being looked after, being saved, even though they were dead. She took them with her everywhere that term, tucked up in the matchbox and zipped into her pocket. That's how hard Lisa played. 'Everyone wants a perve and a whiff,' Lisa said. And it was true, they all asked for a look. The box smelt strongly of formaldehyde when she slid open the lid. She had made a bed of soft cottonwool for the babies to lie on where they floated on a little cloud, head to toe. 'They're in heaven,' she said, and they did look like newborn angels. She was clever like that, with detail.

Glory overheard two teachers speculating on playground duty what might become of Lisa when she left school, only to agree they really had absolutely no idea. 'Lisa is her own girl,' they said. The teachers were huddled together on a bench behind the library, more interested in gossip and hot pies with sauce and the smell of each other's shoes, than on keeping an eye on the playground caper. 'Will you look at her now?' The teachers looked like they had never graduated beyond senior themselves, with their headbands and polished nails, as if they had gone straight from year ten into teacher's college and back into school. 'She's too worldly for this school,' they muttered. 'She'll end up in a ditch.'

For all that, for all Lisa's interest in dissection and preserving bodies, Glory couldn't tell her about MotherJoy and the anatomy lessons at home around the kitchen table. How lessons in Pressing Meats turned quickly to Naming Parts, sexual parts at that. The two of them would sit with each other at big lunch sunning their legs with their uniforms pulled up high to expose their thighs (Glory following Lisa's lead). They walked together between classes. They sat out of swimming lessons on the pool benches with stories in their mouths about heavy periods and popping Codral and iron tablets. They became a study pair in the science lab in junior, did experiments together with a single Bunsen burner, and wrote up each other's notes. They graduated to dissecting a rat together and spilled the formaldehyde all over their uniforms with a plan to stink out the train on the way home. The science teacher agreed she'd never seen such a good skinning for a grade ten, even though it was pinned the wrong way. Lisa named the rat Ringo Starr after her favourite Beatle.

Being around Lisa made Glory feel different, but it was unlike anything she'd experienced before; it was a different kind of difference too. When she was with Lisa she forgot about being a Solider. With Lisa things went everywhere, haywire.

In the science lab the two of them loved shifting matter from one state to the other: solid to liquid to gas. A favourite experiment was to grow copper sulphate crystals. The two of them grew lots of crystals, the bigger the better. Glory liked the way organic chemistry worked, how each element and compound had to match up and be accounted for—$CuO + H_2SO_4 = CuSO_4 + H_2O$—how nothing could simply disappear. Everything mattered.

Once, Glory and Lisa grew the most brilliant, deep-blue crystal, with the smoothest of sides to its triclinic shape—the three, unequal, oblique axes. So big, so pure, so perfect that Lisa wore it as a jewel on a leather thong around her neck. Blue vitriol. A prize-winning crystal. They both received blue certificates in the secondary school science section at the Ekka, the annual Brisbane Exhibition. Lisa cut hers up into tiny little pieces like confetti and showered Glory with it, laughing at her duck and weave, and then together they danced on the spot in a trance.

Glory hadn't known people like Lisa existed. Everything about Lisa surprised. Glory loved being close to her, loved the idea of being liked as a friend, of being caught in the middle of a circle, a circle in the shape of Lisa. Glory promised herself to make sure they were inseparable.

Still, there was so much between these two girls that remained unspoken. Enough to make Glory wonder whether they really were friends. She didn't want to probe too much into what it was that brought them together. She didn't dare ask questions, not questions of the big, unsettling kind anyway, for fear of dissolving the illusion, evaporating into a gas herself. Did Lisa really like her? It never occurred to Glory that their friendship was because they were both outsiders. This thinking comes later as she writes this story. For the time being, one thing was certain: in Lisa's presence the threat of breaking up into little pieces, as Glory often thought she might do, retreated into the background. Lisa was as good as Quiet Time in the mornings, praying on her knees beside her bed. Lisa created stillness in Glory and Glory began to rely on her as she did her own breath. Glory wonders now as she writes this, what happened to Lisa? What would Lisa make of this Glory-story if ever she chanced to read it?

52

ONE DAY IN ENGLISH things did go haywire. But it wasn't because of Lisa's doing; they weren't conducting a science experiment. It happened because Miss Keynote was in charge.

Miss Keynote, the head English teacher, made it her business to know the girls in grade ten. She said she liked to prepare them for what was to come in the senior years. She insisted on readings and recitals, comprehension. She made her girls memorise great chunks of the best writers' work in English Literature insisting, too, on its capital-L status and authority. 'By heart,' she said, 'put the words in your heart.' Just as she was able to recite whole passages from *Macbeth* and *The Tempest*, decades after learning them herself at school, she wanted these girls to have their own set of favourite recitations: the closing sentences to F. Scott Fitzgerald's *The Great Gatsby* for example, Atticus' instructions to Jem about shooting blue jays and not mockingbirds, and Lucky's and Pozzo's confusion and anxiety when waiting for Godot.

Miss Keynote believed in what she read. She wanted to open the minds of her girls, to take them beyond themselves; out of their provincial Brisbane lives. This kind of learning became conspiratorial, a way of speaking in whispers to each other. She had faith in great writers. She believed that the carefully crafted words and their arrangements harboured meaning—*as a way to live*. She set very high standards.

When Miss Keynote first met Glory Solider she said: 'I know who you are.' She could have been saying it simply as a matter of fact; perhaps their paths had already crossed on a roll call or report card. But her tone suggested something more. *Don't you forget it*, she might as well have added: *Don't forget who's in charge*. All the girls knew Miss Keynote did not like to be crossed; she came to their classroom with a reputation. Something more was going to be said, this was certain. Glory was destined to become the centre of Miss Keynote's attention. In some dread then of what might transpire, Glory practised making a deadpan face in front of the mirror while plaiting her hair in the morning. This is what happened, how this story goes.

The teachers must have known exactly who Glory was the day she arrived. News would have travelled fast around the staffroom like the puff of cigarettes. Miss Keynote might have even announced something: *I'm going to have to say something. Just watch.* After all, her English syllabus was under threat. *Give her to me and I'll tell her what's what. I'm happy to wait, there's time, but I will get her.* In any case, one afternoon after lunch, early on in the term, she swept into the English classroom all puff, hot and red in the face: 'Stand up, girl.'

Glory and Lisa sat in the back row, as they always did. Their uniforms were a mess. They had been fighting each other through lunch, play fighting in the quadrangle in the sun. They had tried to be the first to rub orange quarters through the other's hair, to see how far they could go before getting caught. On the sound of the bell, they smartened themselves up, straightened their uniforms, but still they looked skew-whiff, amuck. A pair of frights. When they heard Miss Keynote shout out, they automatically smoothed down the pleats over their knees as best they could. You could still see orange pith in their pigtails, hair strands were stuck together like glue. It would have been really quite funny except that now Lisa and Glory were obviously in trouble.

'Stand up, girl. Do you hear me?'

There was something different about the way Miss Keynote spoke this afternoon, how her body swivelled into the room. You could almost feel the heat she was giving off. She said the word *girl* in the singular form, so it couldn't be both of them. And it was *how* she said the words too: *Stand up, girl*. It wasn't in the usual *I-must-discipline-you-naughty-girls* kind of way; in the usual *girls-must-demonstrate-decorum-at-all-times* way. Or even that *this is my job, this has to be done, and this is what I have been trained to do*—said with a yawn. No. What she was saying, and the manner in which her whole body was saying it, suggested this mattered more than anything: it was about Miss Keynote herself, her sense of self and identity. Her voice shook too, as she nailed the words in place.

The air prickled with heat and Glory's skin pricked with the sweat of her body. Lisa gasped—Glory heard it, close range. Everyone guessed, without it being said, which girl Miss Keynote was referring to. This was the confrontation Glory had been waiting for. But for some reason and unpremeditated at that, as she heard the command shoot her way, as the space between her and Miss Keynote filled with the smell of rocket afterburn, Glory pretended she didn't know who the English teacher could be referring to. Almost—if you could believe this—that she didn't hear the command at all. *How extraordinary*, she thought later: *how did I do that?* She did hear Miss Keynote's voice from afar, of course, from way off, a shot from the door, the coming of something, yes, but not at her, not *for her*. That was it: Glory delayed her reaction though she knew in time she would have to react in some way. She let the words hang in suspension. Glory insisted, in her own silent way, that Miss Keynote reveal herself more, *with more*.

She did.

'There are some parents in this school,' Miss Keynote elaborated, 'who think they know best how to educate young people, who are adept at the theory and practice of modern teaching, who dare to want to take our place.' She said the word *dare* as she would strike a high C if singing an aria. All throat. A lifted soft palette. Quintessential control. With that word she raised her eyebrows knowingly, as though they were two cats putting their bottoms and tails into the air about to pounce. She cast her gaze around the room across the heads of all the girls, her captive audience, before settling pointedly on Glory.

'Your mother, Glory. I'm talking about your mother. She says the sort of education we are giving our pupils is *defilement*, do you hear?' Miss Keynote pointed a stick of yellow chalk in Glory's direction. Her body was so rigid with her hand extended she was near breaking herself in two. She was casting out evil spirits with this move. 'Now stand up girl when I say,' her voice wobbled on this command, betraying something else: did Glory detect nervousness?

'Your interfering mother thinks she knows best.' Snap. The chalk broke in two, fell and bounced on the wooden floor between her legs like something rude. 'She dares to interfere in Our Literature. She says it is sex-saturated. You've only got to read the letters to the papers—"Mother Disgusted with School Books", "Immoral Books Third-Rate Gutter Trash", "Be Wary of Homosexuals".' Miss Keynote must have learned the lines by heart. 'Your mother says you are not allowed to read the book *Improving on the Blank Page*. Dr Joy Solider says you are not allowed to meet the wicked Holden Caulfield under any circumstance. She says that these books—books on our very own reading list, do you hear?—are pornographic.' Miss Keynote was flying now all around the room, full throttle.

When the girls heard the words *sex*, *homosexual* and *pornographic*, they started to snigger, they couldn't help it. Miss Keynote made a mocking face like a clown. As she grew in confidence, they laughed more noticeably. She liked to control their emotion, she was good with words, they were her preferred instruments.

'And she's saying these things in public, on radio, for everyone to hear!'

With a flourish, she tugged at her hair and to the surprise of everyone, yanked off the black curly wig she was wearing to reveal grey wisp pulled back neatly in a maroon velvet bow. She did it with a single deft swoop of her hands.

'What do you have to say for yourself girl? Stand up when I tell you!'

None of the girls knew Miss Keynote wore a wig. Until then they'd always seen her with it on, had always thought this teacher had luscious black hair, the sort you put into hot rollers each night. Not this smooth, straight greyness. Had she planned to take it off in this way, had she rehearsed? Was it because the room was stifling hot—which it was? Underneath the false curls her neat grey hair looked like a skullcap, glued flat to her head. Everyone gasped. They'd never seen her like this, *in the flesh* so to speak, in such a theatrical act. There was something almost obscene about it, Miss Keynote *disrobing* in public and mouthing those rude words at the same time. The girls were glued to her like a pantomime audience, gasping, oohing and aahing. They shouldn't be watching this sort of thing but they *loved* it. Their very own peepshow. It was exhilarating.

That was when Miss Keynote started to laugh. But it was a very different laughter to the sort Glory was used to. It was an us-and-her laughter kept for special occasions and the girls wanted to join in. The noise was such that a Sister wandering the school peered through the louvres to see what the commotion was about. When she saw everyone laughing, she smiled, waved her hand about, and laughed in a funny way too.

Poor Glory wet her pants. Not dramatically. But a trickle enough to know; suddenly too before she managed to control it with a blush, but not before she wet the top of her legs. She was all sweat behind the knees too where the elastic garters squeezed her folds of skin. She tried standing tall, standing *up* as Miss Keynote commanded—thinking, hoping and *wishing* this would pass quickly.

She wished too she could look down at Lisa beside her. Lisa would know what to do. Lisa could guide her. But Glory couldn't look anywhere except stare straight ahead. She was paralysed, stunned. *Holden Caulfield*? She didn't really know who he was yet; she thought the reference was to some kind of car. *Pornographic*? That didn't sound good.

Suddenly, Glory astonished herself. Instead of being submissive and compliant, waiting for the next command, Glory banged down the lid of her desk. It thudded into the commotion of laughter and exclamation, wood smashed against wood. One minute Glory had the lid in her hands (she'd been looking for a textbook in her desk before the lesson began), the next thing she let it go. MotherJoy would have been proud—wouldn't she?—if it were true the things Miss Keynote was saying. It was like an explosion.

All the laughter in the room evaporated. Everyone in the class held their breath. What would Miss Keynote say next? She stood, mid gesture, unsure how to proceed. She tipped her head as if thinking up a plan, smoothed down the line of hair on one side of her face, the maroon velvet ribbon the only extravagance. She had flawless skin, faintly red heart-shaped lips, but her eyes stared at Glory like two gun barrels staring, ready to return fire.

If this were a duel, it should be Miss Keynote's turn to respond. But before the teacher said anything Glory pulled words from deep inside her throat and out across her tongue through nearly clenched teeth.

'Children don't go to school to learn to think,' she blurted out. 'They go to school to learn to spell, do maths.'

Glory amazed herself with this utterance. She turned pink. What made her dare challenge this particular teacher, like this? Not only slam the desk lid shut, as if that wasn't enough, but to say such words? Was it with the same spirit that drove her to stand up for Jesus? There was no going back. Her classmates sat frozen in their seats, staring straight ahead. It was that quiet, you could hear the ladies in the tuckshop faraway cleaning up. Then Miss Keynote spluttered in response: 'Where on earth did you get that idea?'

53

All Glory kept thinking for the rest of the day was that perhaps, for this one crazy, heart-choking moment, she had not so much lost herself, lost her capacity to think straight, think solidly, to forget who she was and where she was, *but* (dare she think this?), she had rescued her mother. She knew how to resuscitate a body, didn't she? She was a Bronze Medallion, owned a cute metal badge with her name engraved on the back. It was an act of allegiance, surely, not madness. A composition—an *intervention*—of love.

54

Come night, Glory crept into the lounge room to watch her mother from a distance. Something must have startled the girl awake. It was past midnight yet how bright the sky glowed. So too the light from a single lamp in the kitchen, which fell in a cone of off-white around MotherJoy, who sat at the kitchen table with her midnight feast. She was snacking on toast and melted butter spread with Onward's homemade cumquat marmalade. The citrus shone like shiny glass jewels in a crown. Like costume jewellery, the sort MotherJoy took a fancy to.

MotherJoy couldn't have known Glory was there beside the freezer, keeping watch because Glory was as still as a church mouse. Sometimes MotherJoy paused mid bite, staring into space—as if out into a void in front of her, praying. Her other hand was clasped in a fist across the open family Bible. It looked like the Good Book was open at the beginning of the Old Testament, given the thinness of the left-hand side of the book compared to the fat right-hand side. The collected edges of all those pages all silvery too like a beacon. The whole vignette a soft palette of colours.

Glory slowed her breathing to watch, to wait. Not make a noise. She watched MotherJoy take her time with the cumquat toast as if she had all the time in the world, as if she had the power *to still* time no less, to savour the flavours in her mouth. Wasn't this the joy of eating? *I want some too*, Glory nearly called out, *I want what you're eating*. Midnight feasts tasted better, Glory thought, better than ordinary feasts in the ordinary part of the day during the dust of routine. After midnight the tastebuds opened up, the tongue was more vulnerable then, more delicate, ever sensitive to the subtleties of flavour, especially the taste of marmalade, those cumquats. *Take your time*, MotherJoy might admonish, as if she never, never wanted to finish her last mouthful also. *Don't chew too fast, make it last*.

Glory watched, waited, touched by what she saw, by its simplicity: MotherJoy eating and praying in the dead of night, for what, Glory could only guess at. Imagine, for a twinkling Glory thought, if she could write this little scene for others to observe and hear so that it unfolded through the simplest of music scores for the human voice, to be played and replayed. How beautiful, how delicate the sound: 'Loves divine, all loves excelling', as Charles Wesley himself would say, the great hymn writer. People listening would wonder at its inspiration, would draw close because it resonated with something deep inside them, as though they too could have written such a thing—*as if it were always present*.

It was then, as she observed this little tableau, that Glory felt MotherJoy's powerful presence within her, could taste the sweetness of Onward's sugared citrus on her own tongue, smack on her lips, juicy and wet, feel rounds of fruit twinkle between her teeth. After everything that had happened that day. She was pleased she'd done something for MotherJoy at school; she was dying to tell her, the sweetness of this thought edging her tongue against her teeth like searching for a sugar grain wedged between fillings. But she decided not to interrupt; besides she couldn't find the right words. Glory didn't want to disturb the music tickling her ear.

Nor did she say anything when the school report came home at the end of that term with the words *SILENCE IS GOLDEN GLORY* scrawled across the bottom in capital letters. It was written in the spidery handwriting of the Sister-in-Charge with flourishes on the *S* and *E*'s and *G*'s. A calligrapher's hand. 'You're not causing trouble, I hope?' MotherJoy queried as Onward raised his eyebrows across the table.

On the night of the cumquats, Glory had crept back to her bed, careful not to step on the squeaky Masonite floorboards she knew by experience were outside her room, a dead giveaway when everything else was hushed. She thought better than to puncture the reverie of her mother, the warm blood centre of her midnight view. Glory nursed the flare of this new nativity in her belly. Rocked herself to sleep.

55

'Didn't you know your mother says that kind of thing on radio?' Lisa asked Glory the next day, the day after the Wig Affair. Lisa was swinging her bags high into the air like a Ferris wheel. Glory was remembering how she'd wanted to run out of the class early to go to the toilet, but had to wait for the bell.

'What kind of thing?' Glory wondered if they'd still be friends.

'That thinking thing. That children don't go to school to think. Did you see Miss Keynote's face?'

'I wasn't looking at her face. I couldn't.'

'You don't really believe it, do you?'

'Oh—,' Glory smarted. 'What do you mean?'

'That children don't go to school to think? That they only come here to learn how to spell, how to add up?'

Glory didn't know what to say. Hearing what she had said the day before now slide out of Lisa's mouth didn't sound right at all. She didn't know how to respond. She felt caught.

Then Lisa said: 'You're such a dag!' And chased Glory to the front gate.

Shame was a strange thing, Glory decided; it made you feel like a coward and she did want to be brave. Mostly you didn't know what it was when it was happening, when you were caught up in the action, because you were anxious to find out what would happen next. Make amends. When she stood in the middle of the classroom, defying Miss Keynote, speaking her own mind more or less, or at least reciting lines from home, the ones she could imagine MotherJoy repeating with *oomph* and most probably heard her say in fact, it didn't feel right, but she wouldn't have done it differently either. She felt ashamed standing there on her own with everyone looking at her. And shame too, about what Miss Keynote was saying, her disapproval of MotherJoy's oh-so-public ways. Now Glory felt chastised all over again talking to Lisa.

Oh to return to the midnight feast, the comfort of cumquats and marmalade and watching MotherJoy pray for the world. Oh to remain private, to keep feelings secret whatever those feelings were. Not to wish for different things. For her and Lisa still to be friends.

But Lisa didn't seem to notice Glory's discomfort. In fact, she seemed to relish the little altercation, it interested her, caught her imagination (nobody else said anything to Glory about what had happened but she knew they were all talking about her). Lisa said she wanted Glory to get another rise out of Keynote—that was the best part she said. And wasn't Glory clever to elicit such a reaction. 'Did you see how she shot out of the room after, like a cartoon character?' Lisa thought MotherJoy might be a match for Miss Keynote. She wondered out loud if Glory might be able to do it again, if this daughter might be able to channel the anti-smut campaigner like she did yesterday. 'You know, I almost thought your mother was actually in the classroom! That's what it must be like in these meetings that get reported about in the paper. Shit flies, hey Glory? I'd love to know what really happens.' Glory couldn't even imagine such a thing; Lisa was going too far. That was when Lisa lent her the transistor, just turned up with it one day and thrust the little red thing into Glory's hand.

'Here,' she said, 'this is for you, have a listen.'

'Really?'

'We've got lots at home. It won't be missed.'

Lisa showed Glory how to tune it, where all the Brisbane radio stations were located, their frequencies, told her about 4BC and its Open Line. Glory couldn't quite believe it was hers for the borrowing, to take away. The trannie was a jewel in her hand. Its snazzy silver trim sparkled, catching sunlight itself. She did so want to know more. She wanted to know if what Lisa said was true or not, whether she was making things up.

On the train home, Glory turned the red plastic box over and over in her hand. It was small enough to fit in a palm, light as a paper bag of feathers. She ran her fingers over the holes for the speaker, twiddled the silver knobs to tune it, for volume. She slipped her wrist through the silver handle, and put the flat holey side up to her ear and listened to different stations nearly all the way home—4IP, 4BC, 4BH—switching back and forth in delight. She decided 4IP was her favourite; it was Lisa's favourite too. But she made sure she knew where 4BC was on the dial as well. This station was important; it was the one where she'd hear her mother at large.

As she trudged home up her street from the bus stop, Glory could see the Poinciana tree on the perimeter of the Solider house. Nearly there now. She quickly shoved the trannie into the bottom of her port, promised herself not to breathe a word about it, and plonked her stuff down on the kitchen lino. Although the radio was out of sight, quite buried in amongst her books and smelly sports uniform, Glory swore she could see it glow like a beacon, red like the Poinciana flower out the front, see it pulse like a heart.

What Glory didn't know then was how this dear little box of technological cleverness would become her friend, even more of a friend than Lisa. It became a transposition of affection. This trannie told the truth.

56

'Hello Queensland. Tell me what's on your mind.' That's the first thing Glory heard. 'Queensland's a big country.' The transistor, cupped now in her hot hand for listening, fairly crackled. 'This is your chance to talk to this great big mighty country of ours.' Richo was in charge with a voice that showed he was king in radio-land—*I want your opinion, that's why we're here*—King Richo of a very new and weirdly wonderful kingdom of talkback radio. What an operator. And Glory was on a first-name basis with him from the minute she first heard his introduction, just like all the other listeners in Brisbane.

When she then heard the next lot of words 'I must speak my mind', Glory nearly choked, then held her breath so she could hear what happened after that, strangely impatient for what she knew was about to unfold.

'Okay, okay,' came Richo's smooth reply.

Richo knew he was onto a good thing, a ratings winner. His recipe worked. He had callers who wanted to talk (good talent), he had public agitation and unrest about social and political issues (good content), and he had an ear for what his listeners might want to hear (and fast fingers to stop a caller if the timing wasn't right). All in the raw, even with the obligatory seven-second delay. Talkback radio was STOP and CARE's preferred method of influencing public opinion. Didn't his listeners just love it?

Whenever she was sick these days, and sometimes she deliberately faked being 'poorly', Glory tuned in to 4BC; it was addictive. It wasn't that hard persuading MotherJoy she needed a day at home either. Whereas at school, Glory learned to act fast, without rehearsal, at home, sickness brought rest. MotherJoy waited on Glory, gave her what she wanted, fed her flat lemonade and packets of chips for afternoon tea to help cure her sore throat, and sometimes, on special occasions when MotherJoy had had a particularly buoyant day, she bought her deep-fried sugar-coated pineapple fritters snug-fit in white paper bags from Toowong as a treat.

Sometimes Glory missed Lisa, but she put the speaker of the trannie against her ear whenever she did, sensing her friend's presence.

The familiar voice came on part way through the song 'Raindrops Keep Falling on My Head'. It was MotherJoy, she knew, this voice insisting on an audience with exactly the right syntax and intonation, she knew that voice even when muffled. Even though she spoke into the phone with a handkerchief over the mouthpiece as disguise.

'Okay, okay, now tell me,' Richo crooned, microphone at his mouth, fingers on the board of callers lit up like a Christmas tree, able to switch any voice on and off with a flick. 'What makes you think you know best when it comes to teaching, to what kids need to learn?' He paused, working the silence. 'Call me old-fashioned, but isn't that for the teachers and the education department to decide?' He had immaculate timing.

'I must speak up,' the voice insisted. 'It is my duty.'

'So you say...' another silence. 'This is Richo, you're on 4BC, and I've got a housewife and mother of six on the line, and we're talking about the books our kids are reading...,' the silence electrified, 'so tell me, you say you have six children.'

Glory could not quite believe what she was hearing—the detail of the conversation, MotherJoy's revelations. She had the transistor on under the bedclothes, pressed to her ear, the fringe of the blue bedspread tickling her nose. With every word spoken through the little red box she felt the chenille closing in on her—and not for comfort, it felt like her shelter was collapsing in on her, like she was drowning in her own fabric. Glory was in her room at one end of the house, home from school and supposedly sick, knowing MotherJoy—and she really did know it was her by now—was underneath the house at the other end talking to Richo. MotherJoy called that study her headquarters—a little room cut out of the clay embankment the house perched on; a little room behind French doors she held shut with a sturdy padlock when she wasn't there. Not that Glory would ever venture in there without invitation. It had a set of louvres facing out the back that created a breezeway with the open door, to ward away stuffiness. This little room was to become an intensive care unit for all the children of Queensland.

Glory could hear MotherJoy's heavy breathing into the phone. Then her licking of lips with her tongue, it was so clear. Lisa's transistor, lying with Glory in her bed, glowed under the covers with her. Richo must know what he was doing. He began: 'There must be a bit of a story here.

Kill! Kill!

So tell us, you've got one child who's in "mortal danger" you say. What does he think of all this? Should we ask him?'

No. No. Glory wrapped the bedspread around her body like a parcel, even more tightly, curling the radio into the soft part of her belly, wanting to disappear into the stuffing of the mattress, hide amongst the metal springs and fibres, hoping now beyond all hope that nobody was listening.

'Children don't go to school to think,' came the reply in a flash. 'To err is to sin against the Almighty God Himself.'

The voices pulled at the very air Glory was swallowing. She could taste acid.

'I speak the truth. Let God be my witness.'

The little red trannie swollen now against Glory's belly very nearly burst the metal casing. Glory had to remind herself that she was grateful, glad to hear what was going on. She knew the flavour of MotherJoy's day would permeate everything. MotherJoy would remain distracted. The Soliders would eat cold burnt sausages for tea and hardboiled eggs tonight.

57

THE SISTERS AT school didn't know what had hit them when MotherJoy decided to barge in, unannounced, full volume. The English curriculum was a matter for the English teachers and the department. Despite that MotherJoy flew in with batted wings, into the small white rooms at the front of the school, agitated, demanding answers. The Sisters tried to catch the words on the front of the book she waved about to at least get a head start. You wouldn't want this kind of altercation to leak back along the corridors and flood the playground.

Bang, bang went MotherJoy, book in one hand, beating it with the other as if she were playing a tambourine. The cover shone back silver, glinted in the fluorescent light like a mirror. The thing was, the Sisters thought they had already pacified MotherJoy in the very first interview when Glory enrolled, when they made it clear what families could expect from this good school. They thought they'd come to an understanding. *We'll look after your daughter's education. You can trust us.* This kind of fracas was far from polite. MotherJoy: a fly in their Christian ointment. Because here she was, right now in the Sister-in-Charge's room with the other Sisters lending moral support from the other side of the wall, holding breaths the lot of them, pressing their hands together in prayer. Anything to help.

The clock must have stopped too. Even the lavender-smelling secretary with the flat chest in the waiting room held her breath, open mouthed, poised above the typewriter keys, fingers curled mid sentence afloat the official letterhead. Her hands were like two small creatures, waiting to be told what to do next. To know where to land with the soft pad of paws.

MotherJoy said: 'Don't you have any shame? Do you know what children at this school are reading?' She waved the silver cover about some more, stared at the book as though she could right then and there tear the book apart in front of them, page from page, limb from limb. 'Have you read this filth?'

It was a terrible noise she was making. *Bang! Bang!* The pages bent and wilted with this treatment. The book itself seemed to shrink.

'Well? Have you read it? What that horrible Salinger says. He should be ashamed of himself.'

What was there to say? Sister-in-Charge smiled back at MotherJoy's distress. Her small hands were invisible behind the fall of her starched robes, clutched in her lap perhaps, gripping a string of rosaries that hung around her waist. Perhaps she could feel the reassuringly hard surfaces of each wooden bead dig into her stomach as she pulled at them around her body in sequence. Perhaps too she mumbled a prayer with each tug, careful though not to attract attention.

'I thought this was a Christian school,' MotherJoy continued. 'But I'm not gutless,' her high-pitched voice running on, 'if you won't do anything about this moral pollution, I will.'

The Sisters on the other side of the wall squeezed each other's hands.

'I insist on Glory staying out of class and you can't stop me,' as if in threat, 'I mean business.' With that, she threw down the book at Sister's feet, stormed out. 'Mark my word. It will happen,' she threw back, over her shoulder. The pages of the book fluttered, in protest.

58

No other parent came to the school to buy the books on the booklist. They all did it in the same way you would order lunch with a paper bag in the morning and with the right change if possible: a simple transaction. Not the Solider family. Glory dreaded the beginning of each term. It was MotherJoy's chance to get as close as possible to what it was she was talking about, it was a way of doing her research, fishing for information. The small musty basement beneath the school hall full of textbooks became the boiler room for her campaign. MotherJoy insisted she come to school to buy Glory's schoolbooks and not just for what Glory would be reading in English that term, but for all the other years as well, for all Queensland children. These books gave her all the ammunition she needed for Richo and his radio listeners—'I know what our children are being force-fed. You just have to glance at my daughter's booklist to know it's filth!'

They were all there, stacks of them, books for all the years across the English curriculum, from grade eight to grade twelve. Perfect. A campaigner's dream warehouse, with the smell of new books about it, new ink, cut paper, unspoilt covers. Virgin pages, never opened.

The youngest Sister of all manned the makeshift bookstore. Sister Elisabeth had told the girls she was only a little bit older than them, told them lots of stories, such as how her real name was Meredith, that girls should go to university, how it was better to say what you think, rather than remain mute and powerless. How she went into the religious life to be an independent woman she said, because she didn't want to become a wife. Lisa said she was the only one in the school who understood her. She said she and Sister E (that was her nickname for Sister) had similar aspirations; they were one. Sometimes Glory thought Lisa might end up in a religious order.

On the afternoon the Soliders turned up, there was Sister Elisabeth sitting at the basement door with the cash box, ready to make up the receipt book with figures and sums. She was having a little rest, reading.

The girls knew she loved this time of the term; it gave her a chance to catch up on her own list, uninterrupted. On this particular day, it was Kurt Vonnegut Jr's *Slaughterhouse-Five*.

Sister Elisabeth had told them she loved the way Vonnegut played with form, with the very idea of writing—how his book was part science fiction, part history, part memoir—he was ahead of his time. How inventive he was, how this made her feel differently every time she read him. Anything—*everything*—was possible between these pages. How she imagined Vonnegut might land next to her at any minute. Listening to Sister Elisabeth made Glory wonder. Lisa was good at getting Sister to talk about these things in maths; she'd even get her to recite her favourite lines. Sister Elisabeth was always talking about how human we are, not as a failing but as something to be celebrated. How to be human is to err, usually out of curiosity, that that was the point of it all. She said we always want to know what we're told we're not to know, what we shouldn't know. Glory decided she didn't believe this last bit.

When Sister Elisabeth saw the two Soliders bearing down on her along the corridor, she slid the yellow cover of *Slaughterhouse-Five* under the desk. There wasn't much warning, although thankfully for Sister Elisabeth and Glory alike, MotherJoy's court shoes clacked loudly on the cement pathway. Glory could see Sister Elisabeth hide the book— she saw everything happen that day, slowed down—and she read the guilty look on Sister's face as well, as if she were being called to account, as if she had found herself at the Pearly Gates already, being called to answer St Peter. What if MotherJoy dressed her down in front of Glory? Sister Elisabeth of all people, it wasn't funny. Over and over in her mind, Glory repeated the phrase: *Please, please, please don't make a scene.* As if her lungful of pleading could make any difference. As if her stiff-body longing would help.

As if MotherJoy cared what her daughter yearned for when there was a treasure box to plunder. Fat chance.

Glory was in a set dance now with a fixed partner, her *only* partner, locked into position to pirouette up and down the aisles, to try and navigate her way around the books and safely back to Sister Elisabeth. Could she do it in one breath? Past all those stacks? The Sister's presence at the door gave Glory an inkling of warmth, confidence. Glory felt sure she detected a smattering of pity in Sister's look as well, which Glory snatched hold of with gratefulness.

Trouble was, MotherJoy was determined. Glory had to try to find a way to thwart her. Glory had to work out how to cover up the authors' names and titles, the dangerous ones, the ones she thought MotherJoy would question. Glory took wild guesses, looked for particular covers, speed-read the authors' names and titles of their books, imagined how bad it could be, moved her body into position to shield these books from sight, twirled on the balls of her feet. MotherJoy's eyes darted everywhere.

It didn't matter, MotherJoy was crafty, while employing a studied politeness. Glory could tell Sister Elisabeth was impressed. Later, she said to her: 'Your mother is quite a warrior, Glory. She's clever, doesn't miss a trick. And you might think this strange for me to say, but I like her independent thinking. If only she put all that energy—all that gumption she has for this campaign of hers—put it to better use, to things that really mattered and could make a difference, she could do a lot of good. Pity she doesn't see it that way.'

59

MOTHERJOY MUST HAVE picked up a book from every pile in the basement that afternoon, all of them now squashed against her body, many more than the number Glory needed for English. She looked like she was coming home from the butcher with an assortment of meats. The books in a squeeze against her bosom leapt about. Burned hot. Especially the pig on the Faber cover of Golding's *Lord of the Flies*. Those eyes. That mouth. All orange and white, saliva and mucus. The illustration made your heart race just looking at it, and this was before you opened the cover to read, if you had the gall. The mucus from the swine's snout seemed to drip out of the bottom of the book in MotherJoy's grip, it was so real, to slide over the skin of her bare arm, and slime its way down the middle of her body, branding her with its mark.

Maybe MotherJoy *was* right all along, right about how the words from inside these books can come alive, can slide out of the pages in their ones and twos, tens and hundreds, to coagulate in pools of sludge, to contaminate and indoctrinate. Home would come this meat to sort. *Kerplonk! Fleur-lap!* Parts of the pig's head alongside the female anatomy marked out with pins and flags. The taste of tongue. And blood. Glory imagined MotherJoy typing up passages from these books ready to distribute in pamphlets, to warn parents what their children might be reading.

Quickly—'here, let me help'—Glory whisked the offending books out of MotherJoy's arms—'there's a dear,' replied MotherJoy—and Glory squashed the books into her own body, a necessary press of the pig's head and all. Sister Elisabeth gave her a supportive look, racing to catch up. And before MotherJoy had time to question what her daughter was doing, with what speed, Glory took the books out to the Holden parked at the front of the school. Out of sight, out of mind. Glory hated to contemplate what the Sisters prayed for that night before bed, what the words amounted to, whether they took her body to lie with them in the lap of their God.

60

Glory went to sleep thinking about books. Not the content of books or what she might find between their covers, but how they looked together on shelves, in a library, a bookshop. How once at primary school she helped pay for some books for the new library with a swimathon. She got pages and pages of sponsors when she went door-to-door up and down the streets around home, not just for one or two cents a lap as suggested, but for five and ten. She told everyone she wasn't a very good swimmer—she didn't think she was—that she would be lucky if she did two laps of the pool. They believed her, and the promises rolled in. On the day itself, Glory kept on swimming and swimming and swimming, lost count of the number of turns. Lost count of the numbers of books this might mean. The sports teacher had a mechanical counter she pointed at Glory's head for each time she tipped the wall at the shallow end. It turned out she did so many laps, the counter flipped over at twenty and returned to zero to start counting all over again.

At the end of the swim Glory felt at one with the chlorinated water, as if she had grown scales and fins. She couldn't stand up. Felt a bit sick and had to lie down with a headache in the afternoon in sickbay. Glory ended up doing more than fifty-five laps of the twenty-five-metre pool (more than a kilometre in all) in her summer-new tie-dyed purple Speedos. She even went past the bell for the next class. The swimming teacher was impressed and didn't tell her to stop until Glory stopped herself (the people who owed money didn't seem to mind).

Each time Glory went into the new library after that, opened by the premier's wife at the school's centenary, she thought about her swim. She wondered how many of these books belonged to her. Five? Ten? She loved the library's cool dark spaces, the order of books on the metal shelves, the scent of fresh paper, the sniff of *story*, and the very particular state-school perfume of this library, the new books with old: thick plastic covers and glued-in pockets for lending. She'd wander up and down the shelves during big lunch, running her fingers along the spines of the books to make music, a repeating *blip, blip, blap ... blip, blip, blap*. It was as though she had her own rhythm just like swimming the lanes with long strokes, opening and closing the pages upon pages of all the hundreds and thousands of books collected there, the millions of words all in a spill, afloat with her in the blue summery water. Sluicing back and forth she went in a great wash, her body one with the bigger body about her, there was no difference. It felt too good to be true. '*Swim* = be covered with liquid; seem to be whirling or waving; be dizzy—.' Yes. She was dizzy with it, whirling proudly.

Perhaps that's why Glory ended up working in a bookshop.

Not that she read any of the new books in primary school: she couldn't remember borrowing a single title. No. It was the *idea* of the collection, the look of them there altogether, the presence of so many actual, *real* words, real stories. Each swimming lesson from then on made her think again of books. She wanted to get stuck there between them all. The weightlessness of all those tomes in the water. To be buoyant with the ruffle of pages, fingers flicking along the mix of spines. Music announcing the spinning of pleasure. A recipe for threading together her fantasies.

Glory slept dreaming of books.

If only she could return to this innocence, and not remember the trail of slime down the front of her mother. *Kill the pig*. Perhaps Sister E could time travel with her, and Kurt Vonnegut too for that matter, to get back what she had lost. To feel again the weightlessness of swimming breaststroke. The fearlessness that comes with floating, cheeks and mouth and nose above the surface of the water, with being able to tread water without thinking. With all those free-spirited pages and stories swaying about in the current like seaweed.

61

MotherJoy banned Glory from English, just like that. Glory didn't hear the news from home. There was no special advance warning. Instead, Miss Keynote told her one morning in English before little lunch: 'Out on the verandah, Soldier.' She must have thought she was in the army, on a parade ground inspecting the troops. 'That is an order!'

This was the beginning of Miss Keynote's new way of addressing Glory so that, at first, Glory didn't realise who she was talking to. Soldier! Who's *Soldier*? Everybody looked at Glory then out through the louvres to a single wooden desk parked on the verandah with its face turned towards the courtyard, away from the classroom.

'Keep your ears covered,' she mocked, 'otherwise Soldier, you'll die.'

There it was again. Everybody laughed. Glory imagined herself in uniform.

'Your mother thinks you're impressionable, did you hear that? Thinks you will surely d–i–e if you listen in to what we are saying in here! Did you hear that, class? We might have a murder on our hands, girls.' Miss Keynote spelt out the word D-I-E for Glory in capital letters in case Glory didn't get what was really at stake. 'Your mother says you'll be corrupted, go to hell. That you'll be burned *a-l-i-v-e*.'

Everyone knew then. Every English lesson thereafter, Glory sat on the wooden verandah overlooking the school quadrangle with a view on everything outside, everybody inside with a view on her. She had her own reading list too, Shakespeare mostly, not that Miss Keynote went to any trouble. The English mistress thrust different texts onto the desk from time to time without explanation—*Hamlet*, *Much Ado About Nothing*, *King Lear*—and set special exam questions for Glory, away from the other girls. 'We can't have Soldier Glory cheating now.' Miss Keynote made sure the classroom had lots of air too, made a point of opening the windows at the beginning of each English class, with a flourish, so that her voice drifted audibly through the open louvres as she recited passages from her list. She'd make pronouncements: 'That's how we like it, isn't it, girls?' The girls recited great chunks of *The Catcher in the Rye* after her in unison 'in a nice loud voice now' while she stared out at Glory perched precariously on her bench. At least the air was more pleasant outside than in, Glory thought.

Out on the verandah there was so much to think about. Not that Glory listened to what went on back through the louvres, or at least she tried not to. Best to block it out so that none of Holden Caulfield's sensibilities leaked into her. His openness scared Glory. She was nervous of his casual spunk.

Glory didn't want to die, but thinking about it she decided there were different kinds of death. There were little deaths and big deaths; a death when you're still alive, like sitting here for everyone to see, for instance; and the capital-D death, the final sort, the one that took you to heaven or hell (the one she sometimes very nearly wished for). There was another sort too, the sort of death that happened while taking note of the likes of Holden Caulfield, even by mistake, listening in to his voice, taking in the view of his world when you weren't meant to, fixed on the verandah like this as target practice—desk, chair and body nailed to the floor.

62

Once, on the septic tank in the backyard with Gracie, Glory poisoned her bad dolls, killed them off in a bunch. *Kill! Kill!* The septic was a good place to do it. That was where the Little Girls made up stories about each other to laugh and cry about. They brought their pillows and rag dolls with them to make the septic all comfy and, together like that, the Little Girls would play for hours. The dolls took on stories and subplots of their own. They played hospitals, mummies and daddies, and teachers and pupils. When the dolls were good, lined up in formation as if sitting in pews in church, or in rows in the classroom, all stuffy, they wore flowers in their blue wool hair stuck on with sticky tape.

But when the dolls were bad, Glory poisoned them with the white sap of the frangipani sucked up with saliva into baby syringes from Onward's hospital supplies. You could squeeze the sap from behind the grey felt bark of the tree, bark that looked like an old man's bottom. It dripped out from under this skin like oozy warm honey except it was white and sticky and easy to suck up into the capsule. Onward said this tree could kill you: 'Be careful to wash your hands,' he'd warn. Glory knew she had to watch that none of it got onto her hands and into her mouth and onto her tongue. Sometimes it went oh, so very close. Sometimes she thought she might actually poison herself. On purpose. Be silly like that. Then MotherJoy would take notice.

Glory cried at all the little deaths, held funerals for each of the dolls. Not that she had ever been to a proper funeral to know how one went, but she had read about Lazarus and knew what happened to poor Jesus on the cross, off by heart.

This happened.

She wrapped up the dead dollies in tea towels and hung them by knots and string from the frangipani branches. The trussed-up packages swung like that in the breeze looking like the crazy fruit bats in the palms. Imagine MotherJoy trussed up like that in a tree. What about all the schoolgirls doing English? Miss Keynote too? Funny how thoughts congeal like sap.

Big Glory can still hear the Little Girls out on the septic singing. Stray voices like acacia pollen. The two Little Soliders stayed out there for as long as they could, until it was almost dark, singing and swaying, wrapped up tightly and hanging by knots off the corners of the house, fluffed up by the song of hymns.

63

Glory's English class kept staring at her through the louvres, sometimes passing inconsequential notes to her through the glass, more to amuse themselves than out of sympathy. It was like touching a bruise that annoys, they kept poking her to see if she squirmed. She was a spectacle. Lisa sent a note or two trying to help. They all resented her being singled out like this, her specialness. The way Glory hijacked Miss Keynote's attention, and all the other teachers for that matter. They began to think that Miss Keynote cared more about Glory than she ever cared about any of them. And that was before Glory turned up in the newspaper, before Miss Keynote made a thing of it in class.

The verdict, according to these girls, as they sucked on their cigarettes and paddle-pops behind the toilets during little lunch, was that this charade was taking the silly book thing too far. They'd find a way to make Glory pay; they'd make her pay for everything. Their resentment grew like wildfire.

64

In Brisbane, everything grows everywhere. And speedy fast too. It's fecund, wild and unruly, restless. Roots break up footpaths, shrubbery hides houses, branches block views. It's only really on the river that you get a chance to see some distance, get perspective.

I took this photograph in 1975 looking towards Toowong up the West End and St Lucia reaches. Or, could it be the other way, towards the university—I vaguely recognise that building on the right—is it a motel? The skyline has changed so much I can't really tell. In any case, this view of the river takes me back, to breathing in lungfuls of air, to feeling the breeze on my face, to the pleasure of crossing the river in the ferry. It is about speaking directly from the past, listening in to Little Francesca.

And this one: this is where I grew up.

I can't remember when I took this photograph exactly, but I do remember owning a little Kodak Pocket Instamatic. You can imagine me aged fourteen or fifteen, coming home from school in a trudge up the hill with this canopy as greeting, skidding my port across the kitchen lino floor, huffing out of breath, thirsty and hungry for afternoon tea: fruit bread and homemade Swiss roll. The scarlet red umbrella of this Poinciana flower gets me close to imagining I am there, places me under the tree next to the letterbox with a click of the shutter.

It was a big house too, an old Queenslander on stilts.

See here: one of four palm trees that grew like sentinels at the four corners of the garden. How they sway now in my imagination, give me a view. How the fruit bats talk away up there at night, freehold with the yellow fruit. What a great pandemonium.

And this is a view from my bedroom, looking out through the louvres. An odd choice to share, you might say. It's very grainy and out of focus. You're thinking: really, it's too dark to see properly.

What I like about this bedroom view is that it's not just about looking outside—to the sky and vegetation, which happens to be a large dormant frangipani overhanging the septic tank where my little sister and I used to play—it is about going from one setting to the other and mixing the two. The dark of the room and the light outside are a coupling: you can't have one without the other. What happens of course is that now as I look through these louvres, I become fourteen or fifteen again, awake and lying on my bed salvaged from the hospital, at the back of the house, gazing up to the outside, to the Brisbane sky, beyond. I figure I smell the coming of summer flowers and dream of a future.

65

I FOUND LITTLE FRANCESCA in my mother's scrapbook, a book bound in red ribbon that kept the pages together. There wasn't much to do with her campaign in there. It was more of a family affair celebrating precious things: photographs, letters, baby teeth. When we moved Angel and my father into the nursing home, we moved the scrapbook with them, stored it away for safekeeping in the Japanese box. That's where I found Little Francesca, stuck into these pages next to a photograph of my mother: *Courier Mail*, 7 February 1975, page three, under the headline 'School Textbooks Slated: Rebel Ideas, says Mother'. It was my mother all right, a slip from the generic to the particular. She was dressed in the batik caftan she was rather fond of wearing in those days—*it covers a multitude of sins*, she liked to say. Imagine the feeling when a newspaper headline about a generic mother is your own particular mother staring back at you. Then this, the first paragraph—

> Mrs Angel Rendle-Short, of Brookfield, said yesterday that a book given to her daughter, Francesca, as an English text-book at school would teach her to be a permissive rebel.

It also said that I was willing to sit out of English classes in order to protect myself from the danger of being corrupted—

> Francesca, a grade 10 student, is now willing to sit out her classes ... teenagers are incapable of discerning and making a judgment about what they read, especially when they have nothing but gutter standards.

I look up the words *permissive* and *rebel*, wonder what one might look like. *Permissive* meaning tolerant, liberal, especially in sexual matters, from the Latin *permissio* as in 'permit'. And *rebel* meaning a person who fights or resists control and authority from the Latin *rebellis* or *bellum* as in 'war'. Permissive rebel. *Permissio rebellis*. Permit war. I like the way these words look in the newspaper, the black and white print, how the typesetters spaced out the letters, horizontally and vertically, how the last letter *e* in *permissive* separates out from the rest—the way it accidentally drops below an imaginary bottom line as if it is being set free and riding away.

permissive rebel.

(Tracing 'permissive rebel' in lead pencil reminds me of the tracing and colouring-in we were always being asked to do at school—maps of Australia, rivers of Queensland, and sometimes lettering, but cursive letters, not wonky letters from newspapers.)

There is something strange about seeing your name in newsprint, seeing it *in situ* as it would have been first read on the day of publication all those years ago. I imagine people wrapping up fish and chips with the long-ago pages. I imagine my mother cutting out the words and sentences and sticking them into her scrapbook.

66

On the day of publication, Miss Keynote pinned the newspaper to the English noticeboard and told the girls how proud she was that one of them had got their name in print. 'We have a famous face in our presence,' she said. 'Let's make the most of it, shall we?'

Glory had to listen to more recitation on the verandah that day, but this time, not from *The Catcher in the Rye*. No, Miss Keynote decided that they should read from one of the wicked books MotherJoy had complained about in the paper—*Improving on the Blank Page*. The girls read from one of the first poems in the collection, *Wish Poems* written by students in South Australia. They recited the various lines in a chant. One, two, three:

> I wish my father would fall downstairs and break his head
> I wish my sister would explode
> I wish I had a house of my own, my most prized trophy my mother's head
> I wish my parents would hate me and leave me by myself to rot away.

Big Glory finds a copy of the book on her father's bookshelf when she moves MotherJoy and Onward into the nursing home. She takes it without asking, hides it as a lump under her shirt. Anyway, it is one MotherJoy threw out: 'This book is rubbish. I'm surprised it's still here.'

It is so strange to see *Improving on the Blank Page* again after all these years, looking tired now in its old library plastic cover; plain, too. A bit ordinary. But in its time it heralded a new vogue in publishing—it is a stripped-back selection of poems and photographs by established writers and artists as well as students. No introduction, no explanatory blurb on the rainbow cover, no context for the collection of works. What you see is what you read. It sold more copies than its authors ever dreamed of, helped no doubt by the brouhaha. Banned books do well, people say.

67

LITTLE GLORY FELL APART that day but didn't have the gall to ask to go to the sickbay. Girls she didn't know came up to her, chanting: 'Saw your name in the paper. Ooh! Saw your name in the paper.' Lisa didn't say a word.

When she got home, Glory spread herself out in her bedroom all over the chenille bedspread with her cutting scissors and glue, 2B pencils and daybook, to do some sorting. If only she could put all that she was feeling into her own pages, make a hidey-hole to escape. If she could just distract herself with cutting things up, gluing things down.

Onward's dictionary. '*Blank* = empty, something which is empty as "his mind was a blank" or "a blank cartridge is a cartridge without a bullet"'. What about blank slate then: *tabula rasa* (in Latin translated as 'scraped tablet')? She wondered about this idea of 'emptiness', of nothing being there, a void on the page. Why couldn't Miss Keynote let her go? *Your mother can't keep her mouth shut, can she, Soldier-Soldier?*

She searched her bedside drawer for the most recent whole-of-year class photograph, the official one. She found it, all thirty-two girls smiling in that artificial way of posed photographs. And there was Glory, plumb in the middle in the back row, the tallest in her year. Glory with tight plaits framing her face.

She took her Gillette shaver and with one of the blades, punctured this face clean through. Her scissors made little snipping noises as she cut around her cheeks and jaw and hairline. She threw away her eyes and nose and mouth and glued the remainder into the pages of her daybook, a headless body, hole and all.

68

Forget Richo, forget the newspaper—Glory's classmates wanted to get even and they knew exactly how they were going to do it, with the help of the famous books themselves.

'Shit-here has a prying mother does she?' The prefects at the school gates were in charge. 'Wants to get involved does she?' Out here in the end-of-day crush, with the whole school as witness, Glory didn't know what to do. She hadn't rehearsed this bit. 'Thumbs the naughty bits does she?'

Glory tried to not listen. At least back in the classroom, the walls and the verandah she perched on like a caged bird contained the commotion, even when the girls blew hot air through the louvres. At the gate, it took on a grander scale. 'She's going to get arrested. She's going to get arrested.' There was a nasty edge to it. This was no soft game; something big was at stake.

'Listen to this everyone, listen up—'. The one with crimped hair bleached white and perfect teeth called out—'Who's got a copy, any copy?' They knew what they were doing. 'Ooh, look at this … Listen to Holden,' and she started to recite passages and excerpts. 'Is this how your mother does it?'

They must have scoured the book all lunchtime in the library to find these passages, mark them up. All the girls were fascinated. A sea of straw hats turned skywards, faces expectant. How daring! They wanted to swallow every word. They didn't mind being late out of school, missing their trains; they wouldn't pass up this show for anything. Perhaps they felt that they themselves had been written into the Holden Caulfield story, as walk-on parts; that J. D. Salinger was thinking specifically of them as he wrote. That their presence was a necessary part of the narrative.

Girls giggled uncomfortably, involuntarily, shocked at the display. Books weren't meant to be read in this way, were they? Holden Caulfield's oh-so-rude meanderings should be read with a bit more care, in a private setting. Doing it like this, out in the open, multiplied the size of the words and their meaning, didn't it? By a factor more than ten.

'Hey Soldier Girl, are you going to jump out the window? Are you a lesbian? A flit?' They guffawed at that. Everyone stood transfixed, aghast yet mesmerised by the spunk of these older girls. What would the teachers think if they could hear?

The girl reading took trouble with each word, such care with the page numbers too. She stood on the authority of the book: chapter and verse. She knew instinctively that it was easier to say difficult things if the words were not your own. Easy to borrow Holden for her role: put him on as disguise. Allow him to express her inner longing. Let him speak up for desire. Had Salinger invented a new genre for a new generation? Did he know the goings on in the heads of these Queensland girls? 'Listen to me,' Holden insisted, 'see it my way.' Certainly they were very quiet as they listened to his voice. They lapped it up and made it their own. Holden Caulfield allowed them to feel a million things at one time, to go off, altogether now, like fireworks on cracker night.

Not Glory Solider. She knew what she had to do: hold her breath, not snap back, and wait for this thing to pass. At home over tea, MotherJoy would ask about her day: 'Anything to report, Glory dear?' And Glory would pretend again: 'No, nothing happened today.'

69

They could always blame Holden Caulfield—he was the one with all the good ideas. You can read about it in the beginning of *Catcher* too, where Allie, Holden's brother, writes on his baseball mitt. He writes poems in green all over the fingers and pockets and everywhere. So he had something to read in the field, Holden said. That's how the schoolgirls found themselves at Roma Street Station in the city in the boys' toilets, Glory in the middle of the scrum. They decided to give Glory something to read without needing to open the covers of *any dirty* pornographic book. It wasn't the prefects' idea; they'd already had their fun and gone home. This time it was the younger ones, the juniors, Glory's classmates and their friends. They had to punish Glory for what she and her mother stood for. Blame Holden.

70

THE DAY IT HAPPENED, the station was awash with uniforms, like any other day: red and grey, blue and white, green, maroon, even gold. Private or public, it didn't matter, everyone flirted, everyone fair game.

Glory Solider very nearly made her escape down the staircase and through the tunnel towards the bus stop. She decided to catch the ferry this day, take the longer route home. But they got her in the middle of the station, on the platform, got her in the space near the toilets where it was empty of passengers, where it was damp. It smelt. It was the bit of the station everybody usually tried to avoid. But today was different. There was a great huddle. The girls grabbed Glory by her bag, then dragged her into the boys' toilet, boyfriends standing guard. These girls knew Glory wouldn't say anything, they felt protected. They were punishing her for this very silence.

Just before they got stuck into her, Glory looked around for Lisa. Surely she must be there to rescue her friend? Wasn't that her, joking to lighten the mood? She could hear her saying: 'They're only playing, dag features. Don't take it personally. You know what girls are like.' Glory thought she could see her, tall, at the back. Glory strained to get her friend's attention. She tried calling out Lisa's name, but her small voice was so far away in her own head it sounded like it came from someone else. But no, it wasn't her.

'Where's your mother now to defend you?' A sudden coarse whisper.

'Yeah, where's your mother now, Soldier-Soldier?' The chorus chanted. 'Who says we're not old enough?'

Then someone pulled out a big black texta from their pocket and started to write on Glory's arms, write quotes they'd learned by heart from *Catcher*. They took turns. While one read out something from the book, another wrote the lettering up and down Glory's bare arms and then up and down her legs: *sex maniac, backasswards, flits, lesbian, whore.*

And then the poem from the other day: *My most prized trophy my mother's head*.

'You'll never get this off,' they laughed. 'This will be on you forever.'

Glory realised suddenly it had all been prearranged.

'You won't forget.'

Glory thought about trying to resist, but she was trapped like Piggy on the island when the boys all turned. If she could bury herself deep enough, dig down into the clay, perhaps then she could shut out this horribleness. She wanted to disappear, crawl away for solace, into her bed; pull up the eiderdown for cover. Her nails scratched helplessly across the floor.

'Try showing this to your mother, Glory Solider! Love to see her face!'

Glory tired to wriggle her arms and her legs free. She wanted to make the letters go haywire so the words didn't make sense. But the girls, very clever at anticipating any resistance, anchored her more tightly. They knew what they were up against.

'Glory! Whorey! She'll have you arrested you for this.'

What if her mother turned up unexpectedly? In a great cloudburst? To rail against the principalities of darkness? Her voice would leap about like flames; scare them all away. For a millisecond Glory wished MotherJoy *was* there. She wished she was holding her hand, dragging her out of the middle, even if it did hurt, yelling—*Get thee behind me, Satan!* That would make them stop dead.

On cue, as if choreographed in preparation, it was the boys' turn now. This was the horrible part but you wouldn't have guessed that by looking at all those girls' faces. They were almost radiant with expectation, like some of those clowns you get at the show. And Glory felt sure she could see Lisa's face clowning with the rest—could this be true? She so wanted Lisa to tell the boys: *Let Glory be!* Boys listened to her. Instead, they thrust a jar of peanut paste into Glory's hands, unzipped their flies. 'Come on,' they said, suddenly all go, bravado. 'Show us what you can do, Whorey Glory. Cover us up and think of your stupid mother,' they taunted, out of control. 'Now lick it off, you bitch! All of it!' Their pink penises dangled in front of Glory. A damp smell of sweat, dirt and old urine. Their scrotums lay pinched and divided, squashed against the teeth of zips, unsure whether they were part of the display—in, or out. The boys groaned with a kind of unspent desire. They pushed themselves forward, their bodies instructing them what to do. The girls behind them were suddenly uneasy, turned away.

Kill! Kill!

All this probably took no time at all, in real time, the boys probably flicked their penises out and back in all of a few seconds, if at all. Pretend spunk. It really was a joke—to see how far they could go. Because in a flash everyone disappeared. Including Lisa, if she had been there at all as well, she simply stopped being her friend, dropped off for good.

All the way home, Glory's mouth was a round O, the shape of eternity. All Glory wished was that she could spread her body thin and gaseous into outer space. Dilute herself like that—*Glory*, 'the intransitive of light'. Her jaw ached as if peanut paste glued her tongue down, as if she really did have a mouthful of it, pieces of nut caught between teeth. She tried to spit everything out over the side of the ferry into the river.

Don't ever tell

71

ELSIE CALLS OUT: 'Look what I've found!' She's laughing.
Big Glory comes into the corridor of the rented apartment to find her oldest sister standing legs apart, book in hand. The cover flashes silver in the Brisbane sunshine and Glory's throat lumps up. Elsie is saying: 'Isn't this strange? This is the same book I have just been reading on the plane coming out here—*The Catcher in the Rye*—and here it is on this pew.' She points at a book lined up alongside others on the wall, then holds up the book she's been reading: exactly the same. Flashes them both at Glory who's speechless. 'Do you think it's a sign?' Then she laughs to break the tension. 'Funny old Queensland? It's a weird place, isn't it?'

Glory, Elsie and Ruthy are staying in the middle of Brisbane. They'd had to line up a place at the last minute. They weren't sure what state MotherJoy would be in, how long they would need it for—but it had to be big enough to fit them all. It's an old Queenslander in Auchenflower, down the road from the Wesley Hospital where MotherJoy now is, so near, very practical. And it is only a couple of blocks from the railway line, and with a view across Coronation Drive to the Brisbane River. At dusk Glory can see swarms of bats against the gloaming sky. Ribbons of light flash up and down the river as CityCats pass. Everything they need for the next few days (weeks?) is within reach as they wait to find out what is the matter with MotherJoy. Is she going to die?

'Isn't this the book Mum got in a flap over?' Elsie asks. 'You know the one.'

It had been Ruthy who had phoned—'Glory this might be serious.' There was something about the tone of her voice: 'Mum can't speak. She says she can't swallow.' This time, Glory thinks, this time I might not go home until the end—and it only took four months in the nursing home, like they said. It seems that MotherJoy's mended heart is still going strong, but now her muscles are fading. Three of the sisters are standing guard. It's February and the weather is muggy and hot. Even at seven in the morning as Glory strides up to the hospital the sun is baking on her face, and she's wondering how to keep cool in the waiting room. Glory is distracted beyond measure; everything is colliding. There will come a time in the next few days when she will forget what it is that she is writing, how it mattered once, very much. She will forget to eat too. Dying and death are never convenient. But why is Elsie reading *Catcher*, of all books, just now?

The Catcher in the Rye was the most frequently banned book in schools between 1966 and 1975. MotherJoy counted some seven hundred and eighty-five 'instances of obscenity' inside its two hundred and twenty pages. She told Richo as much. The book was originally published as a serial, then in book form by Little Brown complete with a red and white cover and gold lettering. It was dedicated and inscribed by Salinger: 'To my mother'. On publication it became an instant success and still sells some quarter of a million copies each year. Glory flicks through the pages. Looks at the small typeface on yellow pages. She can still feel Holden Caulfield's words all over her skin, his way of putting things, word for word, bite by bite. She wishes she'd been able to wash it off properly.

72

In Brisbane, kids were always stripping off to keep cool. When I was small, we used to go to the Centenary Pool in Spring Hill, near Herston where my father worked in the Royal Children's Hospital. The pool complex, a sophisticated modernist design, had a fifty metre pool as well as a diving pool, the only one of its kind in Brisbane at the time—not that we were allowed to swim in the diving pool. Visiting the complex was a good way to keep us all quiet, my mother said. The Big Girls were told to look after the Little Girls, to keep us from drowning. You can see my father's hospital buildings in the background here, the nurses' quarters perched on top of the hill like a piece of Lego.

What I remember as I gaze at this photo of me beside the pool is the feel of these togs; how they hugged my body with a kind of roughness, how sometimes they made my skin red with scratchy lines. Do you like the stripes across my tummy, how they run with the contours of my body? My lovely thick thighs—people say I take after my father; I have his legs. Do you read uncertainty on my face? See my little sister running away?

These togs were impossible to slide off when wet—they pinched the skin and made rude sucking noises. It was easier to strip off under the water in the pool, if the truth be told—not that I would ever be caught doing that, stripping off in public. I remember how the back of them perished across the stretch of my bottom and weathered away, so that little holes began to appear in the elastic weave, little holes big enough to poke through with little fingers.

After each swim we had to have a bath too, those were the instructions. I can hear our laughter and splash and then my mother's voice calling out crossly: 'That's enough now! Out you get!' In my family we were lucky; we had baths at either end of the house—growing up in Brisbane, you washed every day. I remember boasting about this fact at school, about my luck of having two baths. I didn't have much else to boast about. At school I tried to forget about home and at home I tried to pretend I didn't go to school. But sometimes, just sometimes, things slipped out when I didn't mean them to.

My mother liked to bathe in the bath at the front of the house near the street because the bathtub was shallower and wider and neater; she could make more noise that way. I could hear her, walls away, sloshing about. It was such a tremendous noise I imagined the whole bathroom was full to the brim. She had no shame, unlike us. I imagined she was singing her way to heaven on the wings of baby angels, her head ceiling-ward, exclaiming. I imagined Jesus grilling her at the celestial gates, asking her how many children she had saved that day. Baths made my mother happy, made her triumphant. Hymns sprayed forth in fountains from her mouth—'How Great Thou Art' and 'Beneath the Cross of Jesus'—as if the bath were a church. I recall catching glimpses of my mother's naked body coming out of our old bath, water flipping drips across the linoleum, wet hair in a veil across her face. I see her round belly and her tired breasts that fed us all and I feel her determination.

Funny how we remember things as if they were only yesterday even though some forty years has passed. Funny, too, how we remember through our bodies, through a sting, a pinch, the rude noise of *little holes* and togs sliding off in squelches at the swimming pool, the feeling of needing to run to the change room urgently to do a big fat poo before it is too late. The suck of wet skin.

Memories bite us, scratch and dismay: memories big enough to poke and prod with messing fingers.

73

WHEN LITTLE GLORY GOT HOME that day from Roma Street, she vomited behind the septic tank. It hurt to swallow. It really did. All she could hear was MotherJoy's Bible voice in her temples with the *lob-lob-lob* of her own heartbeat: *For we wrestle not against flesh and blood but against principalities, against powers, against the rulers of darkness of this world, against spiritual darkness in high places.* She did it for MotherJoy, Glory reassured herself. *Blessed are they which are persecuted.* Her mother, of all people, would understand this.

After that came the diarrhoea and, as she sat on the toilet in the pink bathroom, for a second or more she lost herself, fearful she was backsliding. She didn't feel right. Haven't I accepted the Lord as my own personal Saviour? Don't I love going forwards for Jesus, singing with the archangel? But something inside Glory had come unstuck, one of her internal organs perhaps, a pancreas or appendix, her stomach or intestine or worse. She was imploding all loose and down the toilet bowl. But the relief too of not holding back—not that the Soliders ever talked about bodily functions in this way, out loud. Only within the strict privacy of medical diagnoses.

She tried to scrub off the writing. She stood underneath a hot shower with a bottle of methylated spirits she'd found under the house, the acrid smell burning her nostrils, her skin going from black to grey to pink. She covered up the stink with a lather of Vintage Velvet soap. That should do the trick. When Little Glory dressed up for tea that night, she covered up her red legs in a long cotton wraparound skirt in navy blues and slipped her arms into a long-sleeved shirt: the one with yellow and white checks and baskets of appliquéd pineapples. MotherJoy harrumphed at her and Onward said: 'You do look nice,' eyebrows wriggling, 'I must say.' He almost beamed. 'Terribly grown up, Glory dear.'

But Glory-dear didn't feel anything. She was worried the words would peep through the material, leak out somewhere at the seams. That someone would be able to read them through her clothes. That Holden

Caulfield would make his presence felt around the Solider tea table—his voice superimposed over hers. That he would introduce himself then and there; announce she had invited him to tea. That MotherJoy would ask what happened that day. And Onward would say, trying to save his daughter in this instance (or this was what Glory might hope): *Don't you know ink like that on your skin is poisonous?* He always leant towards the technical, if he said anything at all. Then MotherJoy would read a Bible chapter and pray before doing anything else, as a safeguard, as protection, for you never knew when God would call you to account. Holden Caulfield would have to bow his head and close his eyes as well.

Or…perhaps not.

Glory sensed she was very, very close now to making a scene. How finely balanced her body was, eating spaghetti mince, thinking these things. She sucked up the long strands from the plate through pursed lips, sometimes slurping a single straw between her teeth—the gapped ones at the front were especially good for this kind of thing—swinging it around like the Octopus ride at the Ekka. Was it Holden who said *don't look back*, whispered those words into her ears, made her internal organs whooshy with the purr of his breath? Must Glory learn to live with the wild jabbering over her skin? One thing she knew for sure, whatever came next, her mother *must not know* what happened that day on the railway station. Still, Glory wanted to be punished. If only she could get into some sort of trouble. Then, she could feel guilty for something concrete.

That was why she started to eat untidily, spraying sauce over the edge of her plate and onto the tablecloth, hoping to goad her mother into a reaction. She wanted MotherJoy to lash out: *Eat nicely now, Glory-girl.* To be told off for making too much noise. *I don't have to tell you twice, now do I?* To be admonished.

But MotherJoy didn't take the bait. No amount of sipping and slurping and sucking on Glory's part made any difference. Not a sound, not even a look. MotherJoy spent the duration of the meal chatting—*chatting*—about how she'd been asked to play the organ the following Sunday in church, an old Hammond organ. How she'd do her best with the double keyboards but couldn't make promises with the foot pedals. Some of them were bunged up, to use her words. 'Do you think God will mind?'

74

Later that same night, Glory saw the same look on her mother's countenance that had been printed all over her own spaghetti face. She was downstairs, peering at her mother cutting up books in her study. Glory had squeezed through a small gap in the side of the clay embankment under the house, crept to where the louvres let the air in. To watch, wait, observe. This was the way to see MotherJoy at work in her headquarters. Catch a glimpse of *something going on*. She needed to know more. 'Knowledge is power,' Lisa once told her.

The louvres were always open. MotherJoy loved to throw the whole house open whenever she could, to let in the garden, she said, the sounds of her ducks and chooks. Down here, there was a smell of clay. When she was younger, each afternoon after school, this was the place Glory came to do wees, when she was busting because she hadn't gone all day but couldn't make it upstairs fast enough. The smell of urine and orange clay was sometimes so comforting—such relief.

Like now.

There she sat, almost comfy with her bottom on a ledge of the dirt, toes pressed against the weatherboard, watching MotherJoy busy at work cutting up pages and sticking them onto sheets in a scrapbook. Her mother kept flicking the pages of the various books over and back as though trying to decide, Glory thought, which passages to cut out, which lines to paste down, which ones to type up to go into her pamphlets. The print was so small she had to peer at the pages. If you didn't know her, you'd think she was nearly blind. As she read, MotherJoy mumbled to herself, incoherently. It must have been about what she was reading, the content of these pages, because there was an exultation of colour along the line of her jaw across her cheeks. Did she read these books because she *wanted* to? What would she say if she knew Glory was watching? MotherJoy's face was the colour of being caught out.

75

I WONDERED WHETHER my mother Angel read the books on her death list. There were so many typos on any list I found it was hard to say whether she knew the books and authors she was talking about. Either that or she wasn't very good at transcribing.

But I do know this; Angel did read *Lolita*. I found a reference to the book in one of the pamphlets she sent the Governor General; it was a reference a librarian rang me about to ask if I might be interested in it, a file entitled 'Individuals—Requests and Complaints Received From People Within Australia' at the National Archives. The file was full of letters and pamphlets.

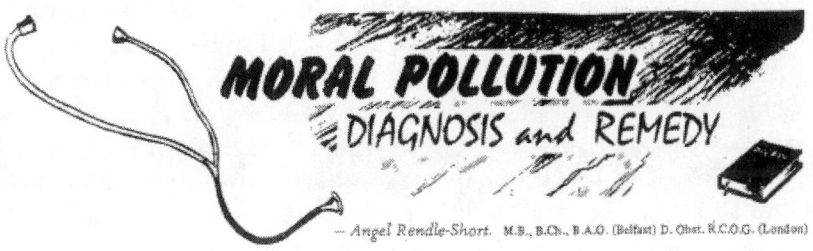

My mother was still alive when I received that phone call and when I dashed to retrieve the file, to read it for myself. In fact, I've just realised now, writing this, that once she died, I didn't find anything else of interest—did I uncover everything in the nick of time?

In this '*Lolita* file', Angel confesses to Sir Paul Hasluck to being 'thoroughly aroused and anxious and inquisitive' when she set out on what she called 'a long and laborious path of literary research' that included the actual reading of books. I try and imagine my mother reading this 'sheer unrestrained pornography' by the light of her lamp, surreptitiously, while the family slept. I try and imagine her imagining Humbert Humbert and his very own 'Lo-Lee-Ta'. Then, I imagine her trying to understand what it was that she had just read, ordering her wild and 'anxious' thoughts. And it is to these very thoughts that I turn, to her particular way of putting things, to the register and tone, her notion of causality, cadence, and breath. This is what she wrote:

> I was thoroughly aroused and anxious and inquisitive. I therefore set out on a long and laborious path of literary research. I was astonished to find that Salinger's *"Catcher in the Rye"* (PARENT HAVE YOU READ IT?) which had once been questioned, was no longer controversial and is used extensively and generally in Brisbane schools: state schools and Church schools. Moreover, this book is in the Junior section of our local municipal library (PARENT HAVE YOU READ IT?). I discovered that boys of 16 and 17 from our great Church schools were reading *"The Group"* and *"Lolita"* — both of which have come under national censorship in Australia and New Zealand. Parents reading this should obtain from their local library both these books, and read the second chapter of *"The Group"*, and the first few chapters of *"Lolita"*. The theme of *"Lolita"* by Nabakov — a prescribed author for English undergraduates at the University of Queensland — is the passionate attachment of a middle-aged man for a lovely little girl of twelve. Because one sin leads to another, the book ends in murder. There is no pornography in this book, moreover it is **beautifully** written. But it is **a rotten** book, and fit only to be burned.

She would have taken her time composing this response. But there is no mistaking: she really did think *Lolita* was good writing, not pornography. My hands hover over the page, fingers tracing the words, reading and re-reading: **rotten, beautiful.**

76

MotherJoy was kneeling on the seagrass matting in the middle of the room surrounded by books. It looked like she was praying. But there wasn't that usual stillness. She was all fluster, there were multiple sighs. MotherJoy couldn't get it right whatever it was she was trying to do. The job overwhelmed her. She must have made mistakes too because at one point she pulled up something she'd just pasted down. She had to lick her fingers to help stick it back in its new position, smooth flat the curl at the edge of the paper. All this looked more difficult than any cutting and pasting Glory did on the blue chenille bedspread. Glory collected words for relaxation and amplification, to discover things, whereas MotherJoy was doing this with such urgency, such impatience, in the same kind of frenzy with which she hammered the death list to the front door of their house.

MotherJoy was concentrating so hard that she didn't notice her skirt was riding up over her thighs. That was how Glory really knew this all was very, very serious—MotherJoy never *didn't notice* things like bare skin. But how magnificent her bare her legs were; those folded knees without stockings like great big fat sausages from the freezer before they were barbecued by Onward, here out in the open, flaring white. Oh, and look: the bottom of her white girdle, the bulge of flesh at the top of her leg where the elastic cut in. Glory wanted to run her finger over the bump of skin and muscle to feel the distortion, its topography. She could even feel her mother's hand now pressed all warm against her roaming one, making her stop but somehow letting her do it too.

So what of all these books? This 'indecent' literature? At a glance it appeared as though MotherJoy could be drowning, the books lapping at those folded knees, at her round bottom, the flare and bulge of all that white skin. Pages flapped open. Rose up around her torso. And what was that? A great rustling of talk, of story. The words themselves were coming alive: this was their chance, they seemed to be saying to each other; this was the opportunity they were waiting for, to get out of there.

Little Glory was thinking about how she could rescue her mother, very nearly calling out to her through the louvres: *Careful Mum, I'm here to help.* Because wouldn't her mother be arrested for this? For possession of pornography? Wasn't there talk of the police being suspicious of these anti-smut campaigners for 'harbouring filth', for peddling 'salacious' pamphlets? Queensland was a tough state to live in if you were on the wrong side of the law. Imagine the police in their blue uniforms marching up the front steps and in through the front door. Imagine MotherJoy in a clink of handcuffs. Dogs barking. The hiss of neighbours. Imagine what Lisa might say, if she heard about it—maybe one of her parents would be in charge of MotherJoy in goal. How could her mother be saved from this?

It looked like MotherJoy was going under, it looked like she was short of breath. It wasn't the same at all as nailing up the death list. Then, MotherJoy was in control, determined, eyes fixed on the jewels in her crown, the ones that would get her to heaven. Now, Glory saw something else altogether. And this thrumming sound in the voice coming out of her mother's body, a voice like an animal's—it hurt to listen. Glory could smell it, smell her mother's suffering, there, in that small room—a smell of confusion mixed with the smell of earth, and with the memory of those stale puddles of orange-clay urine too that Glory suddenly felt ashamed about all over again. They were crying now, mother and daughter. Was this what a drowned body looked like? Glory wished she'd never squeezed along the wall to witness her mother's distress. To spy.

Glory quickly left; this was too much to stomach. She sneaked around the front of the house past the letterbox and raced up the concrete stairs two at a time then across the porch. No one must see her. She washed her face in the pink bathroom, patted the cats on her bed, played with the dolls—sat them upright against the wall in a row—and thought about the tastes she would give them for tea, she could almost smell the meat and boiling potatoes. Pineapple too.

77

T HE HOUSE I GREW UP IN, in St Lucia, was a big rambling old Queenslander with lots of rooms to fit us all in.

I still think of my mother sitting on this porch at the top of the concrete stairs, her feet bare and her favourite housecoat buttoned up to the throat, with an open Bible the size of her lap. She liked to watch the world this way. I imagine her here now, ghostly in this out-of-focus photo from my Pocket Instamatic, as though she were a phantom, even though the house where we lived does not exist like this any more, even though my mother is dead.

The house we call 'Durham Street' was on stilts with a big space underneath. Things went on there—*under the house*. It was where I went to hide and cry as a child, where we kept the Coke bottles filled with homemade ginger beer for fear of them exploding, and where we cracked macadamia nuts with hammers on the cold pitted cement floor to release the soft white fruit. It was here that my mother did the ironing, where she stripped back second-hand furniture with Black & Decker sanding machines, and where she went to pray.

In the far corner of underneath she had a special room kept private with a padlock and key, and, in case you did glimpse inside, red velvet curtains that were pulled across a wall of shelves running ceiling to floor, full of medical things, her sewing, *and* books. Secret stuff. Stuff to do with her activism and campaign.

Down there, the concrete floor muffled sounds, so too the seagrass matting and dirt walls on the topside (our house was buried into a rising hill). My mother was never able to really air out her study even though she opened the bank of louvres to lay them flat. It was always dank and musty. Always dark except where the light flared when she read late into the night. I never dared go into her room without being invited.

I can see her there now, secretly reading books, transcribing passages on her typewriter and pasting them onto roneoed foolscap sheets ready for distribution. She made up pamphlets—'confidential, for parents only'—with lists of suspect books and reasons for her objection, complete with transcripts of what she thought were the obscene bits, not to be read. I helped her collate the pages around the kitchen table upstairs and then we would head out onto the streets of Inala and Goodna, Wynnum and Sunnybank, Rochedale and Redlands to do a letter drop—I never knew why she chose to enlighten those particular suburbs.

There is a photograph of us both my mother kept in her study, taken when I was not yet one-year-old, taken before my parents migrated to Australia from England, in happier times—she gave me a print years later. It reminds me of her, reminds me of her special room. It sits on a small wooden bookcase, one of her sanding projects, a bookcase housing a collection of all those books she wanted to burn. I have been collecting this 'death list' over time, reading the books she objected to, wondering with each one why, exactly, she took issue.

This photograph is the first one I know that exists of us together, just her and me. It's part of a series of slides taken in Sheffield in front of a green velvet curtain in the house we lived in before migrating to Australia. Everyone in the family had their portrait taken in different combinations and poses in front of this curtain except my little sister who wasn't born until we got to Brisbane.

Looking at photographs is a bit like reading books. They invite such acute feeling, such intimacy—you want to laugh and cry. I imagine the grip of her hands holding me firmly around my ribcage, the smell of her hair, the artificial sweetness of hairspray, and her laughter. She is beautiful, don't you think, has the smoothest of skin? I don't remember her wearing that dress, but I do recall the big fat cushion covers she made later out of the silver brocade material, the ones that dressed the special couch in the lounge where we sometimes lay when we were sick.

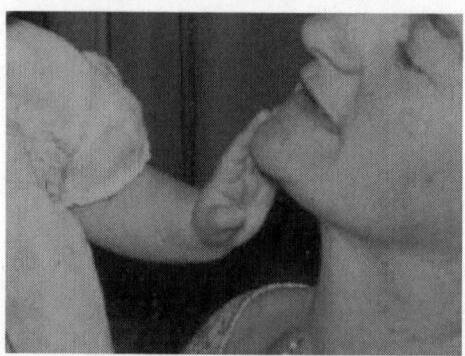

Looking more closely, I see and *feel* something else—there is a bridge between the two bodies. See the child's left hand resting on her mother's face, her fingers flat across the chin and close to her mother's open mouth? I fancy I feel my mother's breath puffing across the space between us both to blow warm on my skin. I feel my hand steady on her body—she does not resist either. Her face inclines my way; her chin reaches out to me.

78

THE PROGNOSIS ISN'T GOOD. MotherJoy has cancer, an anaplastic cancer at that, the most malignant of all kinds, the most aggressive. True to form, she makes her intentions very clear: no resuscitation, no gastro-nasal tubes, only a little oxygen and a morphine driver. The surgeon cuts away what he can from her chest and throat to let her breathe more comfortably, but nothing else can be done. There is talk that she might have to have a tracheotomy but the surgeon wants to avoid this because of the chance that the cancer could grow into the tube at her throat and then outside her body. Glory imagines MotherJoy with cancerous wings growing large and sturdy either side of her throat, white wings for sure. She imagines MotherJoy literally flying to heaven.

'Don't forget to look after Onward now, will you?'

Onward, lost and bewildered, trapped in the nursing home one hundred miles away up north, unable to move now, even in a taxi to visit, to say his last goodbyes.

'We won't,' the girls promise.

Her funeral plans are in place; she has left instructions for everything from the choice of hymns and Bible readings, to the colour of the roses the Solider girls must purchase to make a cross-shaped wreath to lay on the white coffin. MotherJoy is bound for glory, without question, nipped and tucked into her chariot.

79

Little Glory smelt it first. A presentiment. It wasn't the normal scent of an ordinary bonfire under the mango tree in the backyard, that almost sweet-burning, sappy smell of order and wellbeing, of tidiness—a clean-up-the-garden kind of Saturday smell. Or the comfort smell of an open fire in the drawing room—the one Onward lit to remind him of England, but had to open all the windows to let the cool air in because here, it was too hot. No. This was something else, more like the smell of a house burning, that kind of magnitude. Big. The pulling fuel of trees, of wood, of paper, of carbon. A whole paper mill burning. *En masse*. Not that Glory had ever experienced such a thing, but if she did—and after today she hoped she never would—she knew this was what it would be like. It sucked you in.

Such heat.

Then Glory saw MotherJoy, who else? She was down behind the bougainvillea and next to the mango, awash in her nightie, the fabric all breezy about her bare arms and against her bare legs. Even though it was late in the afternoon on this Wednesday, there she was in her night gear, with her favourite housecoat over the top, the one with red buttons in a line down the front like a clown's costume and red ribbon threaded around the yoke front and back with a bow, the one she kept on a metal hook behind the bedroom door for special times, the fancy one she slipped into on Sundays. She had slippers on her feet, and she was stamping them like a small child, left foot then right, on and on in a crackling rhythm, a drumming music, as she hurled book after book into the fire, the bougainvillea's magenta flowers like a sea of swirling purple flames above the real fire.

Finally: MotherJoy was burning books.

When Glory realised what was happening she wanted to call out: *Stop! You shouldn't be doing that!* Instead she found herself running towards her mother, asking if she could help.

MotherJoy turned with a start and Glory was startled by her expression. She'd never seen such a look. The only way she could explain it to herself, as she tried to do later, was that MotherJoy had the fear of God on her face, in her eyes. Everything seemed overlarge, exaggerated, portentous. As if the licking tongues of flame from the bonfire had jumped into her mother's face, to flicker beneath her very transparent skin, a million eyes as a warning. This was what it was all about, Glory knew then, what everything was about; everything she had learned to that point about God and hell and damnation. It made sense: there was a line in the sand after all and you had to make sure you were on the right side. If not—and this was the terrible news embedded in the smell and the heat and also in her mother's now peculiar face—you'd go to hell. MotherJoy was making a choice. She was cleansing herself with fire.

Bang, bang went the books. There was nothing for it but to help.

Glory bent and picked up book after book from the boxes at her feet, blood heavy, and hurled the pages and covers into the flames, a gulp behind her mother. She drowned out the noise of the fire and her questions by clicking her tongue on the inside of her mouth—to make it raucous in her head. Sweat dripped sticky from the usual places: down the back of her neck, behind her ears, behind her knees. And from secret places too: from between her legs where her bottom touched the top of the back of her thighs, between her small breasts. It was such hot work. Glory felt as though she was melting away, praying to Jesus all the while to make things right, to notice. Surely Jesus must have smelt their righteous work.

Bang, bang, bang went the books. *Yes, yes, yes* went Glory in her head, nearly audible too with her lips. *Click, click, click* went her tongue. *Bleat, bleat, bleat* her temples.

Some of the books were ones Glory knew about: *Lady Chatterley's Lover*, *To Kill a Mockingbird*, *Lord of the Flies*. Glory could have recited the authors and titles as they flew into the flames. Then there were others, the ones she hadn't heard of yet; books she didn't know existed let alone what they might contribute to the world. There was Donald Horne's *Lucky Country*, Aldous Huxley's *Brave New World*, Radclyffe Hall's *The Well of Loneliness*, Mary McCarthy's *The Group*, and Virginia Woolf's *Mrs Dalloway*.

To help them burn faster, mother and daughter now tore at the books and the pages and the covers in unison. They made such a mess. Cardboard covers got mangled. Pages fluttered everywhere. Paper flew about like birds circling the lights of a city. The fire ate everything they fed it, unceasingly hungry. All those chapters upon chapters, all those hundreds and thousands and millions of words, many factors of ten gobbled up. The jibber-jabber of paper and words. Even the birds in the chookyard joined the din, honked and quacked about in protest. It all filled Glory with a kind of horror but there was something irresistible about it too. She smiled at her mother and her mother smiled back. For what she loved was this: the way the paper glowed yellow and orange then red and black. The fire was like a giant mouth gobbling, flames like red chillies. How the cinders flew upwards to heaven, delicate, each cinder a miniature boat sailing away, twirling and swirling in the uplift.

Glory immersed herself. A self baptism if you like. Not the deep baptismal waters for the full immersion of adult baptism, the ritual she witnessed her sisters doing in church with the minister, rather this was immersion into the belly of her mother's way in the world, into MotherJoy's thinking. Such was the character of fire; Glory was being transfigured. From now on, things would be different. Her thumping heart was in an elegant dive, not down to the front altar this time, but rather upwards in a reverse tuck, chasing those little cinder boats 'glorywards'.

80

GLORY WONDERED ABOUT the writers who had written these books. How would they react if they knew they were being burned on this day in the Sunshine State in Queensland in the Solider's backyard? What would they say? Did they sense what was going on that afternoon? Did they feel this catastrophe in their marrow, even though they were far away? Had their tongues swelled in their mouths with prescience? 'Like murdering children,' Sister E once said in Modern History, when the subject of book burning came up. 'What would make anyone do that?' Her voice wasn't angry; she just wanted to know. Would Sister Elisabeth understand if she were here?

'Don't even think about it,' MotherJoy said in a coarse whisper under her breath at one point, as she swung a book into the fire like a shot-put.

81

These two Soliders were unstoppable that afternoon. As the sun sank to the west with the bougainvillea and reflected light forming a halo of colour above the two of them, and as the smell of burning something untoward leaking across the suburb on the rising back of a Brisbane evening sea breeze, it was as if their hands were doing the burning: fingers and palms. They had to finish what they had started. Urgently. It wouldn't be over until it was done.

The Soliders raced against time, or at least Glory did—*like murdering children*. She was rushing back and forth from box to flame so that paper and books sloshed everywhere, so that sometimes she had to scramble over the couch grass on her hands and knees to pick up the orphans and widows, the fallen strays. She lost all feeling in her legs. She stumbled. Her lungs puffed up, swollen like beach balls. She began to make little huffing sounds from the back of her throat.

Until now, Glory had never realised the strength of feeling inside her—an inside out sort, if that made sense. As though MotherJoy had lodged herself now *in her daughter*—this was the only way Glory could explain it to herself—as though Glory was actually harbouring her mother, her mother's body swallowed within her own, with Glory's outside skin stretched oh-so thin to encompass them both, very nearly to tear, to bursting. Things weren't right but they couldn't be better. So that if someone were to interrupt, to question her about what was going on—*what's all this?* Glory's answer would be in her mother's voice. The girl she thought she was threatened to dissolve. Her feet were sweaty, slipping and sliding in the Robin lace-ups, her socks quite soaked. What bones and muscle she possessed was now melting away. Very soon her body might actually change state, vaporise.

Then it was over.

Boxes empty. Books thrown. Glory slumped hard to the ground, threw off her shoes and socks, crouched there on her haunches rocking back and forth in a squat. Her throat was sore as though she had been shouting at the top of her voice all afternoon. She made sobbing noises in her chest. She wiped the tears on her face with the palms of her hand.

82

MotherJoy seemed a different person too. She plonked herself down on the ground beside Glory, let out a fat sigh with the flap of her nightie and housecoat, clapped her hands three times and held them clasped in front of her, in a gesture of prayer. Glory wriggled close and wedged herself into MotherJoy's side, took one of her arms and wrapped it about her shoulders. She laid her head on her mother's lap pleased to feel the thickness of her mother's thigh flat to her ear; she was exhausted. She could fall asleep like this, as she sometimes had done when she was very small, in church. MotherJoy could carry on praying and singing for as long she liked, secluded here in the backyard.

83

There is a slide my father took of me kidding around in a pool in the backyard in St Lucia, in our Clark Rubber special we were very proud of—I hear shouts and carry-on, feel the splash of water.

I found the box of family slides in my mother's Japanese trunk, while clearing out her room in the nursing home after her death. I always liked to imagine that this particular trunk was full of chocolates, because my family never had treats like this. Instead it was full of papers and memorabilia, including this old Kodak slide box.

The red and black and white box is falling apart. It was once held together with sticky tape, unsticky now and yellow, with the words 'Royal Tour' across the lid in what must be my mother's handwriting although it doesn't look quite right. I have no idea what Royal Tour it might have been. My parents were monarchists; I do know that. It's certainly not my father's writing, even though he was the keeper of the slides.

Don't ever tell

    This little girl must be me surely, the hair colour is right, even though it is wet. I don't remember the ducky rubber ring, it seems so frivolous for us, but there is something about the way this little girl holds her head that I recognise. A familiar pose. Her cheek, the kick of her jaw, the wrinkle on her neck. If only we could see her face: I wonder what she was looking at?

    I loved to play in the pool with my little sister each day all through summer into the toes and fingers of cooler weather and for as long as we could until the soles of our feet and palms of our hands wrinkled up like prunes. Look at how clear the water was too—we worked hard to clean the pool of slime and mould at the beginning of summer. See the outline of the girl's body beneath the surface, how she is positioned in the water, toes pressing into the blue plastic floor to stay stable, how she keeps her head afloat. Look at the angles she makes with her body, the shape we see now in the water. How her right leg is cocked sidewards like a memory: a picture of what memory might look like, perhaps—the trace and shadow of a known body, somatic recognition. Little girl: do I know you?

Here, swimming in this backyard pool, a little girl and her rubber ring make music in the water with a leg cocked sidewards, a face angled skywards. Here in these words, she comes alive in story. Together, she and I become more than simply a portrait of what once was. As the story gets going, the two of us swim together with only a slit of indiscernible Brisbane daylight between—depending on the slant, the hold, the poetry. Water drips through our hair.

My little sister and I would stay in the pool all afternoon if we were allowed. We liked to play a game we called 'doing the whirlpool'. We dragged the blue water around the perimeter of the pool with our bodies to make currents. We would begin on opposite sides of the circumference from each other and then around and around we would go while holding onto the top metal edge with our hands pulling ourselves along around the rim, with our feet running and cavorting and dragging behind us along the bottom where the edge of the blue plastic sloped upwards. I can still feel with my toes the flaps of folded plastic along the pool floor. 'Let's do the whirlpool,' we squealed, as if calling a bush dance. The blue current caught us up in its arm to do-se-do.

How hard we worked: toes holding on to get a grip before letting go like rubber bands, like jumping jacks, like penny bunger rockets. Faster and faster we went with the water, around and around, with what speed. How we laughed and guffawed with the swing of the water, the whirl of our bodies, and with the slap and slide and clap of our voices. How we bumped and skidded and thumped the metal sides. Sometimes the current was so fast we had to let go of the sides and the bottom and just let the water take us wherever, however. Sometimes, our legs and arms got caught and twisted together so that we spun around in a cheesy hug like a giant octopus doing water aerobics. We glided and floated like that, the water keeping us in shape. I can hear us now, years later, hear the pitch and register and cadence of our voices—unaffected, innocent, joyous—spinning skywards in girly compositions, us, aglow in the watery outdoors. It was the only thing that mattered: the only meaning that existed. The sound of our laughter and pleasure was so pineapple sweet it was infectious. I wonder if my little sister remembers in the same way as I do?

84

Whenever Big Glory first comes into the palliative care room with her sisters, she watches from afar. MotherJoy is so little lying there in the middle of the hospital bed in the middle of the Queen's Suite—that's really what it's called. All Glory can do is stare. Besides, there's so much bustle and flair already, with sisters carrying in paper bags full of clothes and personal belongings, things to sort into cupboards and bedside drawers, things to put away, nurses checking too. There are so many practical, little things to attend to when waiting for someone to die.

MotherJoy is curled towards the light of the window, and still, all Glory can do is gape. Listen to her mother's shallow breathing.

'Is she okay?' Glory asks no one in particular.

MotherJoy looks like a baby. Unrecognisable.

'She's sleeping, she'll sleep a lot I think,' Ruthy says, who had once been a nurse.

'What happens at night?'

'The nurse said we could sleep here, keep vigil.'

'What—really?' Glory asks. 'Here? Overnight?'

'Do you want to?'

'I think so.' Glory surprises herself with her answer.

'Let's take turns, do it in pairs, keep watch.'

That's how it comes about that Elsie goes back to the apartment and Glory and Ruthy stay on that first night, the night the nurses dish up the morphine. It happens quickly too. Suddenly MotherJoy can't breathe. It's as though she already has a foot on the stairs to heaven, but she never conceived it would be this tough, didn't think she would have to swallow knives to get to glory. The gasping yanks Glory into the room. She finds herself holding her mother's hand. It's a turning point.

Ruthy goes to get help. Suddenly, shockingly, Glory is on her own with MotherJoy. She hears herself talking: 'You're doing fine,' she whispers to her mother, 'you'll be okay they'll be here soon with something to help I'm not going anywhere I'm with you you'll be okay I won't leave you you'll be okay I'll stay with you you're doing fine I'm not going anywhere.' The seconds drag and what must only be ten minutes or so stretches in every direction to the horizon. Glory stops breathing herself. Her whole body leans her mother's way because she aches for the suffering before her.

Afterwards, just before MotherJoy falls asleep at last—the only thing to do after such terrible exertion—she turns to Glory, grabs her hand, holds it tight so that their rings click, metal against metal, and she says in a little voice: 'You'll stay with me won't you, you give me strength, you're strong you know.' Glory's hand turns numb, pins and needles.

Glory and Ruthy keep watch all night, listen to their mother breathing. To stay awake Glory writes by the light of the blue night lamp, scribbles into her notebook using a broad-tipped black pen in order to read the words in the ghostly light. The book is black this time with an elastic bookmark to hold it together and the word *blank* written in gold on the cover—she likes the irony. She's perched on the steadiest and quietest chair she can find, and as close as she can get to the bed, to look down on her mother's sleeping body this way, right there, beside her. She finds herself counting the number of breaths as the minutes tick by very slowly (there are no clocks on palliative wards), tallying them up in her book with sticks and slashes like a third grader doing elementary maths. She watches MotherJoy's top lip quiver like a puffer fish (Ruthy swears it's the morphine), breathes along with the rise and fall of her mother's chest, the shape of MotherJoy's ribcage around her lungs and her heart. These organs are working hard, harder than they ever have had to do in her eight and a half decades. What a difficult thing it is to die, how we resist. Is she waiting for all of her girls to be beside her bed—does she know the other three are on their way? Does she want a grand finale?

85

At daybreak, when she opens her eyes, MotherJoy stares at Glory leaning against the sun-white window. 'Do you think I could have scrambled eggs for breakfast?' She smiles in a watery way at her daughter, crawls her fingers across the sheets to reach out to touch her. She holds Glory tight. She fiddles with the toggles of her woolly cardigan now on Glory: 'You look nice in that jumper. It suits you.' Then she adds: 'You really are very strong you know.' She squeezes out the word *strong* before floating back to sleep again, so that the 'you know' bit of the sentence comes out an octave lower and Glory wonders if her mother heard her own words.

Overnight the Solider girls have kept themselves warm while on their death watch by taking turns to wear MotherJoy's cardigan. It's the jumper from Vinnies, the one MotherJoy cut up for her quadruple bypass at the Prince Charles more than two years before. The one with different colours, split up the front with the edges bound in black satin ribbon, stitched into place with red embroidery thread (Glory doesn't remember this detail from the last time she saw it) and black toggles as buttons, a soft black crocheted collar to comfort the neck. All MotherJoy's handiwork: her 'hospital jumper'. Here it is again being put to good use, making another appearance in another hospital. It still smells funny. At the beginning of this stay MotherJoy had said: 'This is the last time I'll use this creation, isn't it?'

During the day MotherJoy is cold by turns and asks for the cardigan to be put around her shoulders. The daughters oblige their mother, sometimes put their arms around her as well, to warm her up. They grow adept at little ministrations of love even though this is something they're not practised at with their mother; they've never done anything like this before. They hover around her bed like butterflies. Step really very close. Take it in turns to sit on the bed, on the armchair, to stand. Take it in turns to fluff up her pillows, bring her jugs of ice, clean nighties, boiled lemon sweets to suck on. They stitch themselves into place as though they are part of her surgery, no one can send them away. Glory cuts up her meals into tiny bite sizes, feeds her spoonfuls of scrambled egg sprinkled with salt (the nurses say she can have anything she wants), and adjusts the oxygen tube snuffling into her nose. She sometimes helps MotherJoy arrange her clothes in order to cover the wound on her neck and throat. MotherJoy naps on and off, sleeps amongst the cushions, nestled in her knitted rainbow of a cardigan.

Glory wears it too whenever it's free, even though she keeps wondering who wore it before this, who might have thrown it out for charity the first time, and who will wear it next when it ends up in a charity bin after this. She pulls the cardigan tight around her as a way to pull MotherJoy into her breast, hold fast. She's getting closer now, purl stitch by purl stitch. Not that Glory can openly show affection—*not yet*, she tells herself—not even a peck on the cheek to say hello or goodbye (she doesn't notice how easy or difficult it is for the others). It's not that she doesn't want to kiss MotherJoy—in the way a daughter kisses a mother—her desire for this natural affection nearly peels her organs apart. But she needs more time, even though time is fast running out. She wants to dissolve the wedge between them, this resistance, this thing that's lodged in the space between her body and her mother's.

Once, when the others having gone out to get a bite of lunch and Glory is alone in the room with MotherJoy sleeping, she opens the locker drawer beside the bed to look at what her mother has hidden there, what treasures she chose to bring into the hospital with her—for this, the final move of her life. Glory feels a little sneaky doing this, knowing it's premature, even though this kind of clearing up has to happen very soon—for before long MotherJoy *is* going to die, and then all her belongings will need to be sorted and disposed of by Glory and her sisters, in some way or another.

Right now, she has to be quick, the others mustn't catch Glory when they return, nor MotherJoy if she were to wake. Glory doesn't pause to consider what she will do if she finds something she doesn't want to know about.

In fact, what Glory discovers are two purses: a small, embroidered one with beads, and a plastic blue pencil case doubling as a purse for coins. Inside the beaded purse, there are nylon scarves in different colours, some jewellery, a pair of nail scissors, and torn up pieces of paper. Glory reads: *But we—beholding the Glory of the Lord—are changed into the same image, from glory to glory, by the Spirit of the Lord—changed from glory to Glory, till in heaven we see Thy face*. The passage is in MotherJoy's characteristic handwriting. She always had the habit of annotating and underlining words on whatever paper she could find. If Glory threaded together all the different notebooks and Bibles and *Daily Lights* her mother had written in, she feels sure she could trace MotherJoy's plea for grace and salvation. *He will not let us SUFFER beyond that which we are able. Suffering is not to be compared to GLORY which is to be revealed.* Glory winces. Her name always comes up, one way or another. And her mother's voice, even on paper, is so distinctive. It scratches at her like sandpaper.

The other thing Glory finds, snuggled underneath this scrap of paper, is a bit of a photograph, face down, torn from something larger. She turns it over. It is one of Glory from years before and probably taken by Onward. It was from when Glory was still at university—married then, hoping that might make a difference—in her 'vintage punk' phase if those layers of skirts and black silk knickerbockers are anything to go by. Glory remembers wearing this outfit on a visit home. It takes her back, and yes, there had been a scene; there was always a scene. Boy, it's hard to breathe.

Glory remembers how MotherJoy was almost speechless, didn't know what to hit on first: 'I'd be a hypocrite if I didn't say something. I must.' She remembers Onward shouting at MotherJoy to *stop it*, and apologising the next morning to Glory, how his face was distorted on uttering the word *sorry*—but how he did find a way to say it, the sorry word. He disappeared then, straight away, and MotherJoy took to her bed, refused to say goodbye. Still, why is this scrap of photograph here—out of everything her mother could choose from? On the reverse side she reads: *He will not let us SUFFER beyond that which we are able*.

Glory quickly slips the photograph back into its place, shuts it all away, and puts the purses back into the drawer. Just as she flops back down on a chair, a nurse breezes in to check on things. Glory feels sure the nurse knows something is up, her face must be the colour of blood.

'Is everything okay, you don't need anything?'

'We're fine,' Glory says, although in her heart she knows she's not—don't ever tell, *you'll go to hell*. If MotherJoy is true to form, there'll be a scene before it's over.

Later that night, as everyone else is saying goodnight and Gracie and Mary are lined up with pyjamas and toothbrushes in hand, determined to keep vigil, ready to sleep in the hospital sofa-bed, take their turn, Glory dares herself to do something she's never done before: act in defiance, not to say something, but to *do* something. There's no time to reflect because instinctively Glory is falling, falling towards her mother, kissing her goodnight. Smack on her cheek. It is a lightning decision, where she is not even conscious of doing it. She's given her mother a kiss in a way she's not kissed before, a Big-Glory kiss. From standing tall beside the bed in the room she freefalls into space like an open book for everyone to read, flutters down towards her mother's body as it lies there, in new lime green pyjamas under the covers. Such a simple thing too, once you do it, *because you want to*. To really kiss. What exhilaration. To learn how to fall *by falling*. She wants to laugh.

The turn of surprise then in MotherJoy—well, more like her mother doesn't curl away. There is stillness about her. MotherJoy receives her daughter's felicitations in a neutral sort of way, without demonstrable pleasure but without disgrace either. Could this be right? Does Glory detect a twin-point sparkle in her mother's eyes too despite any reservation she might have, despite herself?

'Goodnight Mum, I'll see you again in the morning.'

Her mother asks: 'Do you think we should ask a nurse how long I can stay?'

Glory replies: 'Don't worry. You'll be okay.'

Back at the apartment, lights sparkle the river water. Before going to bed, Glory leans on the windowsill, staring out. The warm Brisbane air massages her bare skin. She's bursting in her chest a great hullabaloo but it's after midnight, she must keep the noise down. The quiet of the night with a few circling bats for company doesn't stop her going over things in her head, writing it all out again on her organs in big fat lettering. *I kissed her*. It doesn't matter what anybody says now—as far as Glory is concerned something magical happened with her mother tonight. To smell the aroma of nearness, the pink musk soap of her mother's skin where the perfume sticks to you, its particular chemistry.

The miracle is that Glory feels the kiss still, her mother's soft, soft cheek against her lips—the physicality of an ageing body, warm fleshiness—so much so she believes *it can happen again*. She's greedy for more, for lots of kisses—*one thousand times*. With this one brave gesture Glory finds herself passing from 'before now' to 'after this'. She can't wait to see her mother again.

Wings ablaze

86

A FRIEND ONCE SAID to Glory, 'Forget those other books. There's only one you need to read: *Fahrenheit 451* by Ray Bradbury. Was it on your mother's list?' He gives her a copy and Glory nearly chokes on the pages. How it shakes her up. As if she is a real book being burnt alive, just like all those books Guy Montag burned.

And what about the book refugees? The ones who escape by running into the woods? The ones who store whole literary works in their heads, memorised word for word, because they have to. It keeps them alive. They stick themselves into the pages, name themselves after their favourites: E. M. Forster's *A Passage to India*, James Joyce's *Portrait of the Artist as a Young Man*, Muriel Sparke's *Prime of Miss Jean Brodie*. These Book People witness terrible goings on. *Fahrenheit 451* makes Glory tremble. She imagines all the escapees from her Queensland burning more than thirty years ago, imagines them wandering around as nomads somewhere in the outback scrub. Imagine that: a squadron of Queensland Book People from that time, out in the Simpson Desert, at Lake Eyre, Carnarvon Gorge.

Glory rereads *451* again. Feathers and squawks and hullabaloo; words amok. So how will this story end?

87

MotherJoy started it, by laughing of all things. Little Glory couldn't believe her ears. This was no laughing matter—they were burning books, you could smell it everywhere. Her mother might be arrested for harbouring pornography. What if the *Courier Mail* got a whiff? What if a reporter heard the hilarity now on the breeze? It would be a front-page story, headline in large caps, impossible to miss: BOOKBURNERS LAUGH: CARELESS ABOUT WANTON DESTRUCTION. Glory didn't want to consider possibilities. But MotherJoy was saying: 'Look at us, will you? Look at what we've done. It's a funny old world isn't it?'

For together, still entwined, having plonked themselves on the ground and Glory very nearly asleep on her mother's lap, the two of them exhausted from the exertion, they were laughing, gently at first. Glory could feel it through MotherJoy's housecoat, in the tickle of the red ribbon. She could feel the rising jiggle and roll from deep in her mother's intestine, the rocking muscle movement of her mother's stomach. Before long they were sitting side-by-side, almost gasping for breath, holding their stomachs. Such abandonment.

Glory loved to hear her mother let go. Where the laughter flew out of nowhere. Suddenly there. It was free of restraint, made the skin shimmer. All sparkle. They were like Catherine wheels popping off at cracker night. MotherJoy's laughter seduced Glory and Glory dared herself to give in.

88

M<small>Y MOTHER LIKED TO LAUGH</small> too—Angel was very good at it. It was always unexpected, so out of character we thought, but always very welcome when it erupted.

Even though she's now quite dead, I can still imagine her way of letting go like the coming of summer rain. Best of all, if I gaze at images of her, I catch her easy self, her uninterrupted self; I sense some joy at living. But it takes some concentrating. And I ask myself: Angel, what went so wrong?

When my father married Angel as a young woman he was in love and the war was over and they went to Donegal and County Cork for their honeymoon to swim and dive in the sea and kiss the Blarney Stone. They were over the moon, so the story goes, my mother always laughing, so he said. Things looked simple. She looks so happy.

There is another one of her I've found in an old brown box of photos and slides I keep under my bed, a different box to 'Royal Tour'. I like this brown one because it's got my father's handwriting in notes on the lid, different iterations corresponding with different times of his life and his evolving interests. He must have kept this box behind closed doors in his study; I've never seen it before. There's the reference to my grandfather and his writing—'Some of Father's note books and sermon notes'—crossed out. Then there is a note on the narrow edge of the box about autism and genetics that must relate to my father's research into infantile autism and the importance of early diagnosis. He was a pioneer in the field. And the lovely word *keep*, in his oh-so-familiar wobbly handwriting.

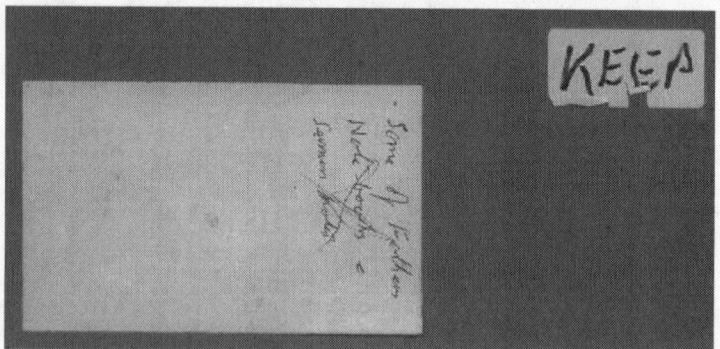

I wonder what my father was preserving when he labelled it this keeping way.

I pull out the photograph I am keeping of my mother, the one taken in the kitchen in Durham Street.

We brought this gas stove with us from Sheffield when we migrated to Brisbane in 1961, a place my mother only knew by name on a map. It was one of forty-two pieces of luggage that accompanied the family of five children with one on the way across the oceans in the ocean liner the *SS Siberia*. When my little sister was born a month after arriving in Brisbane, my mother couldn't understand what the nurses were saying to her, it was as though they were speaking a foreign language she said, even though she knew they spoke English. The new migrants settled in the suburb of Norman Park, close to the Brisbane airport, such as it was then, in a house so full of cockroaches my mother said the walls were black when she turned on the light in the middle of the night to feed her new baby. Queensland took some getting used to.

I remember taking this photograph for a school photography project when I was in high school. I like Angel's smile and the slant of her head and how she wears her watch skew-whiff up her arm. She does look happy, if a little bit forced for the occasion. See the wild vegetation out the side window in the dark?

89

The fire was hot, the books had burnt fast; they were nearly gone. There was nothing more to be done, only to keep watch to the very end and rake the embers into a pile. To fold the rim of the bonfire into the centre like folding flour over yeast to make bread, careful of ricocheting sparks on bare legs. If the Soliders changed their minds (not that they would) and decided to pull the books back out of the fire, the pages would be impossible to read, a mangle of charcoal meanings. Sentences dislocated. Words disgorged. Imagine after all that burning if all that was left to read were the rude bits? Fire purifies, doesn't it? That's what the Bible says.

'We must beg God's blessing.'

Before Glory realised what she was doing, MotherJoy knelt down and bowed her head and started to pray and Glory quickly squeezed shut her eyes. MotherJoy prayed so earnestly that afternoon her hands wrinkled red. She spoke of God's judgement, the final days when all the earth would be called to account. She asked for God's forgiveness too, then committed Glory to His care, *forever*. Beseechingly. Perhaps after everything, this was the time to believe her mother, to trust her. But all Glory could think about was the crown of jewels nearly on her mother's head, the crown MotherJoy said Glory was helping to make, the sparkly sapphires and emeralds, jasper and amethysts Glory was helping to fashion and glue in place because of her goodness: 'Be faithful until death and I will give you the crown of life,' says the Book of Revelation. Glory was one of her mother's precious stones: MotherJoy promised. All her children were jewels in her crown, MotherJoy said, so she could be like the Holy City itself. While they were praying, Glory imagined a crown on her mother's head; she saw her wringing hands too. She'd look very fancy in a queenly crown. Better to help save her mother with goodness than pluck out the jewels with acts of wilfulness and sin because didn't MotherJoy always say that the sins of the daughters would be visited upon the mother a thousand times? Glory decided on this occasion that she wanted the jewels earned with these particular acts of righteousness to be fashioned in ruby and gold. Then she imagined MotherJoy's heavenly crown all joggly, the jewels jiggling up like the flames. MotherJoy dancing and leaping about with it on, all queenly and royal.

Once the fire was almost dead, MotherJoy's dying prayer mopped up what was left of the mess. What scraps remained of any lightness or laughter was small enough to tangle in Glory's plaits. They raked the residue into the centre, all those books transformed into a small, ring-a-ring-a-rosy.

'Let's go in Glory, have something to eat.'

With that, MotherJoy pulled her housecoat tight around her, fastened the buttons across the yoke, and carefully retied the red ribbon into a neat bow. As Glory followed her mother inside, she thought she could hear MotherJoy singing quietly—'Praise God from whom all blessing flow'—as if in benediction after a worship service. Gracie would be home soon from music. Onward too, working late. Eve was away on a church camp.

But it was all over. MotherJoy was spent.

What Glory kept thinking, as she hovered about laying the table for tea, was how MotherJoy had hugged her back as they sat watching the fire. Her mother held on, didn't she? Glory could feel it, body to body, like she felt the realness of her mother's stomach jiggling with laughter, Glory's red ear squashed against those funny tummy rolls. They had hugged a holding-on kind of hug, a hug to last. A hug smelling of Queensland sweat and burning paper, hairspray and 4711 perfume.

They ate leftovers for tea—spaghetti mince, cold baked potato, mashed carrots—a very ordinary meal, a family tableau. An unceremonious finish to a momentous day. Any leftover laughter, any trills on Glory's skin were gone. Glory wasn't sure what she would say if anybody asked about what happened, if Gracie wanted to know, for instance. She hoped that the darkness of the night would soak up the evidence. That she could forget different parts of the story existed. The thing was, a smell of smoke hung from the palm trees that night, swung about all fat with the squawking of the flying bats in their tens and hundreds. These mammals seemed louder and hungrier than usual this night.

'You're in charge now, Glory,' MotherJoy had said. 'And don't forget to spread the ash first thing, before the sun gets up.'

90

GLORY LOVED THE WAY ash went stone cold, like the wicked gone for good. The smell of it in the morning. How it floated up your nose if the direction of the breeze was right. Gobfuls of the stuff, as fine as icing sugar. You could poke it and swear nothing was there. All air. It moved independently at the end of Glory's stick, breathed a life of its own accord, shivered perhaps but as a mirage. But that was it—all that life of exotic burning the day before in the backyard, all those words and stories and subplots and characters and voices, sneezes and sweat, were dust today. As though—and this was the bit that astonished—as though nothing solid had been present in the first place, nothing material, nothing to hold onto. So much so it was almost hard to believe—or recall—what the fuss was about.

91

THERE IS ANOTHER photograph in the series my father took with his Retina of us kidding around in the Clark Rubber pool in the backyard in St Lucia, down beneath the bougainvillea and mango. On our slide nights, it always got a laugh. But I can hear my mother's stern voice insisting: 'Next!' The anxiety in her tone. Then how she left the room.

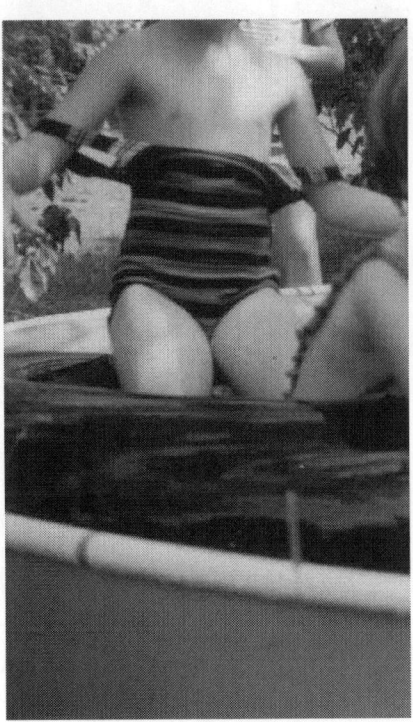

Recollect these togs? The little girl's head is quite cut off: there's no ready facial recognition (my father had a habit of accidentally chopping off our heads). But will you look at her body side-saddle on the black inner tube that she loved to ride? Good at keeping balance, a nice straight back.

How this little girl loved chiacking in this way all day, squealing and carrying on, even when she was turned upside down, dunked under water and had to hold her breath. There'd be a great spluttering everywhere as she shot to the surface in a burst of laughter.

Will you look at her body, those thighs full of shine, glowing muscles. Look at her chest, her strong shoulders: her torso. See the shadows in wings under her arms, her ribcage like the spread of a butterfly. Her nipples: watchful eyes. You can hear her breathing, can't you? The little girl's togs fall off her shoulders; you want to hoist up the straps. But you don't. You can't.

92

Gracie's phone call wakes Glory in the rented apartment.

All the Solider girls are in Brisbane now, have travelled hundreds and thousands of miles to be there. They're all within cooee of the Wesley Hospital, taking turns to keep watch over their mother, even Elsie who swore she wouldn't fly back from England under any circumstances. Gracie is the one sitting beside MotherJoy, holding her hand. She's been there all night with Mary. 'Quick, she's going,' Gracie says. 'Get here as fast as you can.'

What happens next is unrehearsed: her sisters haven't thought this part through. Not the different possibilities or scenarios. Gracie rings is so loud and clanging it must have woken the whole apartment block. Glory sits bolt upright. Dizzy with everything.

All Glory can think about, as she throws on the first set of clothes she picks up off the floor is why this night? Her thoughts are all a muddle but she doesn't say anything to the others. In fact nobody says anything to anybody. *Quick, she's going.* This news takes away their tongues. It breaks up any cohesiveness they have experienced while waiting, while keeping watch, while stitching together a story of their lives in the hope of making a single Solider garment. The silence in the room is unearthly as Eve, Ruthy, Elsie and Glory stumble around to get ready. So too outside the apartment as they walk, almost run up the hill to the hospital. The only noise Glory is aware of is the throb in her ears and the *thwack-thwack* of her flower-thongs on the concrete footpath all wonky with fat Moreton Bay roots. It is still dark although a dawn lightens the sky around the rim of the city. The setting moon is a jewel in the sky. It won't be long now before the sun begins to burn a normal day.

Up the hill Glory's legs ache. How steep the Brisbane hills are in the inner city. Her calves are tight. She has to walk on the balls of her feet, on her toes, to keep up with her heart racing ahead. *Thwack-thwack-thwack.* Why didn't she wear her sandals with the strap across the back? Her Achilles tendons are on fire and she lags behind the others. It would be easier walking up backwards, she thinks. This is it, *really* it. Glory nearly sinks into the earth with the idea. She feels sure her face is glowing in the dark.

93

By the time they get there, MotherJoy has passed away—that's exactly the way the nurses put it and MotherJoy would be rather pleased with their language if she overheard. Mary offers: 'She hovered just a little before she went—perhaps she knew you were on your way—and one of the nurses says she heard a thunder clap on the roof of the hospital.'

'They said she wasn't going to wake up,' Gracie reassures everyone. 'I rang straight away.'

Glory has only just come in through the door, as Gracie says this, stands at the entrance, leans against the jamb to steady herself. How the room assaults her with its impenetrable stillness. It has grown small overnight, like a burrow. She's never faced death before, close up, the magnetism of it.

Still, Glory can't bring herself to move into the room, because somehow that would be declaratory. It would confirm the truth and Glory couldn't believe it is true. She knows her mother has gone. And yet, and yet, how everything stirs within her to say it's not the case. How do you really know, she wants to ask? She wishes she could have a conversation about death with Onward, ask him for medical explanations; he once had something to say about these sorts of things.

From this distance and angle MotherJoy looks as though she might still be sleeping. She's curled like a foetus, face towards the glass of the window. There's time, isn't there? To finish things off? To make things right before it's too late?

There are no words. This seeing of MotherJoy's dead body *for the first time*—her mother's real body but without voice, without movement; without even the flicker of a sleeping eyelash or the sway of a hair against her temple. Nothing.

A nurse interrupts, gently. She tells them they need to straighten out MotherJoy in the bed, in preparation for laying out her body. She says they can watch if they like.

94

THE NURSES LAY HER OUT. They whisper side to side, turn her over and back, wash her blueing skin with large warm cloths that flap and sag and pool. They talk to her as though she can still hear human voices. They are deft. Practised. Sponge soft. They take their time. They know what they are doing; they've done this before. But they are gentle too, as if this is their first time, a once-and-only time performed just for MotherJoy. As if they really care for her.

They hand MotherJoy's watch to Glory, her rings and gold bracelet still strangely warm. They brush her hair too with her favourite fake gold brush. Brush it off her face in long strokes as if massaging and soothing her scalp to make it feel good, and after, lay the brush in Glory's open palm, mirror side up. A stray grey hair tickles the skin of Glory's hand as if it has come back from the dead.

One of the nurses crosses MotherJoy's hands over her chest and another puts a posy into her fist, a posy of small white orchids with pinky-red tongues taken from a vase on the dresser. They sprinkle petals across the pillow and leave the family to say goodbye, smiling in their ghostly way, disappearing with a clanking of trolleys up the hall.

Then it's afternoon, hours past *the passing*. There is no doubt what has happened because of the seal on MotherJoy's face—it's like a still life with orchids. Glory stands in the space between the bed and the sunny window. Her living face faces her mother's dead one. This is how she wants to gaze at death, square on, with her whole body. She can't believe this mother in front of her is the same mother she remembers from when she was alive. How, even as Glory tries to find a way to describe what has happened, to give mother some kind of shape, make her solid in a current of words, it is all now firmly past tense. Her mother's flesh and blood is turning from living muscle to liquid. Lividity—that's what the doctors call it—where the blood pools. Glory sees the colour in her mother's skin drain. When the nurses turned her, the muscles sagged like blue sacks on the bottom side of her body. Her skin is now yellowy white—what an astonishing transition. And the line is crossed in such a short space of time, too. The realness of flesh and blood dissolves irrevocably into a story of what happened, of what can only be remembered. What *is*, in the now, metamorphoses into *what was*: Glory's mother's life becomes memory, a fiction.

Glory is different as well. Her mother's dying has been written back into the facial lines and shape of her own body. It is over, her new face reads. Finished.

95

IT'S OVER.

When Glory bends to kiss her mother on her cheek she asks the others if she can have a few minutes before MotherJoy is whisked off, first to the hospital mortuary and then to the funeral parlour. Glory wants more than anything to stand in the room of this passing, in the actual presence of death and on her own too, before that opportunity passes also. *My mother is dead,* Glory says to herself. *My mother is dead.* Glory knows it to be true but she has to say it to herself over and over in case this new knowledge slips away. Because it doesn't yet sound right.

It's only then, in the privacy of this silence—how very *loud* is the silence of death—Glory lets out a most terrible cry, hand over her mouth. It reverberates between her and her dead mother. How it erupts from deep within her, a sound like no other. She is truly a stranger to herself.

She kisses her mother once, then twice, three, four times, and smooths her forehead, her hair, and finds herself whispering too, something about life, about its strangeness, about this time going by. She has to lean right over to get the angles right—to make sure she kisses her properly now, face to face. Her tears drop onto her mother's face. Glory wipes her mother's face so tenderly; oh-so-slowly too, wipes across the powdery skin with the tips of her fingers, with the back of her hand, her hair. A kiss on MotherJoy's cheek: still egg warm. Glory wants to get lost there for the last time—*for the first time.*

96

Later that very same day, the Soliders know what must be done—the very next thing, before anyone else gets to him. They must tell Onward what's happened. They have a promise to fulfil to their mother: *Don't forget to look after Onward now, will you? It's going to be heartbreaking.*

When they get to the nursing home, they burst into his double room at the end of a maze of corridors at the very end of the furthest wing. If anyone were to watch them, they'd swear the Solider children are one solid mass, all squeezed tightly together for support—limbs and hearts interleaved. And there he is, their father, asleep just like they thought he would be, with a tartan throw rug covering his knees. His little finger is cocked against his temples. His expression is slack but with a wry mouth. His bushy eyebrows in waves with the rise and fall of his chest.

97

In the collection of X-rays we found underneath my mother's bed, there is one of her chest taken in July 2004, two years after she had her quadruple heart operation and twenty months before it stopped beating altogether the day she died. You can see her heart in the bulge and shadow.

If you look very closely under good lights, you can see the perfection of white ellipses floating upwards along the sternum like smoke rings. Listen in: hear her heart beat in response to each signal—*thrump, thrump, thrump.* Is she sending a message skywards?

Unlike Glory, I wasn't in Brisbane when my mother died, I was at home in Canberra where I was living at the time—because there was a scene. There was always a scene with Angel, especially where her children were concerned, the 'jewels in her crown', and on her deathbed, it was no different. All six children had been at her bedside while she was dying; we all made it there in time, even coming from the other side of the world, pulled in towards her in her last days. But, seven days before she took her last breath, all six of us walked out on her. We had to do it. We looped and knotted our sibling hands and hearts together for support. We grew large and solid with determination.

Once I'd left that room, I didn't want to see my mother again, not while she was still alive. I flew home and waited a thousand miles away, waited to hear the news: *She's gone.* I didn't get on the plane to return until I knew she was really dead.

Simply looking at the label on one of her X-rays from Queensland Diagnostic Imaging with her name and date of birth on it, a bit blurred perhaps, makes my heart race.

98

THE DAY MOTHERJOY DIES, Glory is weightless in the water, legs like soft butter. That day ends with a swim for the sisters in the warm Pacific Ocean, in the nearly dark. Somehow it seems fitting. Glory bobs about. Limbs and hair fluffing, a singsong. She loves swimming in the surf between flags, chest deep, and here she is at the Maroochydore Surf Club. The Solider girls are pretty much on their own; most Queenslanders have already turned in for the day.

All Glory can think about is how relieved she is that it is finished—what a thing to admit. Release oozes out everywhere from the beginning of this strange long day next to the river in Brisbane, to this, with the ocean all about her in a swell of tears. *She's dead. Gone.* Relief that Onward knows too—eventually he did wake up, ready for cake and warm tea, blinking with the news.

Death puts things to rest. Puts a stop. It's a private acknowledgement—this lift Glory feels at being able to admit to the feeling itself. A freedom too at not feeling guilty about any of this, at least not here, not in the warm water with her arms up above her body in exuberance, squealing and laughing, letting go with each roll of the wave, spurting out water through the gap in her teeth. The water makes you go quite silly, she decides, like a little kid again. What did some wise person once say to her? *You can't really let go of something unless you've been holding onto it in the first place.*

To everyone else on the beach it is just the end of another ordinary Queensland day soaked in sunshine. All Glory's sisters are here. She watches them playing a game from their childhood as if they were kids again not women in their forties and fifties. They throw themselves to the floor of the ocean then push off from the soft white sand with their feet to lob up above the surface, spit out mouthfuls of salty water in unison, squawking like seagulls. You'd never guess how suddenly today they are all motherless.

Glory imagines writing something like this onto the page: *No regrets. And I kissed her.* With each word uttered the shadow lifts. Each word sounds better, tastes better—doubles its size—not even the sweetest of cut fresh pineapples could match it. *She's dead and I kissed her, I really kissed her*, she mouths up the throat of the sky. Glory imagines singing across the ocean in peals of arpeggios, playing a church organ, a Hammond, perhaps pulling out every stop, her feet pumping all the pedals. Glory could even be playing a hymn, harmonising with the melody in four parts just like she used to sing in church. Because the thing is, she feels more *in her skin*, akin to being here more than she's ever felt before, not so ashamed about remembering herself, not so ashamed of her mother, if truth were told. Able to sing her heart out for whoever is listening and for all it's worth. If that's what she chooses to do.

All that has gone on before—*blessings on you one hundred times*—has brought Glory to this, Glory to now, to swimming under a giant sky. Something has finished today so something can start, on a beautiful late summer Queensland day too with the smell of frangipani in her hair, with the opening of a new book to follow—Glory hears a flutter of freshly opened pages, smells drying ink.

'This is the day my mother died,' Glory exclaims, but nobody hears.

The roar of the ocean gobbles up her words. Above, the sweep of sky is breathtaking. Clouds mount up on the horizon to the east all hurly-burly—with MotherJoy amongst them for sure, Glory-bound always with wings ablaze and true to her word, unwavering. The angels must be agog at this returned soul, their newest arrival. Heaven will never be quite the same.

99

WHEN MY MOTHER DIED, she was dressed in her favourite pale-blue bed jacket. I had been on standby down south waiting for her to *pass away*, which she did early in the morning, just after sunrise. On hearing the news via a number of text messages, I flew straight to Brisbane on the next plane available. I watched the nurses lay out Angel, seizing upon the bed jacket as a keepsake before anyone threw it out after they dressed her in more suitable attire—*who would want this old thing?* It was an old fashioned garment even for an elderly woman; some would call it vintage, made from the 'wonder fibre', British Nylon. My mother loved to fossick around in Vinnies and Life Line. Over a lifetime Angel gave away as many clothes as she bought.

I like the fine lines of the horizontal pattern in the nylon. How it drip-dries quickly when washed. I like the idea of danger when thinking of the material's flammability—it would never pass today's sleep test: SIZE 20 TO FIT BUST 42 BRI NYLON.

I grabbed my mother's hairbrush to keep it too, the bristles still full of her loose grey hair, the same brush the nurses used to smooth down my mother's hair across the pillow when we said our last goodbye. 'You're morbid, Francesca—did you know that?' a sister says.

Because what I've got to tell you is this. All the time I've been writing this story, Angel's blue nylon bed jacket has been hanging in my wardrobe. But the funny thing is, it is only recently that I've read what it says on the other side of the tag because it has been stuck upside down flat against one of my mother's pink crocheted coat hangers. When I turned it over, I discovered two words: 'Miss Gloria'.

Not that my mother knew about Glory, my Glory-story—I could never have told her what I was writing, she hated me writing. But I can't help wondering: did she ever turn over that tag like I did? Did she know Miss Gloria existed on the other side, did she feel her tucked up and nestled against her neck? Did she, perhaps, buy the jacket for this very thing; did Miss Gloria tickle her fancy?

This Bri Nylon clothes tag takes me back to the Wesley Hospital in Auchenflower, back to my mother's room, to trying to make her body comfortable in her final days. To helping her into this bed jacket early one morning when she wanted to spruce herself up for a bite of breakfast, for mouthfuls of scrambled eggs—her favourite kind of egg, she said. To when I adjusted the neckline, her pleading with me to help: 'I must dress nicely for my family, be presentable.' To when I clipped the sides of Miss Gloria together with a safety pin in order to hide the wound at her throat—'Francesca, cover me up will you, there's a dear, make me decent.' To when I turned the blue frill, just so. 'How's that?' I offer. To a moment of softness, give.

Miss Gloria lifts the ordinariness of a remembered gesture into poetic evocation. Sparks the imagination. The silver and black thread of the tag, the tufting at the edges, the little hole on the 'i', attaches any thinking and feeling about my mother dying beside the Brisbane River to the fabric of words here, the heft and weave of this story.

100

That evening in the surf at Maroochydore, north of Brisbane on the Sunshine Coast, it is warm, dizzy as foam. Glory doesn't want to leave the ocean, doesn't want this day to pass—neither do I. The fingers and toes of Glory's new body are wrinkled like leftover baked potatoes; she could stay out here all night, she reckons. She's good at treading water, can do it without thinking. Carries on in tumble turns, sluicing and sloshing effortlessly in the deep summery blue of this Queensland water, now turning mauve to indigo to a deep expressionist black in the growing dark. Limbs and heart all fizzy pop in the spume.

Bite Your Tongue

Dr Joy's Death List: Burn a Book A Day

'Summer of the Seventeenth Doll' (Lawlor)
'The One Day of the Year' (Seymour)
'My Brother Jack' (Johnston)
'Clean Straw for Nothing' (Johnston)
'Catcher in the Rye' (Ballinger)
'Franny & Zooey' (Ballinger)
'Raise High the Roof Beams, Carpenter' (Ballinger)
'The Power and the Glory' (Greene)
'The Tin Drum' (Gunther Grass)
'Cat and Mouse' (Gunther Grass)
'Greening of America' (Reich)
'Bring Larks & Heroes' (Keneally)
'Farewell to Arms' (Hemmingway)
'The Sun Also Rises' (Hemmingway)
'For Whom the Bell Tolls' (Hemmingway)
'Brave New World' (Huxley)
'To Kill a Mockingbird' (Lee)
'Portrait of the Artist as a Young Man' (Joyce)
'Exiles' (Joyce)
'The Rainbow' (Lawrence)
'Sons and Lovers' (Lawrence)
'Women in Love' (Lawrence)
'Mice & Men' (Steinbeck)
'Grapes of Wrath' (Steinbeck)
'Mrs Dalloway' (Woolf)
'To the Lighthouse' (Woolf)
'Lucky Country' (Horne)
'But What if There Were No More Pelicans' (Horne)
'Who's Afraid of Virginia Woolf' (Albee)
The works of W. Burroughs and E. Albee
'Street Car Named Desire' (Tennessee Williams)
'Glass Menagerie' (Tennessee Williams)

'Baby Doll' (Tennessee Williams)
'Death of a Salesman' (Miller)
'Aftr the Fall' (Miller)
'The Crucible' (Miller)
'A View from the Bridge' (Miller)
'The Fringe Dwellers' (Neno Gair)
'Breakfast at Tiffany's' (Capote)
'In Cold Blood' (Capote)
'Fillets of Plaice' (Durrell)
'The Loved One' (Waugh)
'Decline & Fall' (Waugh)
'How To Be a Survivor' (Erlich)
'Passage to India' (Forster)
'Howard's End' (Forster)
(N.B. it is well established that E. M. Forster was a Platonic homosexual)
'Where Angels Fear to Tread' (Forster)
'Catch 22' (Heller)
'Something Happened' (Heller)
'The Femme Mystique' (Friedan)
'The Female Eunuch' (Greer)
'The Outcasts of Foolgarah' (Hardy)
'Midnight Cowboy' (Horlby)
'The Just' (Camus)
'The Possessed' (Camus)
'Crime Passionel' (Satre)
'Krapps Last Tape' (Beckett)
'Endgame' (Beckett)
'Waiting for Godot' (Beckett)
'Not After Midnight' (du Maurier)
'Portnoy's Complaint' (Roth)
'Slaughterhouse 5' (Vonnegut)
'To Sir with Love' (Anouilh)
'Guess Who's Coming to Dinner' (Anouilh)
'One Flew Over the Cuckoo's Nest' (Kessey)
'Patch of Blue' (Kata)

'First Man, Last Man' (Carson)
'The Drifters' (Mitchener)
'The Pigman' (Zindel)
'It's Like This, Cat' (Neville)
'Under Milk Wood' (Thomas)
'Love Story' (Segall)
'Admission to the Feast' (Beckman)
'Prime of Miss Jean Brodie' (Spark)
'Lolita' (Nabokov)
'Endless Circle'
'Go Tell It on the Mountain' (Baldwin)
'Another Country' (Baldwin)
'Blues for Mr Charles' (Baldwin)
'The Well of Loneliness' (Hall)
'Black Like Me' (Griffin)
'Gone with the Wind' (Mitchell)
'The Godfather' (Puzo)
'Into the Whirlwind' (Ginsberg)
'Lady Chatterley's Lover' (Lawrence)
'The Doll's House' (Ibsen)
'Three Sisters' (Chekov)
'Taste of Honey' (Delaney)
'The Group' (McCarthy)
'English Today III'
'Actions and Reactions'
(English assignment books need special watching!!!)
'Animal Farm' (Orwell)
'1984' (Orwell)
'The Lord of the Flies' (Golding)
'Improving on the Blank Page' (Cook & Gallasch)
'Playboy of the Western World' (Synge)
'The Way of All Flesh' (Butler)
'The Grass is Singing' (Lessing)
'Coming of Age in Samoa' (Meade)
'The Little Red School Book'

List of illustrations

Page 1: X-ray of Angel's hands, c. 2003-2005, Queensland Diagnostic Imaging, digital reproduction by Tim Thomas, 2007

Page 26 and 27: Going to church, Durham Street, St Lucia, photograph by John Rendle-Short, c. 1964

Page 60 and back cover: Playing in the pink bath, Norman Parade, Eagle Junction, slide by John Rendle-Short, c. 1962

Page 167: Brisbane River, West End and St Lucia reaches, photograph by author, c. 1974-75

Page 168: The view up the hill, Durham Street, St Lucia, photograph by author, c. 1974-75

Page 168: Corner of house, Durham Street, St Lucia, photograph by author, c. 1974-75

Page 169: Out the louvres, Durham Street, St Lucia, photograph by author, c. 1974-75

Page 171: 'Permissive rebel', drawing by author, 2011.

Page 185: Beside the Centenary Pool, Spring Hill, slide by John Rendle-Short, c. 1966

Page 195: Angel's medical plate, Durham Street, St Lucia, photograph by author, c. 1978

Page 196: Underneath the house, Durham Street, St Lucia, photograph by author, c. 1981

Page 197 and 198: Francesca and Angel in front of the green velvet, Woofindin Avenue, Sheffield, UK, slide by John Rendle-Short, 1961

Page 206: Royal Tour, digital image by author, 2007

Page 207, 225: Playing in the Clark Rubber pool, Durham Street, St Lucia, slides by John Rendle-Short, c. 1966

Page 219: Angel laughing on her honeymoon, thought to be in Cork, Ireland, slide by John Rendle-Short, 1947

Page 220: Keep, digital image by author, 2011

Page 221: Angel in the kitchen in Durham Street, photograph by author, c. 1978

Page 233: Queensland Diagnostic Imaging, from Angel's heart X-ray of 6 July 2004, digital reproduction by Tim Thomas, 2007

Page 237 and 238: Miss Gloria, worn by Angel Rendle-Short at the Wesley Hospital, Auchenflower, digital image by author, 2007

Permissions

Epigraph: from *Fahrenheit 451* by Ray Bradbury, Ballantine Books, New York, 1953; Flamingo, London, 1993, page 124.

Page 3 and 4: Dr Angel Rendle-Short, Letter to The Rt Hon. Sir Paul Hasluck, Governor General of Australia, 7 August 1971 and 1 June 1972, A2880/1, 2/1/3913, from 'Individuals—Requests and complaints received from people within Australia—Dr A Rendle-Short', National Archives of Australia, courtesy National Archives of Australia and Rendle-Short family.

Page 5: Queensland Parliament, Queensland Legislative Assembly Debates, *Hansard*, Matters of Public Interest, Address in Reply by Mr Hanson, Member for Port Curtis, 7 September 1971, pp. 404–06.

Page 12: Beverley Wood gave me my first 'death list'. She showed me a list of books originally compiled as supporting documentation for a delegation to government under the title 'Concerning the moral pollution of children through literature'. This list was presented to the Queensland Education Department in January 1972 by a deputation of six concerned Christian parents. I have, since then, seen different lists of these 'controversial' books reproduced in various ways for different purposes. For example, *Semper Floreat*, the University of Queensland's independent student newspaper, published a list under the title 'Rona's death list: Burn a book a day', a parody of the activity of another Queensland morals campaigner, Rona Joyner (vol. 48, no. 3, 15 March 1978, page 7). Permission to reference this parody is granted, courtesy *Semper Floreat*, University of Queensland Union. Thanks to all the writers of the books listed in the 'death list', in particular to Harper Lee, D. H. Lawrence, William Golding, J. D. Salinger and Ray Bradbury. This book is really for them.

Page 29: STOP, the Society to Outlaw Pornography, was founded by Rona Joyner in 1971. CARE, the Campaign Against Regressive Education, was inaugurated a year later (*STOP PRESS*, 15 March 1985). *STOP PRESS* was the official publication of STOP and CARE for twenty-one years. It was clearly stated on all their publications that none of their literature was copyright and it might be reprinted if found to be useful. Rona Joyner has an online presence at angelfire.com. The last posting was in 2003.

Page 30: Headline, staff writer, *Courier Mail*, 9 September 1967, page 1, courtesy *Courier Mail*, Queensland Newspapers.

Permissions

Page 57: Joy Guyatt and Greg George, 'Publications of political organisations in Queensland held in University of Queensland libraries', Fryer Memorial Library Occasional Publication No. 2, Fryer Memorial Library, University of Queensland Libraries, St Lucia 1983, page 270, courtesy Fryer Library.

Page 57: 'Textbooks are gutter trash', (Mrs) Angel Rendle-Short, M.B., B.Ch., Brookfield, Letters to the Editor, *Courier Mail*, 6 February 1975, page 2, courtesy *Courier Mail*, Queensland Newspapers.

Page 58: 'Sowing the wind: Reaping the whirlwind', Ms, June 1972, A2880/1, 2/1/3913, from 'Individuals—Requests and complaints received from people within Australia—Dr A Rendle-Short,' National Archives of Australia, courtesy National Archives of Australia and Rendle-Short family.

Page 59: References to 4BW come from the following: 'Women's air talks are untuned', staff reporter, *Sunday Mail*, 9 November 1975, page 16; 'Radio plan loud but not clear', staff writer, *Courier Mail*, 27 October 1975, page 8; 'Women's radio tries again', staff writer, *Courier Mail*, 3 November 1975, page 12; 'Women's radio finds voice', staff writer, *Courier Mail*, 7 December 1979, page 20, courtesy *Courier Mail, Sunday Mail*, Queensland Newspapers.

Page 61: Opinion on a review from inside cover to the 1960 Penguin edition, D. H. Lawrence, *Lady Chatterley's Lover*.

Page 74 and 75: Bible references come from Proverbs 16:31; Hebrews 12:29; Ezekiel 23:43–45.

Page 79: It was Senator Bonner (Liberal, Queensland) who referred to the 'gutter words' in *The Little Red School Book*, 'Gutter words in Red Book', staff writer, *Courier Mail*, 22 April 1972, courtesy *Courier Mail*, Queensland Newspapers.

Page 81: The reference to the triple-O hotline was found in the 'Censorship File' of the Australian Press Cuttings Agency, Newspaper Room, National Library of Australia: 'Hot line to beat Red book', *Australian*, 7 June 1972.

Page 81: Australian Press Cuttings Agency, 'Censorship File', 'Book ban denies a right—Librarian', staff writer, 29 April 1972, page 7, Newspaper Room, National Library of Australia, courtesy *Courier Mail*, Queensland Newspapers and National Library of Australia.

Page 82: Joy Guyatt and Greg George, 'Publications of political organizations in Queensland held in University of Queensland libraries', Fryer Memorial Library Occasional Publication No. 2, Fryer Memorial Library, University of Queensland Libraries, St Lucia 1983, page 222, courtesy Fryer Library.

Page 121 and 122: 'Dr Angel Rendle-Short, examined, who has been in frequent correspondence', from transcripts of public hearings to the Select Committee on Education in Queensland (Chairman, Mike Ahern), Queensland Legislative Assembly, Queensland Parliament, Brisbane, Day 14, 5 September 1978, 11.31 a.m., pp 795–800 (Records [ca. 1978] [manuscript], UQFL81, Box 9, Fryer Library, University of Queensland), courtesy Fryer Library.

Page 123: Ann Draper, 'I oppose the evils of homosexuality, sodomy: 4BW in action', *Semper Floreat*, vol. 45, no. 16, November 1975, page 4, courtesy *Semper Floreat*, University of Queensland Union.

Page 123: 'Are you concerned about your children's moral welfare', Queensland League for National Welfare and Decency, A Public Meeting, Thursday 7 October 1971, 7.45 p.m. St. Paul's Presbyterian Church Hall, Brisbane, report by R. B. J. Wilson, Senior Lecturer in English, Queensland University (FDO Fielding Collection, Papers 1969–1991 [Manuscript], UQFL126, Box 11, Fryer Library, University of Queensland), courtesy Fryer Library.

Page 144: I first came across the expression 'Children don't go to school to learn to think' in the archive in Ann Gowers and Roger Scott, monograph, *Fundamentals and Fundamentalists: A Case Study of Education and Policy-Making in Queensland*, APSA Monograph 22, Adelaide: Discipline of Politics, Flinders University, 1979, page v. Rona Joyner, the director of STOP and CARE, used this expression a lot.

Page 170: 'School textbooks slated: Rebel ideas, says mother', staff writer, *Courier Mail*, 7 February 1975, page 3, courtesy *Courier Mail*, Queensland Newspapers.

Page 172: *Wish poems*, Students at Salisbury East High School, South Australia, in *Improving on the Blank Page*, eds Keith Gallasch and Deborah Cook, Rigby, Adelaide page 3, courtesy editors.

Page 191 and 192: 'Moral pollution: Diagnosis and remedy', Ms, June 1972, A2880/1, 2/1/3913, From 'Individuals—Requests and complaints received from people within Australia —Dr A Rendle-Short,' National Archives of Australia, courtesy National Archives and Rendle-Short family.

Every endeavour has been made to contact copyright holders to obtain the necessary permission for use of copyright material in this book. Any person who may have been inadvertently overlooked should contact the publisher.

Acknowledgments

Bite Your Tongue is part fiction, part memoir. It is a work that has its genesis in life and art but, like any story of its kind, the interpretation is my own. This book grew out of a short story published in *Red Cat Country*. In my novella *Big Sister* (Redress Novellas), the fictional family enjoys making brawn out of a pig's head, and baby mice appear here too, but for very different reasons. In a short story published in *Four W*, my first MotherJoy character (in name only) makes an appearance. Parts of *Bite Your Tongue* have been published in various publications and I thank these editors for believing in the work: *Hecate, Mixed Nerve, Overland, TEXT Journal*. This current work was originally part of a Doctor of Creative Arts at the University of Wollongong.

In the writing of *Bite Your Tongue*, I have so many to thank who have assisted me generously in different ways. A special thanks goes to my supervisor Merlinda Bobis who helped me find the voice to tell this particular story, and to Carrie Tiffany, much later, who recognised that voice and gave me great encouragement. Thanks to all my friends, especially, Alison Dredge, Helen Ennis, Paul Hetherington, Barbara Holloway, Ellen Kleimaker, Helen Maxwell, Fiona Norris, Felicity Packard, Pat Tandy, Biff Ward and Jen Webb. Thanks also to Jeff Rickertt and the other staff at the Fryer Library at the University of Queensland, whose interest in the project gave me a number of new leads, and to the staff of the other libraries and archives where I researched my mother's public persona: National Archives of Australia, National Library of Australia, Queensland State Library. I want to thank the Australian National University School of Art and the Canton of Graubünden, Switzerland, for a residency at Schloss Haldenstein; Gorman House Arts Centre, Canberra, for studio space; and Varuna, the Writers' House in Katoomba, for a week's residency to finalise the manuscript. Thanks too to my colleagues and students at the University of Wollongong, University of Canberra, and RMIT University.

A world of appreciation to Susan Hawthorne and Spinifex Press for deciding to publish this book, and to the Australia Council for helping to make it possible. For all her sensitive work and thoughtfulness, thanks to Sophie Cunningham: no one could dream a better editor. And to Gail Jones and Cate Kennedy for their wonderful commendations.

My family too, I couldn't have written this book without them: thank you for your love. To my siblings: Charlotte, Alexandra and Hume Rendle-Short, and particularly Johanna and Hephzibah Rendle-Short. This is my version of our strange and remarkable family; I am sure they each would have their own story. To my out-of-laws, the extended Horacek family, and to my dear and incomparable children, Kukame and Jaffa McKenzie, thank you all for your support and love. And finally, enormous thanks to my partner Judy Horacek, who understands the very grain of making, and who loves discussing with me the possibility and beauty of everything. To her: boundless, heartfelt gratitude and love.